ORDINARY GIRLS

Also by Blair Thornburgh

Who's That Girl

ORDINARY GIRLS

BLAIR THORNBURGH

HARPER TEEN

An Imprint of HarperCollinsPublishers

HarperTeen is an imprint of HarperCollins Publishers.

Ordinary Girls
Copyright © 2019 by Blair Thornburgh
All rights reserved. Printed in the United States of America.
No part of this book may be used or reproduced in any manner
whatsoever without written permission except in the case of brief
quotations embodied in critical articles and reviews. For information
address HarperCollins Children's Books,
a division of HarperCollins Publishers, 195 Broadway, New York,
NY 10007.
www.epicreads.com

Library of Congress Control Number: 2019932653
ISBN 978-0-06-244781-4

Typography by Molly Fehr
19 20 21 22 23   PC/LSCH   10 9 8 7 6 5 4 3 2 1

First Edition

To Alice

 ONE

Ah! But verses amount to so little when one writes them young.
One ought to wait and gather sense and sweetness a whole life
long, and a long life if possible, and then, quite at the end, one
might perhaps be able to write ten lines that were good.
—Rainer Maria Rilke

I have never been good at beginnings, which is one of my many shortcomings. Starting with childhood seems very romantic, like a true *bildungsroman*, but I don't really *remember* half my childhood due to being a baby, and I'm not about to rely on Ginny's accounts of what I was like, because she did not care for having a baby sister and once covered me in Vaseline when Mom left us alone in the playroom. So I suppose I will start on that sunny Saturday in September when I first realized how acutely I wanted to murder my sister.

For reliability's sake, this is mostly hyperbole. Even now, I am not sure I actually possess the stomach to become a teenage murderess. I faint when I get blood drawn. I can't even watch those extreme plastic surgery shows where people lie on a table like sliced deli meat wrapped in blue tarp and come out with a springy new set of whatevers, because they are disgusting. I cannot, for any reason, abide hospitals. But living with Virginia Eleanor Blatchley, highest of the high-strung, especially at the beginning of her senior year of high school—that would have driven even the most steely nerved and introverted of young women to madness.

That Saturday, September 3, had dawned pastoral and bucolic: Iris Mortimer-Blatchley was dead asleep, probably splotched with oil paint. Almost-Doctor Andrews, our tenant (he lived in the carriage house) was composing music for his PhD course of study. The poodles were lounging on one of our beds, the fish were circling each other in little fish loops, and the chickens were fattening themselves on the crusts of my apple butter toast that I had obligingly dumped into their backyard pen. I was looking forward to an afternoon of watching Home and Garden Television, practicing my French-braiding, or reading Ginny's hand-me-down copy of *Jane Eyre*, which was the summer reading, and which I had already finished but would gladly read again.

Yet soon the morning demonstrated signs of high drama. By ten to noon, Virginia Eleanor Blatchley was clomping around between the tower room, the library, and the kitchen. Furthermore, I, Patience Mortimer Blatchley, found myself occupied with getting Kit Marlowe to come out from the compartment under the stairs—which is a very good place for hiding. I used to climb in there with my notebook when I was a little girl. Now, however, I was too big to fit, and Kit needed to take his heartworm medication or he would probably die.

"Kit." I crouched in front of the little white door, clicking my tongue cajolingly. "Here, Kit."

Kit meowed but did not move. I pulled my phone out of my pocket to use as a flashlight, which made Kit's eyes gleam like marbles.

"Plum?"

From somewhere up on the second or third floor, Ginny's voice rang out. I ignored it and tucked the end of my braid out of the way so it wouldn't get coated in dust.

"Plum?" she called again. Ginny does not like being ignored. "Plum? Plummy? *Plum?* Where are you?"

Where I was was on the first floor, kneeling on the Oriental runner with the stain from where Gizmo threw up my Easter candy three years ago.

"I'm trying to feed the cat a pill," I yelled back.

"Girls, this house is too big for yelling," yelled my mother. "And I have a headache."

I leaned forward so that my head was now in the compartment with Kit, since there was no way I *wasn't* going to get dust on it at this point. It was hot and dark in there, and smelled like old wood and warm cat.

"Come on, Kit," I said calmly. "I mixed it in some spreadable meat and everything."

Spreadable meat was what we had taken to calling liverwurst, our all-purpose pill concealer for Kit and the poodles. You can't even get it at the regular grocery store, just the co-op market where they sell organic coffee in big bins and the natural kind of toothpaste that tastes like rotten strawberries and you're likely to run into the parents of someone you strongly dislike, like Tate Kurokawa. But that was the length we—I— would go to for our pets.

Kit hissed.

"PLUM!"

"You can't hide forever, Kit," I told him, sternly but wisely, in the tone of voice a governess might use to instruct her young charge in the ways of the world. If it were not the twenty-first century, and I were not only fifteen, I would become a governess. Surely, in that line of work, tone of voice is key.

Above my head, the boards of the stairs groaned and squealed, and someone's feet came pounding down. Everything at 5142 Haven Lane groaned, or squealed, or rusted, or just didn't work. It was extremely old and tired, for a house. But it had been around since 1863, and was therefore grand. Not enough things are grand anymore, if you ask me.

"Plum? What are you doing?" came Mom's voice from somewhere outside the compartment. "Why is there spreadable meat on the mail table?"

"I told you," I said, easing out from the compartment. My braid did, in fact, leave a trail in the dust. Cripes. I shook it off. "Kit's afraid of his heartworm pill. Even when I hide it."

"Take care of it later." Iris Mortimer-Blatchley, my mother, was looking stately and columnar, draped in her daytime blacks—not to be confused with her evening blacks—and a midnight-blue scarf. Black, Mom always said, is universally flattering, to which Ginny would always reply that Mom was being morbid and just because she *was* a widow didn't mean she had to dress like one. I thought Mom looked nice, even if she did wear a lot of eyeliner for someone over the age of forty. One time, when I was eight, I called her "a handsome woman of middle age," which was something I'd read in a book and I thought sounded complimentary. Mom did not think so.

"But—"

"He's not going to catch heartworm in the next three hours," Mom said, waving a hand. "Just give it to him when we get back."

"You don't *catch* heartworm, Mother," I said. "It's not like a cold. Which cats can also get, I think."

"Thank you for the veterinary lesson. Will you please go help your sister find something white to wear? I forgot about that thing of hers, and she's having a conniption about it."

Kit, recognizing he had won this round, purred from inside the compartment.

"We?" I said. "Leave for what?"

"The thing," Mom said. "The school thing. With the white dresses."

"Oh no," I said. I knew there was a reason I knew that today, specifically, was September 3. The cream-colored invitation from the Gregory School for the annual Senior Tea had been sitting on the kitchen counter for at least two weeks. "Do we have to?"

Mom pressed a hand to her forehead. "Do you think *I* want to go?"

It was a rhetorical question. Mom did not like socializing with the other Gregory School parents any more than I liked socializing with anyone. Especially any other Gregory School sophomores.

"Plum!!!!" came the shriek.

"She can't find something to wear," Mom translated. "I don't know what to do with her. Can you just—I don't know. Do something?"

"Honestly, Mother, I could not care less if Ginny can't find clothes," I said primly.

Mom pressed her lips together. Although our mother did not believe in *buying* makeup, she did acquire a healthy number of samples every time she stopped in a Sephora, including, evidently, something bloodred.

"Well, you should," she said. "She took some of *your* clothes."

I leaped to my feet.

To get to Ginny's room in the tower, you can either take the front stairs, which are very creaky, or the back stairs, which are very steep, and you are likely to slide down and break your shin if you don't walk slowly. Victorian houses are not constructed for the impatient. Which makes it a miracle Ginny loves living here so much, as she is patience deficient.

Our father used to joke that it was good they named us in the order they did or Ginny would be a living oxymoron.

I took the front stairs, which wound through the pink-red front-hall walls, and creaked into Ginny's room, which was round and painted with a mural. When our mom was pregnant with my sister, she'd spent the last weeks of her confinement decorating the tower bedroom walls with a fairy-tale landscape of castles and bunnies eating ice-cream cones and airplanes trailing little banners like at the beach. It was, naturally, wonderful.

"Don't take my stuff!" I cried.

"Is the cat okay? Is Mom acting weird? Do you have anything white that I can borrow?"

My sister was sitting on her giant sleigh bed, cross-legged in a pile of clothes—none of them white, many of them mine. I flew forward and ripped a pair of corduroys out from under her knob-knee.

"Ow!" she yelped melodramatically. "You gave me a brush burn."

Gizmo and Doug, who were curled up by the pillows like two black standard poodle doughnuts, lifted their heads an inch.

"*Ginny*," I said. "You can't just take my stuff." Two hours ago, those corduroys had been neatly folded and sitting in a laundry basket with their neatly folded fellows. Now they were a rumpled mess.

"We're sisters," Ginny said simply, as if that excused

everything. She rubbed her palm over her knee. "And I need you to lend me something. If it's white."

Lending implied *I* was the one to instigate the action of sharing. But I never was. This was one of thousands of tiny irritating Ginny things pushing me to the brink. "Well, even if I wanted to, I can't."

"Why not?"

I gave her a look that hopefully said, *You are shaped like a forest nymph crossed with a praying mantis while I am shaped like a lima bean.*

"Because the only white thing I have is a sheep costume from the youth group Christmas pageant," I said instead. Gizmo, smelling the spreadable meat, was now licking my fingers.

"Ugh!" Ginny wheeled back her arm and flung a shoe—black, low heel—at the wall. It bounced, leaving a crumbling crater behind.

"God, Ginny, what is wrong with you?" I rushed over to the wall to inspect the damage. The shoe had landed square in the middle of Imperative Park, which Mom had painted full of signs that read KEEP OFF GRASS and ENJOY THE VIEW. The sign that read SNIFF next to a bunch of flowers had been obliterated. "You're ruining everything."

Ginny sulked. "Mom says you should check the closets. In the Hiltiddly Room, I guess."

The Hiltiddly Room is actually the utility room, meaning

a random room on the third floor with built-in closets and a sink and all the exercise equipment no one uses, but when we moved in I mispronounced it in my baby-Plum way and the name stuck. This tendency to misunderstand words is also how I ended up with a nickname that sounds very little like my actual name.

Ginny bounded ahead across the landing, I followed much more sedately, and Gizmo brought up the rear.

"Has Mom been acting weird to you?" Ginny flung open a closet and pushed aside some of Great-Grandmother Eleanor Blatchley's old fur coats.

"What?"

"Has Mom"—she sneezed—"been acting *weird*?" She stopped and rubbed her nose. "I think she might be smoking again. I saw butts in the urns. Haven't you noticed?"

"If you mean have I caught her in the act, then no," I said. "It was probably just Almost-Doctor Andrews."

"Almost-Doctor Andrews can't smoke," Ginny said. "His undergrad minor was in vocal performance. He knows better than to abuse his voice."

"As if I am supposed to know what doctoral candidates in music do or don't do in college," I muttered. It being her senior year, college was Ginny's new obsession. This was part of what was fueling my sororicidal (of or relating to murdering one's sister) fantasies.

"And no," Ginny went on, not waiting for me, as usual. "I

mean, haven't you noticed that she's acting weird?"

"You mean more than usual?" Iris Mortimer-Blatchley was never not weird. For one thing, she *did* wear all black all year all the time, and not just because she was a widow. Also, her hair was pure silver, instead of highlighted to hide the gray, and fell all the way to her waist, instead of ending in a neat bob. She was not going to blend in well at the Senior Tea. "You have *met* our mother, right?"

Unable to provoke sufficient drama with this interrogation, Ginny was back to the closet. "What am I supposed to find in— Ooh." She thrust a bony hand into the closet and pulled out a crepe, knee-length dress with a pleated skirt and a giant, triangular collar.

Her face contorted in disgust.

"It's white," I said helpfully.

"It's old aye-eff," Ginny said.

"It's . . . vintage?" I tried.

"You don't even know what that means."

"Do, too. It's French for *old.*"

Ginny cracked up. "It's French for *ceci n'est pas une robe blanche.*"

"If you say so." French was my worst subject, probably because Mme. Fournier despaired of me for not being as *intelligente* as *ma soeur*, and also because I did not like speaking up, much less in a language that was not my native tongue. This, in a nutshell, was what it was like to be Patience Mortimer Blatchley.

Ginny held the dress at arm's length like it was poisoned.

"I told Mom like three weeks ago that I needed to buy something to wear to this and she totally ignored me," she said. "Then I tried to buy something online, but I think her card must have expired because it wouldn't go through."

"You stole her credit card?"

Ginny waved her hand. "I'm her dependent. It's allowed."

"Well, does it have to be white?"

"*Yes*, Plum."

"Why?"

"I don't know," Ginny said crossly. "For the ritual sacrifice. Cripes, I can't wear this."

We had both started saying *cripes* after a summer spent watching all of the episodes of *Jeeves and Wooster* we could find on YouTube. Ginny had decided I was definitely Jeeves the valet, because I was practical and spoke in a normal tone of voice, and I had pointed out it was only too obvious that she was Bertie Wooster, because she got herself into lots of scrapes and could never remember the words to poems.

"Ginny, you look good in everything," I said. It was the annoying truth. "Just wear it, okay? Who cares?"

"Yeah." Ginny held the dress against her body and swayed a little. I caught Gizmo's collar before he nipped at the hem.

"Is there going to be *dancing* at this tea?" I asked.

"Shut up," Ginny answered, and stopped swaying. "Can you do one of those braids for me?"

I sighed. "Yes, but like, now."

Ginny threw the dress on the NordicTrack and started pulling her clothes off right in the middle of the Hiltiddly Room.

"Were you going to pick that up?" I asked, when she flung her sweatshirt to the ground. She ignored me and yanked the dress over her head.

"How do I look?"

The dress hung off her in a gauzy, not-particularly-well-fitted way. "Well . . ."

She stomped off to her room before I could finish, and, after deciding to leave her jeans where she'd thrown them, I did, too.

"*Merde*," Ginny said into the mirror. We were night and day: Ginny, six feet tall with thin, wispy blond hair and bronze-colored eyes; me, relatively tall, with obstinately thick brown hair and muddy eyes to match. The only thing we had in common was our sheet-white skin. "I look like one of those fairy paintings Mom likes."

"You mean the Pre-Raphaelites?"

"Yeah. Like the Lady of Shalott. Is she one of the ones who drowns?"

"Probably," I said. "They all drown in the end."

Ginny cackled, then closed her eyes, crossed her arms over her chest, and fell backward onto her bed, which alarmed the still-sleeping Doug. "I shall die, Plummy. The stress is too much. Please put my body in a flower-wreathèd barge and

12

push me gently downstream, preferably in the direction of the University of Pennsylvania."

This was too fanciful to merit a response. Ginny only slipped into her sonnet-like pronunciation of past participles when she was irretrievably far gone into a flight of fancy. I sat on the edge of the bed and scratched Doug's butt.

"Plum!" Ginny opened one eye. "Don't you care about my incipient trauma?"

I shrugged. "Why would you still go to college if you're dead?"

"It may be the only way I can get there," Ginny said gravely.

"Well, if you're dead or in college, can I have your room?"

"Do you *want* me to be dead, Plummy?"

I pretended to think about it, partially as a joke, partially not. Ginny, now not dead at all, leaped out of the bed.

"Plum!"

"Okay, okay," I said. "I don't want you dead."

I *didn't* want her dead. But at that point, I would not have minded if she were simply *gone*. As cruel as it sounds, I knew my life would be infinitely easier and more pleasant when my life did not revolve around Ginny's quotidian hissy fits.

"Girls?" Mom's voice called up the stairs. "Ten minutes was over almost ten minutes ago."

"Coming!" we yelled at the same time.

"Here," I said in my governess voice. "Let me do your hair."

Ginny is terrible at doing hair because she is impatient and doesn't have time to spend hours watching tutorials on YouTube because she is studying or spending time with her best friend, Charlotte. I, having neither a particular reason to study nor a best friend, have nothing but free time, and extremely fast fingers besides.

"Hold still!" I yelped. "You're making this impossible."

"Sorry, Plummy," Ginny said. "Thanks."

I continued braiding in silence.

"Oh, wait!" Ginny jumped forward, which screwed up my braid, and grabbed a little velvet box from the dresser. "Here."

"My hands are full," I reminded her.

"Right." She popped it open. Inside was a stack of silver rings.

"I found them when I was digging through the guest room dresser," she said. "You should wear them."

I finished what was probably my fifth-best braid and took a ring from the box, surveying. It slipped all the way to the bottom of my finger.

"See?" Ginny said. "I knew they were meant for you."

I shimmered my fingers in the air. It did look nice. I slid on the rest. "Thank you."

Ginny grabbed me around the waist, and I shoved her off, and then we both went downstairs to where Mom was waiting with Almost-Doctor Andrews, who was probably over to deliver his rent check and a loaf of zucchini bread.

Almost-Doctor Andrews was a slim and attractive man of about twenty-eight with brown hair and a mustache. If he were not gay, and if our mother had any interest in remarriage, I would put him forth as a possible stepfather.

"Oh, there you—" Mom stopped. And laughed. "Is that what you're wearing?"

I looked down at my body, which was clad in a fairly regular pair of jeans, socks that did not match, and a purple T-shirt with a cat that read COFFEE RIGHT MEOW. Plus, now, rings.

"From the tone of your voice I'm guessing that's unacceptable," I said drily. I say many things drily. It is my trademark.

"Ginny," Mom said. "That's a bridesmaid dress I wore in Kathy's wedding in 1992."

"I don't *have* anything *else*," Ginny said, folding her puffed-sleeve arms fiercely. "*You* wouldn't let me *buy* anything."

Mom and Almost-Doctor Andrews exchanged a glance.

"It's vintage?" he offered.

"Told you so," I said.

"And you're just going to let Plum go like *that*?" Ginny demanded. "*Siblings are requested to please dress their best.* It says so on the invitation."

"This *is* my best," I said. "And they split an infinitive."

Mom sighed. "Don't you have a skirt or something, Plum?"

"Senior Tea is only a big deal for *seniors*," I pointed out.

"And I don't have a skirt." Skirts made me look like a tube of spreadable meat.

"Okay," Mom said. "So wear those pants."

I groaned. Ginny cackled.

"What's wrong with those pants?" Mom said. "The gray dress ones with the little cuffs at the end? Aren't those the kind of nice things respectable people wear?"

"Mom," Ginny said. "You are always telling Plum to wear Those Pants."

"What?" Mom said. "Am not."

"You are, too," I said, and ticked off on my fingers. "Church. Your students' gallery shows. Almost-Doctor Andrews's recital that one time."

Mom flushed. "So? They're nice pants."

"We're already late," I said. "I don't have time to get changed."

"Only because *someone* took a long time getting dressed," Mom said.

"Only because *someone else* wouldn't let me buy a real dress!" Ginny cried. "What's wrong with one dress? Are you trying to *deprive* us? Is this why you've been acting so shady lately?"

Mom flushed deeper. "Ginny. I have not been—"

Kit Marlowe cut her off with a hacking cough. An orange-and-whitish blob splatted against the carpet.

It was a cigarette butt.

"It's time to go," Mom said briskly. She flung her scarf around her neck. "Put on a skirt, Plum."

A tense moment of silence followed.

"Forgive me if this is something I should know," Almost-Doctor Andrews ventured. "But is there supposed to be liverwurst on the mail table?"

The Gregory School is among the Philadelphia area's most elite private schools. This means that it is both expensive and full of rich people who spend their summers sailing around various islands in New England and eating lobster. The Blatchley sisters, who spend their summers watching British television from the 1980s and eating microwave popcorn, have never been a smooth cultural fit. Were it not for our being the daughters of Buck Blatchley, I doubt we'd have even been admitted. (Well, Ginny, maybe, but only because she is actually a genius. I might have been able to skate in on my large vocabulary, but I'm almost certain it was just that they didn't want to split up a pair of siblings.) And were it not for the life-insurance policy of Buck Blatchley, we would not have been able to stay enrolled.

Ostensibly, the Senior Tea is a chance to get to know the twelfth-grade faculty, socialize with the other seniors, and kick off the year that would serve as crowning glory of your TGS career. In reality, as Ginny was making abundantly clear on the drive over, it was a viciously competitive session of passive-aggressive one-upmanship, but with cucumber sandwiches. Project utter calm and confidence that you'd be cruising into an early slot at Princeton, and your classmates were likely to crack from the pressure, leaving one fewer competitor in the arena. Screw things up, and—

"I am going to fail, die, and end up at Anthracite Swineherd Academy and Secretarial School," Ginny moaned to the car window. "In that order."

"Don't be classist, Ginny," Mom said. "I worked as a secretary when your father was in grad school."

"Also, anthracite is coal," I said, having studied this in ninth-grade earth sciences last year. "Why do you need pigs *and* coal?"

"I don't know," Ginny said miserably. "For barbecues or something. It doesn't matter." She pressed a hand to her temple like she was getting faint, which, although the air-conditioning was broken, was patently ridiculous.

"You'd better improve that delicate constitution if you're going to become a coal miner," Mom said.

"Or a pig farmer," I said.

Ginny tried to stay pained-looking, but her lips started to twitch between a smile and a fake frown. "This is all a joke to you, isn't it?"

"You started it," I pointed out. "Unless you're serious about animal husbandry. You already have practice from the chickens."

"You would know, *Laurie*," Ginny said, glaring at my skirt. "Excited for the box social?"

As it turned out, I did own a skirt: red with little yellow flowers and with a ruffle around the bottom hem. You see, every year, TGS forces the ninth grade to participate in a production of musical theater. *Oklahoma!* is a musical about farming and cowboys and other things that no ninth grader has cared about since Manifest Destiny. (It is also—ridiculously—spelled with the exclamation point at the end; I looked it up.) I tried to get out of it by offering to paint the scenery, but then I got stuck with double duty: stagecrafting *and* singing the soprano harmony to the title number.

"Everyone is going to know it's from *Oklahoma!*" I said.

"The only thing anyone remembers about *Oklahoma!*," Ginny said, "is that Tommy Wills-Wyatt came onstage with a boner on opening night."

This is true, both that it happened and that that's all anyone remembered. You just don't forget the image of a fourteen-year-old kid with chaps, spurs, and a raging erection.

"I think the skirt looks darling," Ginny said, and reached around to pat my hair from the front seat. "And your hair looks fantastic."

"Just as long as I'm not *embarrassing* you," I said. "Or screwing up your chances at college."

"Please, Plummy. I've already done plenty of that myself."

"You get straight As!" I said.

20

Ginny acted like she didn't hear me.

After five minutes of big houses and bigger lawns, the Blatchleys pulled up to the headmaster's house. Mom made a beeline for the group of parents underneath a plastic tent, where they seemed to have bottles of wine. Ginny made a beeline for her friends. I, having nowhere else to go or hide, trailed behind her to where her fellow High-Strung Smart Girls were circled.

TGS is not a particularly cliquey school. It's hard to develop sufficiently defined subcultures when a graduating class is only eighty people; there is too much bleed-over. Regardless, subfactions occur. Ginny had long been a member of the High-Strung Smart Girls group, which included Charlotte Forsythe, Lily Sweet, Lily Gordon, Ava Kestenbaum, and Julia St. John. All of them had straight-A averages and wore cardigans and ate yogurt together in the alcove under the stairs in the math building.

Behind the HSSGs there was a little garden wall, and, after making sure the coast was clear, I sat down and took out *Jane Eyre*. It was a bargain copy with tightly cramped text, and the pages were thick with Ginny's underlines and highlights and sloppy margin notes, which left little room for me to say anything of my own. So instead of noting, I simply read, and imagined I was on a moor. The headmaster's backyard was very beautiful, though un-moor-like, and extremely suitable for reading. From my place on the small patio, I could see a huge, sloping green lawn with white wrought-iron chairs sprinkled here and there and even a gazebo past a swell of grass. Gizmo and Doug would've gone crazy for it. And with any luck, I would blend right in and no one would notice me.

But apparently I didn't have any luck, because I had barely been reading for fifteen minutes when someone found me.

"Excuse me? Are you lost?"

A mom had discovered me, and, since I could not come up with a valid reason not to be wearing my name tag, led me to a little table stacked with sticky white squares and watched while I filled one out. Then the mom asked me why didn't I join the party and serve some snacks with the other younger sibs. (That is what she called us—*sibs*—which sounds like the acronym for a disease.)

I gave her a look that said, *Because I am very shy and wearing a skirt from* Oklahoma! It did not work. The mom outfitted me with a tray of smoked salmon sandwiches and instructed me to go forth.

My heart sank. I could literally feel it sitting in my stomach. I decided the quickest way to unload as many sandwiches as possible would be the adults, since Ginny and her white-dressed friends were probably not eating much, and so I headed to the parent tent, where the conversation was exactly the sort of things you would imagine hearing from parents of seniors at an expensive private school: beautiful time of year, summer never long enough, Long Beach Island, the Hamptons, the Poconos, the Shore, get together, so fun, visiting a few, not sure, can't believe, grew up so fast, early decision, early action, tutors, counselors, subject tests, not worried, excited, don't know yet, hoping, grades, points, sports teams, applications, working hard, push through, scholarships, football, cross-country, New Haven, Cambridge, Ithaca, didn't your father, know him from work, we'll see we'll see we'll see, laugh laugh laugh.

Awash in grown-up talk, I finally threaded my way to Mom, who was listening to another mom talk about how busy she was.

"It's just so much work, volunteering," the other mom was saying. She gave a quick glance at my plate of sandwiches, which I offered and tried to telepathically command her to eat as many as possible.

"We're trying something so much more *ambitious* at Art-Song this season, but our fund-raising coordinator has been out on 'indefinite maternity leave,' even though that child has to be at least *five* . . ."

"Mm," Mom said.

". . . but it's good to *work*, I think," the other mom finished. "Don't you?"

"Oh, absolutely," Mom said. "At least until we find that room full of money."

The other mom must have noticed that I wasn't smiling, because she smiled very aggressively at me.

"Everything okay"—she glanced at my name tag—"Plum?"

"It's short for Patience," I explained. "Sort of."

"Plum," Mom said. "You remember Tommy's mom."

"Pamela," said Pamela. "Pamela Wills."

"How do you do?" I said.

"Your family is so *artsy*," Pamela said. "I love it. You did those little mouse books, right? The—oh, gosh, what are they called? I used to read them all the time—"

"Five Little Field Mice."

I knew exactly how the rest of this conversation was going to go. I'd heard it dozens, if not hundreds, of times before: No, Mom did not write them. No, she hasn't met the author. Yes, her kids loved them, too. (We did.) Yes, it was fun. No, she hasn't done any other books. They're selling fine, thank you very much. (That was none of anyone's business, but yes, the Field Mice were a perennial favorite of families and continued to make a respectable royalty year after year.)

"You know, I used to paint, myself," Pamela said, chomping so hard her earrings swung. "Watercolors, mostly. So freeing. So delightful." She hummed a little to herself and chomped some more. "Are you working on another book?"

"I teach," Mom said. "At Ferrars College of Art."

Mom did not enjoy teaching. All her beginning art students paid $40,000 a year to paint the exact same things and experiment with hallucinogens. Yet another reason Ginny and I were duty-bound to find practical careers.

Pamela Wills, not listening at all, took another sandwich. "Your mother was just saying that your sister's hoping to major in some kind of science," Pamela said, earrings wobbling. "Are you interested in that, too, Plum?"

"No," I said. "I can't think analytically."

Pamela gave me a knowing smile. "I find that hard to believe."

But she *didn't* know me, and so the knowing smile threw me off. I must have looked stymied, because Pamela elaborated.

"You don't have to be modest," she went on. "I've read what your father wrote. Everyone has. It was just *lovely.*"

I suppose context is necessary. Richard "Buck" Blatchley wrote short stories, a form of creative writing that pays more than poetry but less than novels, and earns you the respect of fellow creative writers and very few others. He published them in good places: the *Atlantic,* the *New Yorker,* and once—and I still find this incredibly embarrassing, even though he is dead and nobody reads magazines anymore— *Playboy.*

But he wrote personal essays, too, and his most famous, "A Treatise on the Astrolabe," was a meditation on the relationship between artists and their children (the title being borrowed from a poem written by Geoffrey Chaucer, Father of the English language, and also a son in need of an astronomical education). In it, he marvels at his two-year-old daughter, "a tiny genius, toddling forward, somehow sprung not from a crack in some immortal's skull but from the loins of a schmuck like me."

That two-year-old daughter was Virginia Eleanor Blatchley. "That's not me," I said shortly. "My sister."

Pamela smiled at me like I was Gizmo dancing on his hind legs for a glob of spreadable meat. "Huh," she said. "I guess it's been a while since I read it."

This woman probably *never* read. Or she only ever read at her Nantucket house. She probably kept a basket of paperbacks with titles like *The Candlemaker's Wife* by the sunscreen.

"I would think so," I said. Mom looked daggers at me.

Pamela was unfazed. "Well, I'm sure you'd rather be a writer anyway. You have the genes."

That was the *thing*, though. Everyone *expected* me to be a writer, and the more they expected it, the less I wanted to do it. It's not that I had any other skills—actually, I had almost *no* skills whatsoever, beyond French-braiding and Kit Marlowe–whispering. But when your father is someone talented but dead, your *own* skill is beside the point anyway. And Ginny was the one with the documented genius.

As if she were reading my mind, Pamela Wills beamed brighter. "I mean, just think about it. You'll have your career cut out for you. I'd think publishers would be falling all over themselves to publish something by Buck Blatchley's *daughter*."

I would like to say that what happened next was an accident.

But—in the interest of total transparency—that is not exactly the truth.

"Ah!"

Pamela Wills winced and rubbed her toe, her earrings swinging frantically.

"Oh," I said, face absolutely calm. "Was that your foot? I'm so—"

"*Plum*," Mom interrupted. "Why don't you get more food?"

There were still five sandwiches on my plate.

"Or give them to your sister," Mom said quickly. "You know how much Ginny loves salmon."

At first I didn't move (we Blatchleys have just never been big fish eaters, or particularly good liars), but then Mom gave me a little shove between the shoulder blades in the general direction of Ginny.

"*I'll* have another one," Pamela Wills said, but it was too late. I was hustling my way out of there, tray in hand.

Ginny was sitting at a little table with a bunch of High-Strung Smart Girls. I thrust the tray at her.

"Here," I said. "Can you just eat all these?"

"Ew, what? Are those salmon?"

"It doesn't matter," I said. "Just take them. It's a sandwich-related emergency."

Skeptically, Ginny unloaded the remaining five scraps of bread onto a napkin, and I thanked her and walked away very fast, past the High-Strung Smart Girls at their table, past the stretch of lawn where the Sporty Senior Boys were playing a game of pickup football, and around the corner of the head-master's house, to where the rest of the snacks were lying in wait.

And I sat down.

And I clenched my fists a little.

And as if things could not get worse than almost severing the toes of a very important mom at your sister's Senior Tea, I was then interrupted in my almost-meltdown by a triumvirate of my least favorite TGS subfaction: the Loud Sophomore Boys.

As the name might imply, the LSBs were all gross for various gross-boy reasons, and these three were some of the grossest. Tommy Wills-Wyatt: aforementioned boner inci-dent. Stevie Vandenberg: squat pug-like nose and eyes that didn't quite go in the same direction, liked to grab girls' butts in the hallway. Tate Kurokawa: rumored to have gotten oral sex in the auditorium in seventh grade, very loud laugh. All of them: stole my notebook in fourth grade, read it aloud, humiliated me.

The three of them banged out of the kitchen door, snort-ing and punching each other and generally acting self-satisfied the way only fifteen-year-old boys in full Brooks Brothers can. I thought that if I stayed still, maybe they would not notice me and proceed to whatever Loud Sophomore Boys things they had planned. But, as had already been established, an *Oklahoma!* skirt did not make for good camouflage.

"Hey," said Tommy Wills-Wyatt. He was a mopey six and a half feet tall, and even when he wasn't wearing cowboy pants, he walked sort of bowlegged.

"You all right, Peach?" Tate Kurokawa grinned at me. He was wearing a blazer and a shirt with the top button undone, and his hair was the color of bister, which is a pigment made from burnt beechwood that's a kind of brownish-grayish-black and comes in conté crayons. Mom keeps a box of them in her studio.

"Plum," I said.

Stevie Vandenberg snickered, probably because his brain was incapable of beading together two coherent words. "What?"

"Plum," I said again, and indicated my name tag. "My name is Plum. Not Peach." Of course, my name is actually Patience. But that was not what I had written on my name tag.

Stevie Vandenberg grabbed two sandwiches from a tray and crammed them in his mouth. I narrowed my eyes in intense disgust. Tate Kurokawa just snapped his fingers.

"Ugh. So close. Knew it was a fruit that starts with *P*."

He also took a sandwich from the tray, which Stevie Vandenberg had now endeavored to offer to him.

"These are pretty good," Tate said.

"Gimme," said Tommy W-W.

"Hey!" I felt suddenly very protective of the sandwich trays. "Those aren't for you."

The three of them looked at one another. Stevie snorted. Tommy licked his teeth. Tate ate another sandwich.

"Relax, Peach," he said. "We're here on official business."

"Wur ferving fuff." Stevie was talking with his mouth full, which did not stop him from cramming in another one. I did some quick sibling calculus—Stevie had an older brother, and there was some Wills-Wyatt girl in Ginny's history class—which must have shown on my face, because Tate Kurokawa nodded across the garden, at a long-limbed curly-haired boy in a salmon-colored polo shirt.

"I'm with him."

"Benji Feingold," I said, "is not your brother."

Tate blinked. "You got me. I'm here voluntarily. I just heard there were sandwiches." He tipped the plate toward me. "Want one?"

I shook my head.

"They're good," said Stevie. Tommy W-W was probing a tray of little toast slices.

"It's liver," I said. Tommy retracted his finger.

"Nah, man," Tate was saying. "This is nothing. The library gives out cannoli at their fund-raiser thingies."

"Yeah?"

"Yeah. And the Historical Architecture Society has caviar."

Because there was nothing for me to add, I took out my

book, which is what I do when I don't know what to say. I retrieved my bookmark, a Christmas-card picture of Gizmo and Doug, from the interior of *Jane Eyre* and set it on the table.

"Hey, that's right," Tate said, right in my ear. He had onion breath. "You guys have the dogs. Two black curly ones, right? Portuguese water dogs?"

Everyone thinks that Gizmo and Doug are Portuguese water dogs, I guess because they don't know that standard poodles don't *have* to get that froofy haircut. Also, the froofy haircut was designed so that the poodles could keep their joints warm in the water when they splashed in to retrieve game. It's actually quite practical.

"Poodles," I said, and explained about the haircuts—warm joints, retrieving game, practical.

"Huh," Tate said. "I never knew that."

Stevie burped.

"I have to go now," I said.

I found Ginny on a folding chair back by the punch bowl, tapping at her phone, with Charlotte craning her neck to stare at the screen. Most of the other High-Strung Smart Girls had dissipated to make conversation with the headmaster or one of the parents. Seeing an empty chair and no parent to rope me back into service, I sat.

"How's the tea?" I asked.

Ginny made a vague *eh* sound.

"It's intense," Charlotte said for her. Charlotte Forsythe does not particularly like me. She told me once that I was too judgmental just because I did not want mushrooms on my pizza and she did. I didn't think this was a reflection of her poor upbringing or anything; I just think mushrooms are gross. But Charlotte also always looked like something smelled bad under her nose, so what did she know? "Ginny's been sucking up to Dr. Maldonado."

"I have not," Ginny said.

"The physics teacher?" I said. "Why?"

Charlotte and Ginny exchanged a look—or, rather, Charlotte gave Ginny a look and Ginny huffed.

"Fine, fine, so I want a good letter of recommendation. Is that so shameful?"

"It's going to be very competitive to try for the science programs," Charlotte said matter-of-factly. "Especially if you haven't taken advanced math."

Ginny twisted the ends of her hair, staring at her phone again. Her poufy bridesmaid dress was sagging a little.

"I'm just saying," Charlotte said. Charlotte "just says" a lot of things; she is one of those people who corrects you if you complain about chemicals in food, because all organic compounds *are* chemicals, as if everyone wouldn't get what you meant anyway. The strap of her sundress, which was a dazzling white eyelet material, slid precariously down one shoulder.

"Your boobs are showing, Char," Ginny said. To be fair, Charlotte's boobs were rarely *not* showing.

Charlotte crossed her arms. "You know I'm right, though."

I was skeptical. "Is she?" I said. "Are you?"

"I'm her best friend," Charlotte said, tipping her head onto Ginny's shoulder. "I'm just being pragmatic."

Ginny closed her eyes for two full seconds, then nudged Charlotte's head off her shoulder and whipped her phone into my face.

"Check it out, Plummy. We all snuck inside to take pictures in the bathtub." She flicked through a few on her phone: Ginny, the Lilys, Charlotte, Ava, and Julia giggling and making duck faces in a huge white bathroom. And at that moment I was struck with a memory, of the day after Ginny's eighth birthday, when our father could not let go of the fact that there had been two Lilys at her party. "It's positively funereal!" he had said. And I remember that was the day I learned the word *funereal,* not that that's even impressive. Anyone can have a big vocabulary; it's just a matter of memorization. But what Buck Blatchley could do was use the right word at the perfect time, so unexpected that a single phrase would knock you off your feet.

That's genius. You're born with it or you're not.

I finished examining the picture. "That bathroom is *huge.*"

"I know! And the toilet actually flushes without a weird pull chain you have to hold on to for fifteen seconds." Ginny

33

pretended to swoon. "How was serving sandwiches?"

"I almost cut off Pamela Wills's foot."

"Oh my God." Charlotte gasped.

Ginny grinned. "On purpose?"

"Well . . ." I squirmed. "She . . . insulted me."

Charlotte made a little *hmm* sound. "Insulted you? How?"

"She just *did*," I said. I didn't want to discuss it, and I certainly didn't want to discuss it with Charlotte.

"And then you stomped on her," said Ginny.

"I didn't say that!"

"But you did."

"Whatever," I conceded. "Can we leave yet?"

"Sure." Ginny sighed. "I'm too hopeless to go on."

"I thought you said we could go to Wawa after," Charlotte whined.

Ginny looked genuinely torn.

"You guys go for lunch all the time," I said. All the HSSGs had had high-enough grades to get advance senior off-campus privilege at the end of last year.

"Yeah," Ginny said. "And I really want to change."

Charlotte raised her eyebrows and took out her phone. "I bet."

Ginny gave Charlotte's shoulder a smack, and Charlotte cracked a smile, and they air-kissed.

"Where's Mom?" Ginny stood up. "Maybe I can bum a smoke for the ride."

I nodded back at the tent, where Pamela Wills seemed to be foisting a business card on Mom. "She isn't smoking."

"Not at the moment, no." Ginny brushed the front of her skirt. I got up, too, but realized with a sinking feeling that something was missing.

"One second," I said. "I left my book with the sandwiches."

When I went back around the house, Tate Kurokawa was sitting at the table, reading *Jane Eyre*. My *Jane Eyre*. Well, technically Ginny's *Jane Eyre*, but almost everything that I claimed as mine had been hers first.

Naturally, I was horrified. I tried to rush over and snatch it away, but I rounded the table a little too quickly, and the stupid hem of my stupid skirt caught on the stupid wrought-iron table, and I fell. Stupidly.

"Nice outfit, Peach," came Tate's voice from somewhere above. "It's pretty O-K."

He leaned down and flashed me the *okay* with his thumb and forefinger. I lay on the headmaster's impeccably groomed grass and wished for death.

"Hey!"

My eyes flew open to reveal Ginny, hands on hips, bridesmaid skirt poufing everywhere. "Is that your book?"

I shook my head. "Don't worry. I can get another one."

Ginny looked aghast. "But that one is special!" She helped me to my feet and wheeled on Tate. "Excuse me. That is *not* yours. Try CliffsNotes if you're stumped. They use small words."

Tate said sorry and backhand-threw *Jane Eyre* at me like it was a Frisbee. Miraculously, I caught it, and Ginny looped her arm through mine with a *hmph* and marched me right out of the garden, declaring Tate an asshole in a not-at-all-quiet voice and giving my *Oklahoma!*-skirted butt a smack.

The fact is, at that moment, I would have actually preferred to spend ten more dollars and several more hours repurchasing and reannotating my own copy than ever have to speak to a Loud Sophomore Boy. But Ginny had her reasons for making sure I kept that copy. Then again, since she was the reason I was at the Senior Tea in the first place, she had also been the reason I'd almost lost it.

Then again, again, really nothing in my life would've happened the way it did without Ginny there. That was just what it meant to be a sister.

A nd yet here I have spent so much time on myself when the *real* thread of the story leads to the Senior Tea's aftermath and the mystery of the cigarette butt.

Nothing else truly remarkable happened the day of the Senior Tea. Or nothing that *seemed* remarkable, especially after the high drama of the Tea itself. When we got home, we were all hot, cranky, and hungry, because no one had eaten enough toast points, so we microwaved popcorn, went to the couch, argued over seating arrangements, argued over the remote, and then fell into a stupid argument over the best film adaptation of a Jane Austen novel. (I like *Sense and Sensibility*; Ginny thought Hugh Grant was miscast. Mom liked the 1980s direct-to-VHS *Pride and Prejudice*—not the Colin Firth one; it's an older one no one else remembers—and Ginny likes the Keira Knightley remake.)

This wasn't an unusual argument; it was equal parts pointless, pretentious, and heated, like many discussions we have.

"The Keira Knightley one has the best soundtrack," Ginny declared.

"We know," I said. "You're always blasting it in your room."

Ginny, when she was in a fit of pique, played classical music and lay on the floor of her bedroom. She was often in fits of pique these days.

"Yeah, well, the eighties whatever version is better," Mom said. "It's more loyal to the books."

"That doesn't actually make it better. It just makes it interminably long," Ginny said. "And it has the cinematography of an episode of *Antiques Roadshow*. And no one has ever heard of it except you."

"And," I put in, "I don't like Mrs. Bennet."

Mom had sunk far back into the couch, with a wounded look. She was staring at the coffee table.

That is one other thing I know about my father. He was a woodworker, constantly scavenging for scraps, bolting and crosscutting things, or so I dimly recall. The coffee table had been a gift for their first Valentine's Day, and Mom always said that was the moment she knew she wanted to marry him, because there are not many men who will spend hours sanding and varnishing a piece of ambrosia maple for you. According to legend, he had been so excited to give it to her that he accidentally put on a leg upside down. And Mom always said she didn't care, because nothing was perfect, but Dad always said he was going to fix it. I don't know if any of that's true, but the leg *is* on upside down.

"Yeah," Ginny said. "There's no way we're sitting through that one."

"Let's just watch something else," I said.

"I know, I always have terrible taste." Mom set her glass down with a loud *clunk*. "I'm a thousand years old and just a mom. So just . . . put on whatever you want. Don't listen to me. I'm letting the dogs out."

"The dogs already went out," I whispered, but the stairs were already creaking.

I stared at the coffee table, at its still-upside-down leg. Ginny flopped her whole tall body on the length of the couch, so that her gross feet were in my lap.

"Get off." I shoved her away, but she just put her feet right back.

"Make me."

I gave up, and instead got up to follow the disappearing sound of creaks. Outside, in the hallway, the glass doors at the end of the landing were still closed. Of course they were. Mom didn't go in the study. Although, on reflection, it's not really accurate to call it *the* study, since that implies communal use. It was—it is? It had been?—our father's. None of us went in, and none of us ever would. No matter how much storage space we ran out of, no matter whether the rest of the house literally caught on fire. Even Gizmo and Doug somehow knew not to trespass.

"I'm putting on *Amadeus* in T minus ten seconds!" Ginny

yelled from the couch. "Plum! What are you doing?!"

"Nothing." I padded back in and settled on the couch. Mozart gushed dramatically from the speakers.

"This is going to be good." Ginny wiggled herself to a straighter seat and adjusted the bowl of popcorn in her lap.

I gave her a look that said, *It's always good, because we watch it maybe once a month.* Ginny frowned.

"Are you okay?"

"I don't know," I answered truthfully.

Ginny nodded. "I know. What did I tell you?" She chomped her popcorn with authority. "Something *weird* is going on."

Salieri screamed.

So, all told, the events of Saturday, September 3, had the following repercussions:

1. Because I had embarrassed the family name by crushing Pamela Wills's toes, Mom had been unable to refuse Pamela's invitation for a coffee date—perhaps subconsciously realizing that it would be a chance to convince her that not all Blatchleys are homicidal and/ or clumsy.

2. Because I had embarrassed *myself* in front of a Loud Sophomore Boy, I vowed I wasn't going to speak to any of them again. (Which, honestly, I did not think would be that difficult.)

3. Because Ginny had spent too much time with the other HSSGs, and perhaps because she had been wearing an inferior party dress, her high-strungedness about college admissions had skyrocketed to near-incapacitating heights.

"Drill me again," Ginny said. This was approximately 5:47

p.m. the Tuesday after watching *Amadeus*, and we were both hanging out in her room. She was trying to memorize a poem by Victor Hugo for French class while folded into the pink armchair with the squeaky springs, and I was flopped on her bed, shimmying my new rings up and down my fingers in a very satisfying way.

"It doesn't count as drilling if I don't understand what I'm reading." I pushed the smallest ring to the tip of my finger, then spun it back down again.

"Well, then just prompt me when I mess up." Ginny closed her eyes and rose from the chair to pace. Ginny was very good at pacing, like she was a movie villainess during an interrogation, but unfortunately her room, in the tower of 5142 Haven Lane, is about six paces across—maybe less, because her legs are so long—so she didn't have very far to go. Also, the tower room gets very poor air circulation, and it was an unusually hot evening for the end of September, so we were both sweating.

"*'Demain, dès l'aube, a l'heure où blanchit'*— Ow!"

I looked up from my sketchbook to see Ginny rubbing her shin next to her armoire. "Damn. Shit. Ow."

"That is definitely not French," I said.

"*Très drôle.*" Ginny straightened and shook out her hands, and wiped off her forehead. "I'm dying in here." She peeled her T-shirt over her head, leaving her in a crisscrossing sort of sports bra that had certainly never seen any athletic activity,

42

and flung herself onto her bed, jogging my elbow in the process. The topmost ring went flying to the carpet.

"Damn it, Ginny!" I rolled onto my stomach to retrieve it.

"I'm going to fail."

I sighed and pushed the ring back on. "No, you're not."

"I am. I'm going to fail French and never go to college and die alone in a cardboard box."

"Shut up, Gin."

"I don't even know how to *do* anything else. We have terrible genes, Plum. Neither of our parents gave us any practical skills."

"Dad could make furniture," I reminded her.

"Oh, *well.* Then *that's* what I'll do." She made an *arghhhh* sound and started to gnaw on a cuticle, which was so gross I had to roll my eyes.

"Ginny. Stop. You're being ridiculous. You've never failed a French assignment *in your life*, and even if you don't go to college, you're not going to die alone because you'll at least have me and Mom."

She *was* being ridiculous. Even for someone as high-strung as Ginny, this was unprecedentedly annoying behavior, and I found myself equal parts exasperated and mystified.

Ginny stopped gnawing and opened one eye.

"And the dogs," she added.

"And the dogs." From the floor, Doug thumped his tail against the floorboards in solidarity. "And Charlotte," I added, because it seemed rude to leave out her best friend.

"Yeah."

"How's the University of Pennsylvania?" I asked. "Do they even *care* if you know French?"

Instead of answering, Ginny curled up into a ball, which made the bumps of her spine stick out between her petal-pink bra straps. For a minute I thought she was going to cry, but then I heard her making fake snoring noises.

"Gin—"

"Asleep. Don't bug me."

"You're not asleep!"

Eyes still closed, she stuck out her tongue, and then smacked me right in the stomach, which hurt.

"Ow!" I rolled away.

"Can't . . . help . . . myself," Ginny mumbled. "Too . . . asleep."

"You are *not* asleep," I said. "You're just being *crazy*."

That made Ginny wake up. And hit me.

"Ow!" I rubbed my elbow.

"I'm *not* crazy." Ginny pushed her sweaty hair out of her eyes. *Now* she looked like she was going to cry. "I'm *not*."

"Okay," I said. "Okay. You're not. You're fine."

Except of course she was not fine. My sister had never been fine a day in her life, and now she was setting herself up for four more years' rigorous study in a field that I knew she did not actually care about. She had burned up countless hours perseverating over what would happen if she *didn't* get in to the University of Pennsylvania, but I wondered if she'd given more than a few minutes' consideration to what would happen if she *did*.

Ginny squeezed her eyes shut again and rolled onto her back. *"'Demain, dès l'aube, a l'heure où blanchit la campagne, je partirai. Vois-tu, je sais que tu m'attends.'"*

Outside, the Volvo door slammed, which made the dogs jump to life and start barking, which made Ginny say her French poem even louder, which made me kick her, which made her leap to her feet.

"'J'irai par la fôret!'" Ginny yelled back. *"'J'irai par la montagne! Je ne puis* something something *de toi plus longtemps!'"*

There was a moment of silence, or a moment where the only sound was poodles barking, which was the closest our house ever got to silence, and then the *trit-trit-trit* sound of dog toenails on the stairs. It was Gizmo, with a paper towel tucked into his collar, which I untucked gently.

Sandwiches here, it read. *Come on downstairs.*

"Gin," I said, interrupting her babbling. "Dinner."

"What?"

"Gizmo-gram." I waved the paper towel. In a house as big as 5142 Haven Lane, shouting does not usually travel far enough to get anyone's attention; therefore, we devised the Gizmo-gram system of sending each other notes on paper towels tucked into the dog's collar. It works almost all the time, unless Gizmo decides he'd rather take a nap.

We went downstairs to the kitchen, where Ginny promptly plunked an elbow on each of my shoulders.

"Who ordered ham-and-cheese?" Mom held aloft a foil-wrapped tube of sandwich.

"Me." I swung out from under Ginny's grasp and took my sandwich, and also took the roast beef and Swiss that was Ginny's and put them both onto the plates with the dandelion designs. Ginny, however, ignored the sandwich when I offered it to her.

"Hi," she said, waving at the screen door. I turned to see Almost-Doctor Andrews holding a big cardboard box.

"Oh," Mom said, her hands streaked with mayonnaise. "Plum, would you—"

But I was already at the door.

"Thanks, Plum," Almost-Doctor Andrews said. He set the package on the countertop and took a seat at the counter. "How's school going? Back with all your friends?"

"It's fine," I said. There was not that much to say about school and even less to say about friends. I did not really *have* friends, except for the Weird Sweatshirt Kids who spent lunch period in the school bookstore playing games that involved notebooks and dice and tolerated my presence. Jeremy Beard, a fellow sophomore the size of a Yorkshire terrier and ardent evangelist for Dungeons and Dragons, had made strong overtures toward me joining a quote-unquote campaign with them, but I simply did not have any interest in Dungeons and

Dragons, nor in Jeremy, who—and please never tell him I said this—smelled like an everything bagel, and not in a good way.

Also, the Gregory School is one of those places where being squarely average brings dishonor on your family name. Especially when your family name is Blatchley and all the teachers say, "Oh, I had your sister two years ago! She was brilliant," and you accidentally forget to turn in your problem set because, to be honest, math is boring. I *was* taking honors English—hence the *Jane Eyre*—but since the Gregory School is also one of those places where an indignant phone call from a parent is just as good as a high academic record, I did not count my class placement as an actual coup.

"It is not fine." Ginny threw herself across the counter, arms splayed. "I am going to die."

"Ginny," Mom said, yanking a paper towel from the flamingo-shaped holder.

"I am never going to make it," Ginny said into the fake Formica. "I am going to be rejected from everywhere and end up alone. I'm going to be the college equivalent of a spinster."

Almost-Doctor Andrews was politely unfazed. I hoped his rent was cheap enough to offset the insanity of his landlord's daughter.

"Did the electricity in the carriage house go out again?" I asked. Mom looked alarmed.

Almost-Doctor Andrews shook his head. "Not yet," he said, and knocked on the wood of his stool. "I just came by because UPS dropped this off at my door by mistake."

"Ooh," Ginny said, and jumped up from the counter, her incipient failure forgotten. "What is it?"

"Opening someone else's mail is a felony," I said, scooping up Kit Marlowe, who had been threading himself through my ankles.

Almost-Doctor Andrews frowned. "I don't think— Well, I didn't open it, anyway." He studied the label. "It's from Halcyon-Haupt Publishing."

Ginny yanked a giant knife from the wooden block, stabbed into the packing tape, and ripped apart the top leaves of the box. Inside were three neat stacks of rectangular hardcovers with the familiar fuzzy faces and our mother's name in block letters, a bunch of brown paper for padding, and a note.

Mom dived forward for the envelope, attempting to hold it out of sight while swallowing a gigantic bite of her hoagie, but Ginny pounced.

"Let me see!"

A brief struggle ensued, with Ginny scrambling for the letter, Gizmo nipping and yapping, and me trying not to drop any sandwich innards onto the ground.

"Virginia," Mom said sternly—or as sternly as she could through a mouthful of salami and hot peppers—"give that back."

But Ginny was already scanning down what seemed to be a tri-folded piece of very official stationery. Her face was very, very pale.

"'Dear Iris Blatchley,'" she read. "'Per our letter of September 1, we have enclosed as a courtesy a collection of FIVE LITTLE FIELD MICE titles from our warehouse. As a reminder, these editions of FIVE LITTLE FIELD MICE will be out of print effective October 1. The final royalty statement will arrive by December 31, and no further royalty payments will be issued beyond that date. Per your contract, the rights to the artwork shall be retained in perpetuity by Halcyon-Haupt. Any questions may be directed to our rights department' at blah blah blah. Sincerely, blah blah blah.'"

"Cripes," I said.

"Oh," said Almost-Doctor Andrews.

Ginny threw the letter down. "What does this mean? What *letter of September 1?*"

Mom stared down at her sandwich.

"Mother!"

"Okay!" Mom snapped up. "They're redoing the books. For the twenty-fifth anniversary. They're taking all these out of print and getting a new illustrator."

"So they're not going to sell yours at all anymore?" I asked.

Mom shook her head.

"Were you going to *tell* us about this?" Ginny cried. "Does this mean we're broke?"

"I don't *have* to tell you about this, Ginny," Mom snapped. "This is none of your concern."

"I knew it!" Ginny said. "I knew it. Your credit card not

working, and the cigarettes, and . . ."

She trailed off, her knuckles white as she clutched the letter. She looked from the countertop, to her untouched sandwich, to the pile of French homework she'd thrown on the counter. And then she burst into tears.

"Oh, for Christ's sake," Mom said. She put an arm around Ginny's shoulders, which just made Ginny wail louder. Almost-Doctor Andrews quietly fished the letter out of her fingertips and tucked it back into the envelope. I slipped a piece of ham to Gizmo, who had been whining.

"We're broke," Ginny sobbed. "We're b-broke and I'm going to fail my French test and I'm never going to get into school and—"

"Ginny," Mom said. "We're not broke."

"Not yet," I said quietly.

Mom glared at me. "Okay. You want to know what broke is? Try your grandmother putting four kids through college. I wasted thousands of dollars of her money on *art* school, okay? I've been broker than either of you two will *ever* be. And for what? A stack of"—she gestured at the box—"remaindered kids' books about goddamn *mice*."

Ginny had started to breathe very hard and very fast.

"Here." I handed her the bag the sandwiches had come in. Ginny disentangled herself from Mom and put it to her mouth but coughed before she could really breathe into it.

"Blech," she said. "It tastes like hot peppers in there." She sniffed, and crumpled the bag into a ball.

Mom rubbed her temples. "Why don't you just . . . take a bath or something? I don't know. I can't engage with this right now."

Baths are a Blatchley panacea, although I think we get it from the Mortimer side. Mom told us she used to give us baths to stop us from crying, because apparently it was the only thing that worked besides a hefty dose of children's Benadryl, and I have to believe her.

Ginny, for some reason, looked at me. I gave a small shrug. "You might as well?"

She nodded, and left, sniffing. Mom sank onto a stool, and Gizmo burped, and I yanked open one of the little bags of chips but realized I wasn't hungry, not even a little bit.

"I apologize for Ginny's histrionics," Mom said to Almost-Doctor Andrews. "She's just very wound up about school." She put her face in her hands—which, like mine, were covered in rings. Somewhere in there, still, was her engagement ring, and just seeing it gleam under her knuckle made me both hopeful and sad. "She isn't usually like this. Right, Plum?"

"Not really. Well, like this, but not quite this *much*."

"I don't know what to do," Mom said through her hands, and looked up. "I mean, Ginny's always had a flair for the dramatic. But now she's so much more . . . what's the word? *Extra*."

I groaned. "*Mom*. Don't say that."

"I'm sorry," Almost-Doctor Andrews said. "I didn't realize. About, er, any of it."

"It's okay," I said. "It's not your fault."

"It's *my* fault," Mom said. "I'm such an *idiot*. I should've known the money from that book wasn't going to last. It's a *book*, for Christ's sake. But did I decide to go out and learn something, or get a practical job, or take that offer on the house so we could live somewhere we could actually afford? No. Because I'm an idiot."

"You were going to sell the house?" I said.

She ignored me.

Almost-Doctor Andrews nodded at the screen door. "Why don't I bring over some wine?"

Mom looked up. "You don't have to—"

But he was already gone. Mom rubbed her forehead, fished a pack of cigarettes out of her purse, tapped one out, and told me not to tell Ginny.

You see, our house was not simply any house. 5142 Haven Lane was a magnificent heap, possessing the following deficiencies and/or shortcomings: weak forced-air heating that came up through cast-iron grates, a capricious plumbing system that could not handle more than three toilet flushes an hour or showers over ten minutes long, walls that were too thick to let a cell phone signal through but that would crumble when confronted with even a moderate amount of blunt force. The only place you *could* get cell phone service was standing next to the kitchen window. There were no light switches on any walls in any of the rooms, so that entering a room after sunset meant tripping around in the dark until you could locate the pull chain for a lamp. It's so old that when we moved in, the city stuffed our mailbox with pamphlets about how dangerous lead paint is and how you should not let your children eat it because it will stunt their intellect. Our parents had thought that was hilarious, until a chunk of ceiling fell from behind the fan and into my oatmeal one morning. Then they read the pamphlets.

Sometimes I wonder if my problem was simply breathing in too much lead-paint dust. But Ginny had breathed it, too, probably *more* of it, and her intellect was decidedly unstunted.

And all the idiosyncrasies were worth it. Mom got her high ceilings, and our father built the furniture: the dining room table that curved perfectly with the bay window, the bookshelves in the library, the bookshelves in the living room, the bookshelves in Ginny's tower, the bookshelves in my servants' quarters room, the coffee table. And he got his office, so well outfitted and well preserved that we'd never disturb it again.

Needless to say, 5142 Haven Lane was perfect. And if we sold it, I knew I would die.

Lips zipped about the cigarette, I took the rest of my tiny bag of chips, dumped it around Ginny's sandwich on the dandelion plate, and headed for the third-floor bathroom. The third-floor bathroom is the cramped-est of them all, possibly because Ginny never cleans it. Instead of wallpaper, our parents had pasted up old-fashioned biological prints of sea urchins and starfish and kelp, which, instead of making the space feel more open, made it feel like the inside of a very tiny specimen cabinet. Also, the bathtub is so small it's practically circular.

I knocked, and waited until I heard a muffled *come in*, and then I came in.

"Hi," I said. "I brought your sandwich."

"Thanks," burbled Ginny.

She was wedged in the tiny tub, her head underwater and her hair floating around her face like a mermaid's. Ginny did not seem to care if I saw her naked, even though the same was definitely not true of me. The air smelled like the lavender bath soaps we'd gotten in our Christmas baskets from Aunt Linda. Aunt Linda sells baskets on Facebook, so she doesn't limit giving out baskets of stuff to just Easter. We get Christmas baskets, birthday baskets, Valentine's baskets, Fourth of July baskets, you name it. Mom says they must *pay* her in baskets.

I stood there a moment, not sure if I could leave.

"We're going to lose the house," she said. "Like, almost guaranteed."

"What?"

"The royalty payments." Ginny dragged a hand through the water. "You know that Mom doesn't make any money. That was what was keeping us afloat."

"You know, you could try not worrying about everything all the time," I said. "It might help."

Instead of answering, Ginny reached up with her foot and turned on more hot water. I set the sandwich on top of the pedestal sink and was starting to leave when Ginny spoke up again.

"We can't live anywhere else," she said. "We can't leave all this stuff."

She didn't have to say which stuff. The furniture was as built-in as we were. Outside of this place, we looked funny and misshapen, but inside, we were perfect. We didn't fit anywhere else.

"We're *not* going to sell the house," I said. "We'll just . . . have to make some extra money."

"How?"

"Well, maybe Mom can take on some extra classes next semester. And I can . . ."

I didn't know what I could do. I had no skills, except writing, which obviously did not count, and no professional ambitions beyond governessing, if that was still a thing.

"Well, I'll do something," I said.

"What will *I* do?"

I gave her a look that said, *You and I both know you could do literally anything and do not be absurd.*

She floated, thinking, for almost a full minute. "Maybe we could be like those sisters who do all the lip syncs. Surely they have some kind of sponsorship deal."

"I think they're German," I said. "And twins."

"Hmph." Ginny burbled. "Well, *I* could do it."

"You'd be perfect."

"Why?"

"I don't know," I said. "You just would."

"Do you think I'm a show-off? "

"What?" I said. "Why?"

Ginny shrugged, sloshily. "Iunno."

I didn't answer for a minute. I didn't even know *how* to answer.

"Of course not," I said at last. "Who said that?"

Ginny popped a blob of bubbles in her fist.

"'*Triste,*'" she muttered into the bath, "'*et le jour pour moi sera comme la nuit.*'"

"You're crazy," I informed her. This time, it didn't even make her angry. She just closed her eyes.

"I am *relaxing*," she said. "Hand me that sandwich."

I did. Ginny set the plate on the lip of the tub and took a bite of her sandwich. I made a face.

"Whuh?"

"Eating in the bathtub is gross," I said.

Ginny took another bite. "Is not. They do it all the time in *Northanger Abbey*."

"Yeah, but that's different. They thought it was, like, a restorative for the nerves or something."

"Exactly. My nerves need restoring."

Ginny swallowed, and sloshed around some more, for emphasis. I had to laugh.

"Just don't restore your nerves too long, or anything. Your fingers will get all pruney."

"'Kay."

"I hope you feel better."

"Thanks."

I closed the door. Some two hours later, from my place in the TV room, I heard the bathroom door open again, and the distant glug-glug of the tub draining. I remembered I sort of imagined it as a metaphorical as well as literal draining, like the water was taking all Ginny's annoying anxieties and whooshing them away to a water-treatment plant.

As with beginnings, it is hard to know which moments to identify as catalysts of change. But over the course of that week, as Ginny repeated her hours-long-bath ritual night after night, I remember a feeling of duty taking root in me. Until then I had been as unremarkable as a fifteen-year-old girl could be, but now I had an opportunity—an obligation, really—to work hard. It would be character building; it would be essential. It required no brilliance or insight, just derring-do and commitment. And though I knew my mother and my sister would do all they could to keep us afloat, it would be mine alone to undertake.

 *TWO*

I care for myself. The more solitary, the more friendless, the more
unsustained I am, the more I will respect myself.
—Charlotte Brontë, Jane Eyre

And so I began to make a plan.

I did not especially know how to save money, mostly because I have never had any. Ginny had babysat for a while, and over the summer she had worked selling flowers in the farmers market on Main Street. I, having exactly the wrong personality for customer service, and no marketable skills, had mostly stayed home and begged off the occasional twelve dollars for a movie (seventeen if I wanted popcorn). But I had done some googling and read the Amazon previews of books with titles like *The Money-Management Bible*. I could figure this out. I could figure this out and we would never have to leave 5142 Haven Lane unless it was totally voluntary.

I got out of one of my thousands of notebooks and sat at the kitchen counter with a can of La Croix, chewing a pencil. Over at the table, Ginny was flipping index cards and muttering things about asymptotes.

"Can you keep it down?" I said. "I'm trying to save our house."

Instead of getting quieter, Ginny started slamming each card against the table when she'd memorized it.

I didn't even bother saying anything, because it would be counterproductive, and decided to double down on my focus. But before I had gotten out a single idea, Mom came down from the back stairs in her huge drapey dressing gown, yawning theatrically.

"Lord," she said. "I feel like I got hit by a train."

"Mother," I said. "We need to save money."

Mom rubbed under one eye. "I'm aware. Let me have some coffee, Plum."

I grit my teeth. I loved my mother, but where Ginny Blatchley was hyperfocused on the future, Iris Blatchley seemed, on the whole, intentionally unaware that the future was coming at all. This would have to change.

"I've made a preliminary list," I said, as Mom put the moka pot on the stove and snapped a burner. After about two seconds, the smell of gas wafted out into the air.

"Mom!" Ginny yelped.

"Sorry," Mom muttered. "Pilot light must be out again." She pulled a lighter from the pocket of her robe and flicked it under the stove grate.

I took a deep breath. "We could start by making more money."

Mom leaned against the countertop, arms folded. "Plum, I've already committed to my class schedule for the year. And it's an hour drive to campus and back. Unless I can find a job that'll let me work two hours in the morning on Mondays, Wednesdays, and Fridays and three hours in the afternoon on Tuesdays and Thursdays—"

"Okay," I said. "Next. We can have a yard sale."

Mom shook her head vehemently. "No. No yard sales."

"Why not?" I said. "We have a lot of stuff."

"We don't do yard sales," she said. "Not around here."

"Yeah," Ginny said, having forgotten her asymptotes. "We might as well put up a big sign that says *we're broke*."

This was proving to be more difficult than I'd anticipated.

"Well," I said. "We can minimize spending. Cut out some luxuries."

Mom looked around the kitchen as if to say, *What luxuries?*

"I saw a list online." I started writing. "No more vacations. No fancy makeup. No more highlighting our hair—"

"We don't *take* vacations," Ginny said. "Mom already cleans out the Sephora ladies for those little packets. And when was the last time any of us got highlights?"

"That reminds me," Mom said. "Did anyone make an appointment for the dogs' day of beauty?" Poodles need to be washed and groomed regularly because instead of fur that sheds off naturally, they have hair, almost like people. Ginny and I both shrugged.

"I mean, I'd just drop them off this afternoon," Mom said. "But now I have the dread coffee date with Pamela Wills."

"You're already drinking coffee," I pointed out.

"Yes," Mom said. "I need coffee to steel myself for coffee."

"Coffee costs money," Ginny said unhelpfully.

Mom turned to me. "Take it out of my hair highlighting budget."

"Nobody is taking this seriously!" I slammed down my pen, which scared Gizmo. He did look awfully dusty. Doug, still lying with his head down, had those crusty things under his eyes. This gave me an idea.

"Don't bother with the appointment," I said. "I can wash them myself." It would save us, if memory served, two hundred dollars. Poodles are not inexpensive dogs.

"Sure," Mom said. "Thanks, Plum."

"Whatever," Ginny said. "Just don't use my shampoo."

So that afternoon, while Ginny panicked over calculus and Mom went out for her dread coffee date, I ushered Gizmo and Doug into the first-floor bathroom, which, like all the bathrooms, had a claw-foot tub. The real estate listing had apparently described this situation as "for your convenience, a tub on the first floor," which our father could never get over. "There's absolutely *nothing* convenient about it," he said. "It's a perversion of the word!"

Not true, I thought, herding the poodles inward, a ragged towel draped over my arm. It was hard enough to get the dogs to follow you upstairs, let alone hop in a tub. This eliminated at least one step.

When I closed the door, Gizmo started yipping his pathetic *free me* yip, which got Doug all agitated, too, and then Gizmo started clawing at the door, and Doug decided to go for broke and drink out of the toilet. Also, I realized, the lip of the tub was too high for them to climb in. It was, in a word, chaos. But a chaos that would save us money.

I did a deep knee bend to hoist first Gizmo, then Doug, into the tub. I ran the water not too hot, dampened them all over, and scrubbed them with a drugstore-brand shampoo I had found in the medicine cabinet and had to assume was safe for dogs, as there was no contraindication to veterinary use printed on the label. The whole time I felt satisfyingly industrious, even a little prideful, of my savvy in eliminating a needless cost to our family. I had visions of other bootstrapping enterprises I could undertake: knitting scarves, patching jeans, darning socks, whatever that meant. We would be just fine, I knew, as I gave the dogs a thorough rubdown with the towel.

Gizmo yipped. The water was now up to the bottom of his belly.

"All right," I said. "Fine." I went to pull the plug in the tub. But then I realized that I had not plugged the tub. The tub itself was plugged.

I breathed deeply, willing myself to a governess-like state of practical calm, when the water burbled. Gizmo yipped again. Doug had started to drink out of the tub. The water burbled again, menacingly.

"Mom?" I heard Ginny yell from outside the door. *"Mom?"*

There must have been some dog hair covering the drain, but I couldn't get at it with the dogs both crowded in there. So, having no choice, I pulled Gizmo's wet front legs out of the tub, then lifted his rear, covering the smiling cartoon sushi pieces on my T-shirt in water in the process.

The water burbled. Then burped. Then the tub began to moil, like its own little sinister whirlpool. My practical calm began to ebb away. I repeated the process with Doug when my sister called down again.

"Mom!" Ginny yelled. "The toilet *isn't flushing*!"

Some inflections in the narrative can only be crystallized in retrospect. But then, watching the tub burp one final time and the water swoosh away ominously, I felt the shifting of the situation drilling down to my very core. I had made—through no fault of my own—a catastrophic mistake.

An emergency plumber was summoned. The three of us stood in an anxious knot as he descended to the basement, only to see him return ten minutes later with the bottoms of his uniform pants soaking wet.

"You've got standing water down there," he declared. Standing water, we learned, meant water that was not only not in a pipe but also not flowing anywhere. It was, generally speaking, bad. The basement of 5142 Haven Lane was no stranger to standing water, especially during hurricane season, because it was poorly sealed due to window caulk that has not been replaced since before World War I. But as it had not rained in over three weeks, this incidence of standing water was extra bad.

"Has there been any unusual stress to the system lately?" the plumber wanted to know, pulling out a clipboard. "Anything that would be pushing a lot of water down the pipes at once?"

A strained silence, in which no one mentioned Ginny's

nightly two-hour bath with repeated tub refills.

"I'll have to get some special equipment for this," he went on. "When was the last time you had work done?"

Mom couldn't remember. The plumber wrote some things on a clipboard and gave her a carbon copy.

The prognosis was not good. Our outflow valve had been overloaded and broken. We could not use the sinks. We could not use the showers. We definitely could not use the tubs. We could not even flush the toilets, unless we want the contents of said flush to contribute directly to the standing water in the basement.

"How are we supposed to *shower*?" Ginny was furiously incredulous, or incredulously furious, and ignoring her egg salad on wheat. We were eating sandwiches for dinner again, because sandwiches do not require running water to prepare and are almost free if you use eggs from your own hens, and sitting at the kitchen table our father had made out of a giant tree-size slice of wood, so it was not a fully symmetrical circle. Even I, usually famished, had only taken two half-hearted bites. For someone in a chicken-owning family, I do not really like eggs.

"We can't," Mom said. "Unless you can think of a way to shower without water going down the drain."

"What if we put a plastic tub in there?" I offered. "So that it gathers up all the water, and then we'll dump it in the yard."

Ginny bugged her eyes out. "Are you *kidding*, Plum?

That's the stupidest thing I've ever heard."

I put down my sandwich and felt my hair, which had a distinct french-fry quality to it, and thought longingly of my last shower two whole days ago. "It was just an idea."

"Where are we supposed to *pee*?" Ginny demanded.

As if in response, a *honk-honk* bleated outside.

"I figured something out," Mom answered.

Ginny and the dogs and I put down our sandwiches and scrambled to the kitchen window. Outside, a lumbering truck with the words *POTTY QUEEN* on the side was backing its rear end into the driveway of 5142 Haven Lane.

With a look of frozen horror, Ginny turned back to our mother.

"No," she said. "You did not."

Mom threw up her hands. "What did you *want* me to do, Ginny?"

"We could put it in the backyard," I said quickly. "So that you can't see it from the street."

This, of course, was ridiculous, because all the little cabins strapped to the back of the Potty Queen truck were bright green. There was no way *not* to see it.

"You're going to make us pee outside," Ginny said. "In a *porta potty*."

"Gross," I said. "Ginny, don't call it that."

Ginny rolled her eyes. "Cripes, what do you *want* me to call it, Plum? A tiny plastic house of shame?" She said the last

69

part with a *Downton Abbey* accent.

"No! God!" I said. "Just don't use those words." The combination of the words *porta* and *potty* is the most absolutely-disgusting-slash-repugnant phrase in the English language. I suspect it's because it forces adults and almost-adults like myself to say the word *potty*.

"Porta potty," Ginny said in a half snarl. "We're all going to have to pee in a *poooorta pooootty*."

That did it.

"Shut up!" I yelled. "This is all your fault. This never would've happened if you hadn't taken all those stupid baths."

"*My* fault?" she said. "You're the one clogging all the drains with poodle hair."

My face got hot. "I'm just trying to save us *money* so we don't lose our *house*. Because *I* actually think about someone who isn't *myself*."

Ginny goggled, then snapped her mouth shut.

"Well, that's *rude*."

"It's not *rude*," I said. "It's *true*." At that moment, all I wanted to do was rip Ginny's hair right out of her dumb head.

"*Girls*." Mom must have noticed the sororicidal gleam in my eye, because she pushed us apart a little. "Not now. Please."

"But it's her fault!" I cried. "She's the whole reason we have to pee in a . . ." I choked. "A tiny plastic house of shame."

"Hmph." Ginny gave an airy sniff and stepped out of the way before I could smack her. Mom looked like she wanted to kill whichever of us would cause the least screaming. The dogs, sensing something was wrong, retreated to their refuge under the butler's pantry table with a whimper.

I did not want to be next to my sister, and I definitely did not want to be there while they installed the (ugh) porta potty, so while Mom went outside to greet the Potty Queen delivery people, I retrieved the dogs' leashes from where they were draped on the (fake) stuffed polar bear by the back door. The dogs, using the selective hearing that cannot compute the word *sit* at any volume but can hear the jingle of a leash or the tinkle of kibble falling into a dish from three floors and six rooms away, bolted right for me.

"I'm walking the dogs," I announced. No one answered, of course. No one cares where I do or do not go.

The door slammed behind me, and after carefully maneuvering around the Potty Queen truck (which was not easy, considering the dogs thought it needed a thorough smell-inspection), I set off down Haven Lane toward Evergreen.

For late September, it wasn't that hot out, but after about seven steps, my armpits started to feel distinctly gummy. I stopped to scoop my greaseball hair into a bun at the back of my neck, and wondered how difficult it would be to shampoo it with a hose. The dogs ambled along, smelling everything and peeing on most things, but I kept tugging them along

71

because, for once, I had no patience. (I do not always live up to my name.) I wasn't going anywhere particular, but I wanted to go there fast.

Practically every Victorian on our block was a historically designated house and had the same very nice sweeping lawn with azalea bushes and mountain laurel and a driveway made up of little pebbles behind a wrought-iron fence. My favorite route for walking the dogs was a two-block circuit—down Haven to Evergreen, down Evergreen to Carpenter, and down Carpenter to Locust until I hit Haven—that kept me completely under the cover of trees. The sycamore branches that curve out over the streets and sidewalks like big leafy cathedral ceilings are probably the best nonarchitectural feature of the Haven Lane area. But by the time I reached my usual turnaround spot at Evergreen, I did not feel nearly walked-out enough, and the dogs were still sniffing, and I was already pretty sweaty and gross, so what difference would it make if I just kept going? So I went an additional block down Evergreen, and then another, until I was so far off my own usual beaten path that there were no more sycamores above me, just a velvet-blue sky and a few teeny twinkles of stars.

It was at this juncture that Gizmo decided to poop, and I, unlike *some* Blatchley sisters, was not going to impede the natural excretory functions of another living being, so I let the dog do his thing. Except my self-righteousness was short-lived, because I realized that in my rush to leave 5142 Haven Lane

I had not brought a plastic bag with me. Panicked, I tugged on Gizmo's leash, trying to at least get him out of the line of vision of the very nice house we were walking past, but Gizmo understandably did not want to be disturbed, and so there I stood, greasy-haired, clutching Gizmo's leash, and hoping I could abscond under cover of darkness before anyone noticed.

But someone did notice. And called my name.

"Peach?"

Well, not my name. What this person thought my name was. Which, in turn, made me realize who the someone in question was.

I froze. Gizmo continued to poop. On the porch of 6800 Evergreen Avenue, a silhouette in the shape of a Loud Sophomore Boy leaped down the stairs. As he approached, I vowed to remain silent.

"It's Plum," I said. Damn.

Tate Kurokawa smiled, as far as I could tell. (It was dark.)

"I thought that was you," he said.

"You did?"

Tate nodded. He was wearing a T-shirt, which struck me as odd, because I did not think that boys like Tate owned shirts without collars.

"What's up?"

I looked pointedly at the crouching Gizmo.

"Oh," Tate said. "Yeah."

"I usually always have bags," I explained, as briskly as I

could. "I don't do this. I'm very responsible. I think it's really gross when people just let their dogs—"

"Relax." He put up a hand. "I gotcha."

He jogged back up to the porch and returned with an oblong blue bag I recognized as a *New York Times* wrapper, which he held over the fence. I took it without looking him in the eye and didn't move. It wasn't that I was actually going to just leave the poop on Tate's next-to-sidewalk lawn strip; I didn't hate him *that* much. It's just that there was no good way to do the deed: either I turned my back and gave Tate a full view of my butt, or I stayed facing him and let him see me put Gizmo's poop in my bag-covered hand.

Finally, once I realized Tate was not going anywhere, I settled for a three-quarters view, blocking the actual scooping action with my foot as much as I could.

I stood back up.

"Most people say *thank you*," Tate said, "when someone helps them not get dog poop on their hand."

I was glad it was kind of dark, because hearing Tate say *dog poop* made me very embarrassed for some reason.

"I was going to," I said—well, snapped.

Tate waited.

"Thank you," I said—well, mumbled.

"You're welcome," he said, and did not go away. The dogs, before so eager to drag me down the street, now trotted up to smell Tate's knees through the fence. For a moment we all stood there.

"So are you always this pissed off when you walk these guys, or is tonight a special occasion?"

"I'm—always?" I tightened my grip on the leashes. "Are you watching me?"

Tate stopped scratching Gizmo's ear and did a palms up. "No way." He pointed at a second-floor window. "I can just see you sometimes down Evergreen from my room. You have headphones on, usually."

"Oh," I said feebly. And then, embarrassed of my feebleness, I straightened up. "If you must know, my sister broke our plumbing system by taking a stupid long bath and I haven't taken a shower in two days so I'm on a walk to escape my house because if I stayed home I was going to commit sororicide."

"What?" Tate said. "You were going to kill yourself?"

I rolled my eyes. "Not *suicide*. Sororicide. It means killing your sister."

"Oh," Tate said. "I know the feeling. My brother drives me batshit."

Neither of us said anything. Then:

"Can you really not take a shower at your house?" Tate asked.

"The outflow valve is broken."

"What?"

"It's . . ." I shrugged in what I hoped was a noncommittal way, because I had suddenly realized how strange it was to be talking to Tate about showers outside at night while holding a bag of dog poop. "Complicated. I don't know. I have to go."

I attempted to rustle the dogs up from where they'd plunked in front of Tate's legs for ear scratching, but they were not having it.

"Do you need to take a shower?" Tate asked. "You can shower here, if you want."

I blinked.

"It's cool," Tate said. "My parents aren't home. I mean—"

"What?"

"—what I *meant* was, they won't, uh . . ." Tate scratched the back of his head.

"Never mind," he said, just as I said, "Okay."

Immediately, I realized how stupid of a decision this was. But having seen Tate Kurokawa, of all people, act flustered, and clear his throat a lot, and look down at the dogs instead of at my eyes, it didn't *feel* like a bad decision. And a shower sounded really, really good.

"Cool." He grinned. "Come on in, Peach."

Obviously, being flustered did not prevent Tate from being annoying. He opened the gate, and I followed him up to the porch, subtly dumping the bag of poop into a big plastic trash can by the steps. I realized, as I followed, that I didn't have clean clothes, and that I kind of needed a comb for my hair, but it felt too weird to turn around. And then we were in the kitchen.

The house was, of course, really nice. The kitchen was

clean and gleaming and had pots and pans that matched hanging from a little rack above the island. There were two sinks and a six-burner stove and no stuffed polar bears or phrenological heads anywhere, and the curtains all matched.

"There's a bathroom up the back steps," Tate said, and indicated a very steep, very white set of stairs. I did not move, because I was still holding the dogs' leashes.

"Oh. Here." Tate took the leashes from my hand, without even asking. "You can just go on up. Second door on the right. There are clean towels in the closet. Help yourself to whatever."

And so I went on up, and opened the second door on the right, and found the clean towels in the closet. Then I took off all five of Patience Mortimer's costume jewelry rings and put them in a little copper dish next to the sink. Then, after only a moment's hesitation, I took off the rest of my clothes.

I couldn't pretend that taking a shower at Tate's house wasn't weird. But I also couldn't pretend that it wasn't nice, either. The shower had a glass door that glided open like a dream, the water was hot right away, there was a delightful assortment of bath products, and the towels were fluffy, sage green, and floral-smelling.

I pulled my (admittedly still dirty) clothes back on in thirty seconds, but took a long time mopping my hair dry because, well, I have a lot of hair. After piling it in a wet knot on top of my head, I even helped myself to a tiny blob of creamy moisturizer in a genie bottle with a gold knob top. Then I took a very long time studying myself in the mirror, partially because I was nervous to go back downstairs and interact with Tate again, and partially because I was wondering what, exactly, Tate would see when he looked at me. And maybe it was just the flattering shell-shaped recessed lighting on either side of the medicine cabinet, or maybe it was the blob of moisturizer, but I looked decidedly okay. A little glowy, and very clean. Presentable. I folded and hung my towels politely over the towel bar, not leaving them strewn on the tiles like Ginny always does, and slowly made my way downstairs.

It was cool and quiet in the kitchen, with nothing but the hum of appliances and some squeaky cricket chirps out in the yard. A stack of dishes smeared with something red and saucy lay in sink number one, and a big wooden bowl offered oranges in the middle of the island. Tate was nowhere to be found, and more worryingly, neither were the dogs. I stood stuck, not wanting to infiltrate further into the house, since I had only technically been invited into the bathroom. I could yell something, but what? My voice seemed to have died. I could make some kind of noise in the kitchen to alert the absent Tate to my presence, but I'd already come down the stairs without so much as a creak, and there was nothing else I could do to elicit sound—well, nothing else *normal*. I wasn't going to start randomly turning on the taps or clanging together pot lids.

Instead, I decided to hover by the refrigerator (which was

next to the stairs) and casually study the photographs with my ears pricked so that if anyone came in, I'd act like I'd *just* gotten down the stairs and hadn't been hovering at all. After surveying the same three photos over and over again (Tate in sunglasses and a life jacket, hanging over the edge of a boat with a rope in his hand; a pretty woman in a sweater set I recognized from the co-op as Tate's mom; and Tate and an older, curly-haired kid in matching white polos and uncomfortable expressions), I had just started worrying that maybe I should've just put my towels in a hamper or something instead of folding them up when someone came thumping down the stairs.

"Eep," I said, not too intelligently.

"Who are you?"

The person was not Tate, or a parent. It was Benji Feingold, the guy Ginny's age from the Senior Tea. From the little I knew of him at school, Benji was not so much a twelfth-grade model of a Loud Sophomore Boy as he was a Burnout Sports Boy—i.e., he ran track but also did large amounts of drugs—which would explain his outfit of a TGS T-shirt, mesh shorts, white socks, and vague smoky smell.

"Um," I explained, but Benji was already craning his neck down the hallway.

"Tate!" he roared. "Is this chick a friend of yours?"

In the distance, there was the click-zap of a TV being turned off, and, to my relief, the familiar clicking sound

79

of poodle toenails on floorboards. Gizmo and Doug came bounding out of somewhere, followed by Tate, who nodded a little at Benji.

"Hey. Sorry, she—"

"Whatever." Benji threw open the fridge, grabbed an entire carton of organic no-pulp orange juice, and slammed the door shut with his heel. Tate and I waited as he went back upstairs, as seemed only polite.

"Uh, yeah," Tate said. "How was your shower?"

"Fine," I said, and looked intently back at the fridge, where I realized that the curly-haired kid in the photo was Benji.

"Your brother," I said.

"Yeah."

"Who drives you, um, crazy." The *um* was because I didn't swear.

"Yeah. I know," Tate said. "We look just like each other."

I didn't move, not sure what to say or do, and Tate laughed. "I'm just messing with you, Peach. Yeah, he's technically my stepbrother. My mom married my dad, they got divorced, he lives in Connecticut, my mom remarried Benji's dad, boom. And she changed her name but I didn't because, you know, I still have a dad I see in the summers or whatever. And my first name is her maiden name, so, like, it's still around."

I got the sense that he'd told that story a lot.

"My middle name is my mom's maiden name," I blurted out, for no real reason. "I didn't get my own."

Tate nodded. "Nice."

It wasn't nice, but I wasn't going to protest, and anyway, at that exact moment, Doug let out a barrel-chested *woof* and knocked right past my knees to the screen door, where I could just see a jogger in neon shorts whipping past on Evergreen.

"Sorry." I lunged for his collar. "They're really badly trained. I mean, they're not really trained at all."

"It's okay," Tate said—or yelled, over the booming barks. I gave Doug a yank, but he wouldn't shut up.

"I . . . I guess I should probably be going," I yelled back. "Um, thanks for the . . ."

"Don't mention it." Tate held out the leashes. "See you around, Peach."

Outside, it was the electric blue of an autumn evening, and the night air felt clean and cool on my newly washed skin. There was a single light on in the carriage house, and faint sounds of piano music drifting down. Inside, the kitchen was empty, and when I went upstairs, I had the TV room to myself. I didn't have to explain to anyone why my hair was wet. I had, I realized, a secret, for the first time in a very long time.

On Monday, we went to school. I always hate when books skip the parts where characters go to school and do homework, but, from my low-level understanding of narrative action, I've also realized that school is just boring. It is not the sort of place where you contend with the profundity of the human condition, unless you are Jane Eyre. It is the sort of place where you contend with vocabulary lists and witness unconvincing assemblies on the importance of self-esteem. And if you describe it in detail, you end up writing the same thing over and over and over again until you graduate or die.

At any rate, we did go to school that Monday, and I was furious, but clean, and trying to avoid thinking about what had happened the night prior. There is a way of avoiding thinking about something, though, that makes you think about it even more.

"How does my hair look?" Ginny poked her lips out at her reflection in the Volvo's rearview mirror and snapped a hair tie around the floppy knot on her head. We were sitting in the parking lot of the Jesus Is the Way Christian Church, which is across the street from the Gregory School and allows seniors to park in its lot as long as they've cleared out in time for 3:00 p.m. Bible study.

"Like you washed it in a plastic tub," I said. Ginny had not apologized for breaking the entire house, and I had not yet forgiven her.

"Plum!"

She dropped her arms and flopped onto the steering wheel, which gave a forlorn beep. That, I have to admit, made me laugh.

"It's not funny," Ginny said, but underneath her pitiful expression she was laughing a little, too. "Ugh. This is the. Worst. We're like Dickensian orphans."

"Except for the part where we still have Mom," I said.

"So we're *half* orphans. Whatever." Ginny stuck the hair tie between her teeth and begun to separate her hair into three very uneven chunks. She was missing a whole chunk at the back.

"You're missing a chunk," I said. "At the back—"

"Ugh!" Ginny slammed her hands down and dug into the car seat so hard that her knuckles went white. "*Ughugh-ughugh—*"

I withdrew. Sometimes, with Ginny, you just have to wait it out.

"Sorry." She shook her tub-washed head. "Sorry. I'm just,

83

like . . . ugh. Our house is falling apart, and I'm never going to get into college, and my hair is a mess."

"You are going to get into college," I said, rote.

"I hope Dad left some tools in the basement. I'll be hewing wood soon. Whatever hewing is." Ginny's knuckles went slack.

"Here." I took the hair tie. "I'll fix it."

Ginny turned obediently back around, and I divvied her hair up into four sections (even size, no missing chunks). I braided in silence for a few seconds before she interrupted again.

"Plum!!" She grabbed me by the wrist, which made me completely lose control of the braid. "Your rings are gone!"

My rings. I drew my hand back—it was naked. I didn't remember taking them off this morning. Usually I only took them off to . . .

. . . shower.

"Oh my God." Ginny gasped. "You *pawned* them!"

"What? No." I clenched my hand into a fist. "I just—I'm not wearing them today."

"You pawned them," Ginny said, "because you knew it was the only thing you could do to save your impoverished family—"

"*I didn't pawn them*," I said. "First of all, I don't even know where to *go* to pawn them."

"Okay, okay, you sold them on eBay," Ginny said. "Same difference."

"Ginny," I said. "You're being ridiculous."

"Then where are your rings?"

"I told you," I said. "I'm just not wearing them today. I know exactly where they are."

This, of course, was not the technical truth. I had left them in their neat little stack in Tate Kurokawa's soap dish, but for all I knew, Tate had thrown them away by now, or swept them out in a litter of used tissues, or sealed them up in one of those Cash4Gold envelopes and traded them in, except that they weren't gold, and he probably didn't need the cash.

"But—"

"Ginny!" I snapped the elastic onto the end of her braid. "Shut up."

She didn't, but I decided it was time to get out of the car.

"Plu-uuuuum!" Ginny yelled at me when I'd reached the parking lot. I stopped.

"What?"

She jogged up to me, her giant backpack bouncing. (The braid looked very good, I was pleased to note.)

"Just don't tell anyone about the whole plastic-house-of-shame situation," Ginny said. "If people find out we don't have a place to shower, I will literally die."

I gave her a look that said *if that were true, you'd already be literally dead, Ginny.*

But all I said was, "Who would I tell?"

"Gin!" Charlotte was walking in from the senior lot, a pair of giant sunglasses over her eyes and a travel mug of coffee in her hand. She never had a backpack, just a peach-colored tote bag, a small gold charm dangling from one of the straps, that was in no way suited to carrying all her textbooks. I was surprised she didn't need some kind of cantilever to keep it on her shoulder.

"God, I'm exhausted," Charlotte said. "I was up almost all night working on this problem set. You have no idea how lucky you are not to be in advanced calc."

"Tell me about it," Ginny said, before snapping back to me and bugging her eyes out. "Just keep a low profile, okay?" she hissed.

"Sure," I said. This would not be hard, because at the Gregory School, I barely had a profile to begin with. I wasn't *invisible*; teachers knew who I was, because they had had my sister, and upperclassmen knew that Ginny Blatchley had a little sister. Absent my sister, though, I had no identity to speak of. I was *physically* proximate to Jeremy Beard and the Weird Sweatshirt Kids and their notebooks and dice and Chex Mix in little Baggies, but that was it. It would be a sad situation if I didn't, in fact, prefer it.

And school was reassuring in its boringness, because at school all the plumbing worked and there were things to eat that were not sandwiches and I did not have to think about Ginny crying in the bathtub or yelling at me or having conniptions over the University of Pennsylvania. Also, it was a Monday, which meant that my first class was English, which was the only acceptable way to start a school day. Unfortunately, my second class was Algebra II, which meant that in five measly minutes of passing time, I would have to scuttle down the back stairs of the Gregory School main building, speed-walk half a city block including a street crossing, and scramble to the second floor of the Greaves Math Center.

So, after forty-five anodyne minutes of vocabulary worksheets, I packed up my backpack and headed into the breach. Ordinarily, the mad dash from class to class was, by necessity, an anonymous time. Standing still to talk slows the tides of the hallway flow and everyone naturally hates people who do that. But that day, fate intervened.

I saw Tate at the outside picnic tables. Not alone, of course; he was flanked by Stevie and Tommy and some other Loud Sophomore Boys whose names were irrelevant.

My heart palpitated in my chest. This was exactly what it had been like, moments before my greatest humiliation. Moments before they'd snatched the notebook out of my fourth-grade hands and read aloud my idiotic verses composed for the class poetry unit, which, in retrospect, was fruitless and lost on most of our fourth-grade brains. The fight-or-flight was suffocating.

But Tate also had my rings, or at least (perhaps) knew what happened to them. And, worse than that, he had noticed me.

"Hey," Tate said. He was grinning. "Come here a sec."

I froze, heart still pounding. What was I thinking? Talking

to Tate would involve, well, a conversation, and that conversation would probably touch on either the dog-poop incident or the no-plumbing situation. Or, worst of all, the porta potty.

"Yeah, come here," said Stevie. "Sit your fine self down." His face contorted with laughter, as if calling me *fine* was the world's funniest joke. Which, I realized, it was.

This was a mistake. I started to walk away.

"Aw, come on," called Tommy at my back. "Don't be such a prude!"

But I turned. Tate was laughing just like the rest of them, and my chest was tight as an iron lung. As the LSBs started speculating on what Tate could have possibly convinced me to do, I unfroze fully, and then I ran—so fast that I couldn't hear whatever else Tate was yelling, so fast that I made it to Algebra II with three point five minutes of passing time to spare.

That night, Ginny went to Charlotte's house to study and, quote, use an actual toilet, so Mom and I watched Home and Garden Television, eating our dinner popcorn as endless iterations of upwardly mobile couples squinted and nitpicked over real estate: too big, too small, not enough yard, too *much* yard, no soaking tub, and so on.

"Jesus," Mom muttered into her wineglass after our sixth episode. "It's just a house."

"Houses are important," I reminded her.

"Mm." She stared ahead, almost like she wasn't looking at the TV. I busied myself petting Kit Marlowe, who had curled up in the dent he'd made in the back of the sofa cushions.

"It's only a few more days," Mom said.

"I know."

"Thanks for putting the tub in the tub."

"You're welcome."

I had enacted my suggestion, despite Ginny's thinking it was dumb, with a plastic tub we had once used for Halloween apple-bobbing. It was not ideal, but desperate times called for a non-Tate shower solution. Even Ginny had used it, although she'd left the water for someone else to dump out.

Kit hissed, and I rolled my eyes. "Oh, come on. You still have a litter box."

"I got a job," Mom said. "By the way."

"What?"

"Pamela Wills," she explained. "She wanted someone with an artistic eye, or so she says. For fund-raising help at Art-Song. It's a chorus or something that she runs. I don't know."

"So what do you do?"

"I think I throw fund-raisers now." Mom gulped some wine. "There's one after Thanksgiving. I said we could have it here, so . . . it'll be here."

"Oh," I said. At least having a fund-raiser in the house meant that 5142 Haven Lane was probably not about to go on the market anytime soon. "Do you know how to do that?"

She threw up her hands. "Well, I *think* I can figure it out. I mean, I learned the basics of mouse anatomy in, like, three weeks. When I was *twenty-two.*"

The Five Little Field Mice had unusually, presumably anatomically incorrect, giant ears, but I didn't mention that. "That's great, Mom."

"Thank you." Mom squinted at the TV, where an ungodly McMansion squatted over an emerald lawn. "I guess this place comes in handy sometimes. You know everyone said we had no business buying this house, though. Your father and I."

"They did?"

Mom nodded, swiping a piece of hair out of her eyes. Without makeup on, she looked older than she was. "At the TGS kindergarten open house. Charlotte's parents, even. Don't tell Ginny."

"Oh." I crunched a piece of popcorn. "That's not very nice."

"They were right, though." Mom shook her head. "They were *absolutely* right. I mean, we have a porta potty, for Christ's sake. We have at least three rooms we don't use for anything. This is not how this house is supposed to be lived in."

"We use the Hiltiddly Room," I said. "We keep the Nor-dicTrack in there. And the office—"

I cut myself off. We weren't using the office, but it had its use. We needed that space to contain everything it contained so that it wouldn't get everywhere else.

"I'm sorry. Thanks for helping us, Plum." Mom turned and patted my knee. "I really appreciate it. And I'm doing my best. We have some old things we can get rid of. Everything's going to be fine."

"Yeah," I said.

"It'll be fine," Mom said again. She sipped from her glass, and twisted her hands. Something was missing.

"You're not wearing your engagement ring," I said.

"Oh, hm." Mom looked at her ring finger, as if she'd just

now noticed. "That's right. I dropped it off to get cleaned."

Iris Blatchley is not the sort of woman who cared about having clean jewelry.

"I hope it wasn't expensive," I said. "We don't exactly have money to spare."

"Oh, no, it wasn't," Mom said quickly.

I gave her a look that said, *You are absolutely lying, Mother,* and in two seconds, she crumbled.

"All right, fine, you win. I'll get it back in two days. It's just a cash-flow issue, okay?"

"Okay," I said.

"They're just *things*, Plum," she said. "Having them or not having them doesn't change anything."

She set her glass on the table with its upside-down leg and settled back into the couch.

Things were *not* just things. And at that moment, I knew that no matter how humiliating it would be, I had to get those rings back.

And so, the following night, I enacted a plan. Fortu-nately, I had a ready-made excuse to leave the house every night, in the form of the dogs. Unfortunately, I also had Ginny, who had taken to staking out the kitchen after dinner and hyperventilating at her schoolwork.

"You're going out?" she said. "You're going to freeze."

"I am, and I am not," I informed her.

"You know what *you* need," Ginny said, a maniacal gleam in her eye. "The Amazing Wonder Jacket™."

"No," I said. "Not at all."

The Amazing Wonder Jacket™—which you pronounce by saying "The Amazing Wonder Jacket tee-em" to make sure your listener hears the little trademark sign—is an old jacket we have that is black on the outside and fuzzy purple on the inside. When we were kids, we used to film these fake info-mercials using random stuff we found around the house, like our mom's old Janis Joplin records or, say, an old piece of outerwear. That is how the Amazing Wonder Jacket™ got its name. Ginny had long maintained her claim that it magically adjusts to whatever temperature you need, like it's a kind of coat-thermos or something. I thought it was warm and relatively lightweight. In any case, the important part was that on anybody but Ginny, it looked hideously bulky.

"Yes!" Ginny cried. "It has advanced therm-adjust technology!"

"What does?" Mom wandered in, a sheaf of papers under her arm, and glanced at the leashes in my hand. "Oh, good. Thanks for walking them."

Ginny pivoted. "Mother," she said, jacket situation forgotten. "Why is there no furniture in the living room?"

She put her hands on her hips. Mom adjusted her papers.

"When were you in the living room?"

"I don't know, *recently*?" Ginny said. "It is for *living*, after all. Except that we no longer seem to own any couches."

I looked at Mom with a look of concern, because I actually *was* concerned, but I was also slipping toward the door. Perhaps this was my chance to flee without the jacket on.

Mom sighed.

"Can we not do this now? I have a wine-and-cheese . . . thing to plan. I'm stressed out."

"Oh, like I'm not?" Ginny said.

"I'm just saying," Mom said. "Cut me some slack, okay?"

"I just want to know where the furniture is!" Ginny said.

Mom sighed again, more theatrically this time. It was easy

to see where Ginny got it from.

"Fine. I had it taken to the resale store."

"What?!" Ginny cried.

"We never go in that room anyway. And it was all . . . I don't know."

"Moldering," I suggested.

"Exactly," Mom said. "Plum, if you're going outside, put a coat on."

Cripes. Trapped. I had made it almost all the way to the door, too.

"But I can't," I said. "It looks stupid."

"So?" Ginny said. "Is anyone important going to see you?"

I could not answer that in honesty. This is how I ended up swaddled in the Amazing Wonder Jacket™.

No sooner had I gotten them outside than the dogs immediately yanked me down the block. This was not in and of itself particularly unusual, but this time they seemed to have a destination in mind, like they *knew*. Dogs are dumb like that, or perhaps smart like that. Gizmo wasn't even interested in biting the leash.

As the dogs sniffed assiduously around the gateposts to the Kurokawa/Feingold driveway, I reaffirmed my executive decision: no matter how embarrassing it was to go up to Tate's house and speak to his face about the matter of retrieving my missing rings, I had to do it. Those rings were important, and I would only have to speak to Tate face-to-face for

95

approximately five minutes, max. And also, the dogs really seemed to like the way he smelled, or something.

So I went up to the back door, knocked, and waited. I stood there in the door-shaped square of golden kitchen light and tried to keep the dogs from eating the semi-mushy jack-o'-lantern next to the welcome mat. Which was strange, as we were still on the earliest cusp of acceptable Halloween decoration season, and stranger still because even in its deflated state, I could tell there was something weird about the face: it didn't have any eyes, for one thing, and the mouth had no teeth on top and a bunch of weirdly shaped ones on the bottom right.

It had been almost five minutes of dog wrangling, and I was about to knock again when something in the kitchen beeped. A series of thumps pounded overhead, and Tate appeared, barefoot and in sweatpants that read NANTUCKET, with his bister hair sticking up on one side. I waved, and he kind of jumped.

"Peach?" He smiled, but also yawned. "Hey."

"Were you asleep?" I asked. I don't know what prompted me to open with this. I think it was something about seeing Tate's bare feet—which were normal feet, just bare, and which makes sense when you think it through, of course. But you just don't think about people like Tate shuffling around in bare feet.

Tate yawn-smiled. "Maybe."

96

"It's five thirty at night," I pointed out.

Tate shrugged. "Yeah. I'm lazy." He looked right at me—or rather, right at the Amazing Wonder Jacket™, into which I had stuffed my leashless hand. "Are you cold?"

"Oh, no," I said. "I'm fine." This was the truth—the AWJ™ was doing its thing.

"Mm." Tate looked over his shoulder, then down at the dogs. "Do they wanna come in?"

It was hard to deny that I was gripping the straining leashes so tightly I was practically getting a brush burn on my right palm. Tate swung open the door, and I let go of the leashes, and Gizmo and Doug vaulted over the threshold and knocked right into the UCK of Tate's sweatpants-knee.

"They probably smell the food," Tate said. "I'm making pizza bagels."

"While you were asleep?"

As if on cue, there was another beep.

"Yo, Tate, shut that shit off!" yelled a voice from upstairs.

"I'm a multitasker," Tate said to me. To the upstairs voice, he yelled, "I got it, Benj."

He grabbed a pot holder—the kind of pot holder you actually buy somewhere, not a half-melted loop-weaving pot holder you make in kindergarten—and yanked open the big silver oven door. It smelled very, very good, in that way that melted cheese always does.

Tate dropped the baking sheet on the stovetop with a

clatter. There were six bagel halves on it.

"You're going to eat six pizza bagels?" I asked. (A stupid question.)

"Probably not," Tate said. "You hungry?"

I was. We had had pasta for dinner, but pasta with just sauce and some cheese, because no one had remembered to buy meat, or, frankly, knew how to prepare a meat sauce. I was probably so hungry that Tate could tell, which is probably why he didn't even wait for my answer before ripping off a paper towel from over the sink and picking two pizza bagels off the sheet.

"Thanks." I took the paper towel and sat on one of the island stools, since it seemed supremely stupid to eat standing up. Tate helped himself to a bagel, too, and as we sat there eating pizza bagels it occurred to me what a weird sentence that was: *Tate Kurokawa and I are eating pizza bagels together.* It was, by the way, an excellent pizza bagel. Not too much sauce.

"How's the shower situation?" Tate asked.

"Good," I said. "Fine. I mean, we are able to shower again, if that's what you were asking."

I did not feel the need to share with Tate my tub-in-tub solution.

"Damn." Tate chewed. "Yeah, I was thinking about it, and that has to be crazy annoying. Like, every time I got in the shower after that I thought about you."

The shock of this statement was immediate. I stopped

chewing. Tate's face went very, very red, like *he* was the one wearing the Amazing Wonder Jacket™, and he started clearing his throat about fifty times a second.

"Um," he said. "I just meant like . . . so anyway . . ."

"Sorry if I scared you," I interrupted, partially because I was worried about it and partially to give Tate a break from all that throat clearing.

Tate laughed, a little uneasily. His face was still kind of flushing. "Don't flatter yourself, Peach. You are not that threatening-looking. Even in that ginormous jacket."

"It's supposed to make me look tough."

"Really?"

"*No.*" I gave him a look that said, *It's a jacket; it is supposed to keep me warm*, and picked up my bagel. "I just meant that you looked surprised to see me."

"Yeah." Tate nodded. "I dunno. Maybe ring the doorbell next time."

I barely had a chance to register the fact that Tate said *next time* before he moved on.

"Oh, shit, of course. Your rings." Chewing, he jerked his head toward the stairs. "I have them. They're upstairs."

He leaped up for the stairs, but paused on the bottom step. Like he wanted me to follow him.

"Um . . ." I looked at the dogs, who were sniffing interestedly around the bottom of the oven. Tate shrugged.

"Eh, they'll be fine."

And so, with my remaining pizza bagel balanced on its paper towel so as not to leave it for dead with the dogs, I followed Tate and his bagel up the back stairs and onto the second floor. I recognized it, of course, from showering there, but this time we went farther down the hallway and to the right, into a room that had clothes all over the floor and papers all over the desk and absolutely zero books. It was surely a breeding ground for bacteria and illiteracy.

"They're somewhere." Tate put his pizza bagel on top of a stereo speaker. "I put them away so I wouldn't lose them."

Judging by the state of the room, which I now realized was his bedroom, I was not optimistic. Also, I was a little embarrassed to be standing at the threshold of Tate Kurokawa's bedroom, especially considering that some of the clothes on the floor were boxers, with little pinstripes and blue and green plaids. But Tate just waded into the mess and started picking things up.

"I didn't mean to scare you or anything," he said. "At school, I mean."

"Oh," I said. There didn't seem to be any good way to tell Tate that Loud Sophomore Boys were, by their very nature, despicable. "You didn't. I just . . . had to get to math."

Tate was silent, and I thought perhaps I should elaborate until he cried out.

"A*ha!*"

He grabbed something off the desk and hopped back over all his piles of stuff.

"Here."

He held out a little velvet bag, presumably containing my rings.

"My mom put them in there," he said. "So they wouldn't get tarnished."

"Oh," I said. "Um, tell your mom thanks."

"Okay."

He was standing very close to me, so close that I could smell the familiar scent of his soap, soap that he must have used in the shower, and I was in the middle of realizing how amazingly easy it is to think about someone showering, even by accident, when a terrific crash came from downstairs.

"The dogs!" I yelled.

I stuck the little bag into my jacket pocket and dashed back to the stairs, Tate pounding after me. When I got there, it was exactly as I had feared—Gizmo and Doug had pulled the baking sheet to the floor and were merrily snarfing up the remaining pizza bagels.

"No!" I leaped forward and yanked them up by the collars. "Bad dogs! Drop it!" I knew these were the kind of things you yell at dogs that were trained, but I figured it was worth pretending.

"I'm so sorry," I said, using all my strength to keep the dogs in check while Tate stooped to pick up the baking sheet.

"It's no big deal," he said. "I wasn't going to eat all of them."

Gizmo burped.

"I should really go," I said. "But thanks for the rings. And, um, the pizza bagel. Bagels. For all of us."

"Of course," Tate said. "Anytime."

With the leashes reclipped, I navigated the dogs out the back door, but I was so focused on not letting them bolt back for the saucy remains of the food that I accidentally stepped into something pulpy and wet. The pumpkin.

"Oh, shit." Tate came out the back door. "Gross."

"It's fine," I said, shaking the pumpkin goop off my shoe. "I think the pumpkin got it worse than I did. Sorry."

"No worries." Tate bent down and picked up what remained of the jack-o'-lantern. "I mean, I was the one who left it under the drain spout. And no one gets what it was supposed to be anyway."

"Oh," I said.

"It's the Sixers logo," Tate said, gesturing as if I (1) knew what that logo looked like, and (2) could discern any intentional design in the rotting orange flesh.

"Mm," I said.

"Our boys are killing it. We're gonna be the best team in the NBA this year—next year, tops. Did you see the game against the Wizards?"

"No," I said. "I don't watch sports."

"No?" he said. "Not even to, like, relax?"

I resisted the urge to roll my eyes. "God, no."

"Oh." Tate regarded his mashed pumpkin. "So yeah, long

story short, I was bored and my mom brought pumpkins home and I couldn't think of anything else to carve."

"Of course you couldn't," I said, before I could stop myself.

Tate stiffened.

"Hah," he said, nodding. "Yeah."

"I have to go," I said, face absolutely burning.

"Yep," Tate said. "Bye."

He threw the pumpkin into the trash, and I clomped down the steps with the dogs, and went out the gate, and hurried myself back to Haven Lane.

Finally, three days later, the plumbing had been mended. Ginny thanked God that she didn't have to sponge-bathe in an empty tub with a kettle of hot water, and Mom wondered if the plumber had used solid gold pipes to repair the outflow valve because *Jesus Christ*, how could it cost that much, and Almost-Doctor Andrews remarked that it would be nice not to have to take showers at the campus gym.

I agreed, of course. I didn't want there to be any cause to leave this house at any time, ever.

Strangely, the one family member who couldn't seem to tolerate a once-again functional water system was Kit Marlowe. Kit has grown into a cranky cat, but typically a quiet one. Now, he had taken to yowling, which I wouldn't have even particularly remembered if it hadn't interrupted a game of Scrabble.

"There." Ginny nudged her final tile into place. "JOGE."

"No way," I said. "Use it in a sentence."

"Hey, look at that *joge*."

We both cracked up. Kit yowled. Then we stared.

"There's something in the water," Ginny said ominously. She clacked around in the bag of tiles, stirring them like they were knucklebones with a fortune to tell.

"What, like fluoride?"

"Huh?" She squinted. "No, I mean, like, a miasma or something. It's making Kit witchy."

"That doesn't happen anymore," I said. "We have filters. I think."

But Kit *was* rolling around with an unusually wild gleam in his eye, and that night, when I retired to bed, I found him on the windowsill outside the office, staring out at the moon, like he wanted to leap out and pounce at it.

Something *had* changed. But then, fixing things does, necessarily, mean changing them, I suppose. You can't go back to exactly how something was; you are only approximating, and hoping the newly fixed version will do you just as well into the future. And there's no way to know but to wait and see how things unfold.

When I woke up, Kit was still on the windowsill, still looking outside.

 # THREE

Safe upon the solid rock the ugly houses stand:
Come and see my shining palace built upon the sand!
—*Edna St. Vincent Millay*

I truly never believed I'd have reason to leave the house again. For one thing, now that the showers worked, and I had my rings back, there was no particular *reason* for me to go anywhere. Second of all, I didn't really like being away from 5142 Haven Lane. The school day was more than enough to get me out into the world and socialize me; the rest of the time, as far as I was concerned, I could be entirely homebound.

Or so I thought, until the November night my sister began another tirade.

"I thought you liked the Forsythes!"

Kit Marlowe brisked himself through my legs and out of the kitchen, and I paused in the doorway, silently as I could. I *had* been upstairs, making a list of possible nonsentimental items we could sell, covertly, on the internet, but had come downstairs to sharpen my pencil in the electric sharpener. In the kitchen, Mom was sitting on the countertop, and my sister sitting on a stool with a predinner bag of popcorn, which she seemed to have stopped eating. Everyone was wearing big sweaters.

"I do, I do," Mom was saying to Ginny. "They're fine."

"What do you mean *fine*?"

"Ginny!" Mom thumped down the leftover three-ring binder from my fifth-grade days that she'd been using to store her wine-and-cheese plan. "Thanksgiving is a time to be with family. They understand that."

"Well, they see me as part of their family." Ginny folded her sweatered arms. "I don't see what's so bad about that."

Mom closed her open mouth with a little click and gave the ceiling a *Someone, please intervene* look. By accident, I had stopped paying attention to my pencil and had sharpened it down to a stub. I would have to go into the kitchen and retrieve a new one.

"I don't see what's so complicated about it," Ginny was saying. "They invited me, and I said yes."

"I just want you here, okay?" Mom said. "Is that so much to ask?"

"Why?" Ginny threw up her hands. "So I can eat dry, frozen turkey with literally three people, assuming Almost-Doctor Andrews shows up?"

Mom deflated against the counter. "*That* was mean," she said softly.

But Ginny was on a roll. "The Forsythes actually know *how* to cook. They don't have to light their stove with a match.

They have actual *food* at their Thanksgiving. They'll have actual *furniture in their house*, can you imagine? And you know what? I'm just sick of being here! I'm sick of dealing with this house, and I just want to be somewhere *nice* for a change. Is that okay with you, madame?"

Mom threw her hands in the air. "What am I supposed to say to that, Ginny? I'm a terrible cook, okay? I get it. I'm not as good a mom as Susan Forsythe."

"And I'm an adult," Ginny said. "So if I want to go there, I can."

I had had enough. "God, Ginny, give it a rest."

It was ironic, I found, how Ginny acted more like a two-year-old at eighteen than she did as her toddling genius self. I'd say she was doing it on purpose, to be contrarian, but that would have required her to have bothered reading our father's essay. Maybe the very existence of the essay put the thumb on the scale, so to speak, and was slowly throwing her off her intended course. Not to cast blame, of course. Just that I wouldn't have been surprised if Geoffrey Chaucer's son had never bothered to learn the astrolabe.

Ginny let her jaw drop dramatically, and her eyes rolled with frightening elasticity.

"Oh, thanks, Plum. I appreciate *you* being so mature. Just because you have nowhere else to hang out doesn't mean the rest of us have to suffer."

The air in the kitchen felt hot and uncomfortable, and not

just because the Franklin stove was spitting out warm wiggly air. Kit, now firmly situated on the kitchen windowsill, gave a plangent yowl at the outdoors.

There is a passage from *Jane Eyre* that I had underlined (well, *Ginny* had underlined it first, but I wrote my own underline over it).

I am no bird; and no net ensnares me: I am a free human being with an independent will.

I was no bird, and I was no indoor cat unable to unlatch the door and escape. I was a fifteen-year-old girl with little air to herself, no particular orders to stay within those walls, and an independent will.

"I'm going to go out," I said quietly. Nobody noticed. But, to be fair, no one usually noticed.

And that's how, five minutes later, I ended up at Tate Kurokawa's back door.

I wish I knew more about why I ended up there. Subconsciously, it may have seemed like the least likely place to go, the one secret that Ginny didn't know I had. I was actually very nervous, and my heart was beating very hard and fast the whole time I walked down the block. I knew that kids at school *snuck out* to go indulge in illicit activities, but I was never really sure what the term implied—in my mind it always involved a rope of bedsheets like in a cartoon. But I had basically just done the same thing, and it was a little scary, but not particularly difficult. It turns out that if no one really pays attention to you in the first place, you can do almost anything.

"Hey," said Tate when he answered the door. He was wearing the same Nantucket sweatpants. You'd think that someone like Tate Kurokawa could afford more than one pair of sweatpants, but who knows.

"Hello," I said. "I came over to watch some sports."

You would think that this would throw him for some kind of loop, or puzzle him—or at least *I* thought that, in the moment. But he simply accepted it, or accepted it at an even lower threshold, like there was nothing to even consider.

"Cool," he said. "Just you?"

"No," I said. "Stevie's just running late."

Tate laughed. "I meant, like, without your dogs."

"Oh." I thought about poor Gizmo and Doug, trapped in the blast radius of Ginny's fury at home. Maybe I should go back for them. But if I went back for them, it would call attention to the fact that I *hadn't* had them when I left, and then Mom might start asking questions. Maybe the best thing was just to go back and not do anything or watch anything at Tate's house.

"I should go," I said, just as Tate said, "Uh, come on in." I did.

"Do you want something to eat, or something?" Tate said. I shook my head.

"You're not doing anything important?"

Tate gave me a look. "What important thing could I possibly be doing on a Thursday night?"

"Homework?"

"Do I look like the kind of person who does homework before two a.m. the day before it's due?"

I conceded that he did not.

"Cool," he said. "Well, the TV room's this way."

Instead of the stairs, he led me down the first-floor hallway, which had very high ceilings that made our steps kind of echo.

"You know," Tate said, echoing a little, "I didn't think you were actually going to come back."

"I'm trying to get into sports," I said. "I've heard sports are relaxing, and I like relaxing."

Tate laughed. "Right, no. I just meant I didn't think you liked *me*."

"Oh," I said, because what were you supposed to say to that? I didn't *not* like Tate, I didn't think, which is to say that I no longer hated him. Which was strange to admit. But I wasn't really ready to phrase my attitude toward him in any kind of positive grammatical structure.

Fortunately, we had arrived at what must have been the TV room—*must have been* because there was not any TV in it that I could discern, only huge floor-to-ceiling bookshelves, a big window, and a red couch and armchair that matched.

"Here." Tate gestured at the couch. "You can sit there."

I didn't know if by that he meant that I could have the entire couch to myself, or that the couch was just the place that everyone sat when they were watching the TV that did not seem to be in this room. But I sat.

"Do you even *have* a TV?" I asked, just as Tate flicked a switch on the wall and two of the bookshelves began to glide away from each other. Behind them was, in fact, a TV.

I felt very dumb.

"Oh," I said.

Tate laughed a little and picked up a remote from the coffee table. "Mom says it's ridiculous to have a TV that big, but me and Benji wanted it, so we compromised."

Remote in hand, Tate zapped the TV on, then paused in front of the couch.

"Um," he said, and didn't sit down. "Hm."

It was totally my fault. Because I had interpreted his *You can sit there* as *you, Plum, will be the only person sitting on the couch*, I had settled such that I was sitting on the crack between two of the couch cushions, more or less in the middle, which meant that if Tate were to sit on the couch *with* me to *also* enjoy the best viewing angle for the TV, we would be well within each other's personal space. I had not done this on purpose.

"Oh," I said. "Um."

My options were few. If I moved toward the couch arm to

open up space, I risked looking like I did *not*, in fact, want Tate anywhere near me, which seemed unnecessarily rude considering I'd just barged into his house. But if I stayed where I was, then Tate might brush up against me when he sat down, the very thought of which made me want to throw up my own racing heart.

While I was panicking, Tate sat in the armchair.

"Your boys aren't playing tonight."

"My who?"

"Your boys. The Sixers." He held the remote aloft and flicked through TV channels so quickly I could barely see which was which. "But we can watch an old game. What do you want?"

"Whichever," I said. "A good one."

Also, by sitting in the armchair, he was actually closer to me than he would have been on the couch. There was more furniture separating us, but in terms of direct physical distance, we were barely half an arm's length apart. If I sat with my back on the couch arm, the end of my braid would touch his elbow. Probably.

"Picky, picky," he said, and clicked on one with the remote. Then he got up and went back to the light switch and turned down the lights so that it was pleasantly dark in the room. Probably as dark as people make it in their living rooms when they have *snuck out* to do things. Which Tate surely did, as we all knew based on his rumored escapades.

He sat back down in the armchair, I sat very still on the couch, the theme song, or whatever they're called for sports, blasted out, and just like that, I was watching TV with Tate Kurokawa.

I couldn't really follow the game, because I didn't even technically know the rules of basketball. But the thing that I did not appreciate about watching television with another person who is not your older sister is that you're not really watching the *program* at all. Your observational energies are occupied elsewhere. You're thinking about this other person, and how he's sitting, and what his breathing sounds like, and how maybe you should've made more space on the couch in the first place, and if *he* is thinking any of these things about how *you're* sitting and breathing. Then you try not to sit or breathe weird.

"You're awfully quiet, Peach."

"Huh?"

Even in the sort-of dark I could see Tate's eyes when he looked at me from the chair, like Kit Marlowe's when he stalks into your room when you're sleeping. Instinctively, I sat up straighter, because somehow in the fiftysomething minutes of basketball that we had watched I had started to sink backward into the couch. My braid had been very, very close to his elbow.

"Just like . . . I don't know, usually when people watch games they say stuff," Tate said. "Like yelling at the players, or whatever."

"That's stupid," I said. "Why would anyone do that?"

"I dunno." Tate shrugged. "Because they think it helps?"

I gave him a look that said, *We are miles away from the arena, and this game has already passed.*

Tate laughed. "Peach, have some self-confidence. You could make Embiid sink that three-pointer."

His grin surprised me so much that I stuck out my tongue—a conditioned response from being teased my entire life—and I was instantaneously mortified. What kind of person did that? What kind of person did that to *Tate*?

But he laughed, and we went back to watching TV, and I forgot to think about my breathing for the rest of the game.

"Do you want to watch another one?" Tate asked, when it was over.

I had to admit that watching basketball with Tate was a lot better than having to listen to Ginny whine and yell. But I also could not necessarily admit that out loud.

"Do *you*?" I asked.

Instead of answering, Tate gave the end of my braid a little flick.

It didn't hurt, but I jolted as if it had. Tate looked like maybe he was going to apologize, even though there was no reason to, and I knew that he had been joking, and actually it was kind of nice to joke with him.

So I said, "Ow." And I smiled. And Tate smiled back and was definitely about to say something when there was a groaning door sound and the whooshing of outside air and the clicking of someone's high heels.

"Tate?"

Now Tate was the one to sit up very, very straight.

"Uh," he said. "Uh, um."

"What?" I said, not particularly intelligently.

"Uh, it's my mom," Tate said. "I didn't know she was—
Shit."

He went for the remote, but dropped it, and I went to pick it up, but then we both bent down at the same time and clonked our heads together, and our fingertips very gently grazed.

But Tate yanked his hand away.

"I'm not supposed to have girls over alone," he said quickly.

"Oh," I said.

It had never even occurred to me that someone like Tate Kurokawa would have rules about something like that. I had just assumed that the LSBs had the kind of neglectful parents who looked the other way when their sons wanted to get up to opposite-sex-related hijinks.

And maybe, also, it had never occurred to me that I was a girl. I mean, I was fairly secure in my gender identity, I just didn't know that, in terms of sneaking out and potential rule breaking, I *counted*. Not in that way. Not to Tate.

"You should probably go," Tate said hurriedly. "Um, just, I mean, go to the kitchen, and we'll . . ."

He leaped to the door and waved me out into the hall, and

I leaped up from the couch and made a beeline down the hall after Tate.

When we got to the kitchen, a short, dark-haired woman was setting a box of groceries on the island. Round Earth Food Cooperative, in the interest of saving the planet by inconveniencing everyone, does not provide bags, only recycled boxes.

"Oh," said Tate's mom. "Hello there."

"Umhi," I said, all one word.

Tate's mom looked at Tate with one eyebrow up. She was dressed very nicely, in one of those asymmetrical gray wrap-sweater things, and had little silver hoop earrings. In contrast, I was wearing a particularly ragged pair of jeans and an old TGS T-shirt from fifth-grade gym class. I felt like a mountain troll.

"Mom," Tate said. "This is Peach. Plum. Uh, she was just leaving."

"Yep," I said. I had never in my life said *yep* before then.

"Peach?" Tate's mom said.

"It's a nickname," Tate and I said at the same time. My face got very hot.

"Um, I do have to go," I said.

"Yeah," Tate said. "Uh, thanks for the homework . . . stuff."

"You're welcome," I said. Then I gave Tate's mom a weird curtsy-bow and rushed out the back door. Once out, I walked with as big steps as I could, and got home in approximately two minutes. (It was much easier to do without dogs.)

Back at 5142 Haven Lane, I slipped into the kitchen with as little screen-door creakage as possible. Mom was still in the kitchen, but Ginny was nowhere to be seen. There was a pause. Mom looked over at the door.

"Hi, Plummy."

"Is everything okay?" I asked.

Mom shrugged. "Ginny is having Thanksgiving with the Forsythes." She made a frustrated sound and swirled her glass. "Am I really that bad of a mother?"

"I don't think it has anything to do with that," I said.

"I try *really hard*," Mom said. "You know there's no school for this, right? I didn't just wake up knowing how to take care of a huge house and feed and clothe and raise two girls."

"I know," I said.

"And I have this goddamn wine-and-cheese thing to plan, lest we forget." Mom groaned. "Like I'm any kind of hostess."

"I know."

"And furthermore"—Mom gestured at the ceiling—"I don't care for all of Ginny's college histrionics. I'm not like, putting an insane amount of pressure on you two. I'm just trying to give you what *I* didn't have."

"I know," I said.

Mom sighed hard enough to sputter her lips. "I guess this is why I have an emergency backup child, right? Just don't go . . . eloping or anything."

"Okay," I said.

Granted, I had no immediate plans to elope. I had no immediate plans to do *anything*, actually, now that I'd done whatever I'd just done with or to Tate. I really wasn't sure *what* had happened between us, actually, only that it really had to stay a secret.

It was kind of nice to have that as a secret, though.

Ginny being gone for Thanksgiving was actually not so bad. In fact, it was everything a holiday should be—calm, warm, involving candles and a dog show on television.

"I think this is the first time nothing's blown up on Thanksgiving," Mom said, thwacking at potatoes with a knife. "Literally or metaphorically."

I did not point out why, but I think we both knew.

Mom made a pretty good turkey, and I made "corn thing," which is a traditional creamed-corn casserole from Patience Mortimer's recipe box that doesn't have a real name, and later in the afternoon Almost-Doctor Andrews arrived at the back door with pumpkin pie.

"Oh," I said. "It has little leaves." I touched the crust reverently.

"I borrowed an egg," Almost-Doctor Andrews said. "From the coop. I hope that's all right."

"Lovely!" Mom said, over the whine of the electric knife. I was keeping my distance, since I didn't trust her not to inadvertently carve her daughter instead of the bird.

"Yes." Almost-Doctor Andrews smiled, but not happily. Something was wrong. He was hovering, rather than offering to find a plate and carve the turkey, since clearly neither of us knew how. His face was flushed.

"Come sit," said Mom. "Come sit! Can I get you anything?"

"Well," Almost-Doctor Andrews said again. "All right."

He sat but did not take off his coat, as if he expected to run out somewhere at any moment.

"Is something wrong?" I asked.

"Well . . ." He looked at Mom, looked at the turkey, scratched Kit Marlowe—who was rubbing his back on Almost-Doctor Andrew's pant leg and leaving behind a festival of tiny white hairs—and sighed. "They cut my funding. I have no teaching assignments next semester."

"What?" Mom set down the electric knife—switched off, thank God. "On *Thanksgiving*?"

Almost-Doctor Andrews shrugged. "I . . . I was actually told at the beginning of the month."

"But you paid rent," I said. "I mean, the check deposited. Mom had me take it to the bank."

"Gigs," he said. "You can always pick up carol sings and maybe a church service or two. Musicians have a love-hate relationship with this time of year. I've been hearing "Deck the Hall" in my head for weeks and it's not even December yet." He closed his eyes and gave his head a little shake. "Anyway, I don't expect that you'll be able to keep me. I understand. But—"

"No!" I said, before I could stop myself. I looked at Mom, who had retreated somewhat into the folds of her Thanksgiving blacks. "I mean, we can't just kick you out."

"You can," Almost-Doctor Andrews said simply. "I'm month-to-month."

"But we *won't*," I said, before even thinking about it.

Mom shifted. Almost-Doctor Andrews wouldn't meet her eyes. Underneath everything, a brass version of "Come, Ye Thankful People, Come" trickled out of my phone.

"No," Mom said. "We'll make it work. I mean, Pamela's paying me, right? And we've literally got food on the table. We can stretch."

And so we settled, the three of us, on three mismatched chairs (one folding, one armchair, one swivel).

"So this is what it's like being an only child, eh?" Almost-Doctor Andrews said, because without Ginny here yammering away, it was indeed very calm. Kind of like the normal sort of holiday normal people have.

"It's not so bad," I said, which was kind of an understatement. I liked it. It was the kind of day I hadn't had in too long—since the beginning of the year, or possibly the beginning of my life.

"Any good projects in the works right now?"

"Projects?" I swallowed my cranberries.

"Books," he said. "Or . . . poems? I'm not sure what you write."

"I don't," I said.

"Oh." Almost-Doctor Andrews blinked. "Well, free time is free time. Better get used to it, right?"

There was even enough pie left for me to have a second slice.

But after the mangled turkey was dumped into Tupperwares and the "corn thing" was secured under layers of plastic wrap and Almost-Doctor Andrews had retreated to the carriage house and Ginny had come back, breathless and chatty and rosy-cheeked from the cold, going on and on about Sue Forsythe's gluten-free gravy (you can make it with cornstarch!) and how much food there was to eat (two turkeys, one venison roast, and eight pies—eight!), dread started to seep into my heart. It wasn't so much the ordinary feelings of getting sucked back into the school drudgery of math tests and sleep deprivation, but more a guilty kind of dread. The guilt that maybe I had gotten Tate into trouble, and I didn't even know how to apologize for it, if I even should. Going up to him at school was out because, Weird Sweatshirt Kid that I was, it would inevitably arouse suspicion. Going back to his house was equally impossible, because his mom also lived there, and after the encounter in their kitchen, the last thing on earth I wanted to have to do was to look Tate's mom in the eye.

Fortunately, I did not have a lot of time to dwell on it. Because that Saturday afternoon brought War and Cheese.

"It's called *Wine* and Cheese," Mom said for the billionth time, and gave her hands a nervous shake. "I don't even get why you're calling it that."

"Because it sounds like *War and Peace*, kind of," I said.

"And because you're acting like a total *sergent de l'armée*," Ginny said.

"Right," I said. "Because we all speak French and know what that means."

"Army sergeant," Ginny translated.

"Ohhh." Almost-Doctor Andrews chuckled. We had roped him in to helping out, since it was a literal all-hands-on-deck situation. "War and *Cheese*. Now I get it."

"Silence!" Mom yelled. She was having no levity that afternoon. "You guys are supposed to be *helping*."

Everyone snapped to attention, myself included.

Of course, after the horrors of the Senior Tea, I was decidedly less than keen to assist at any kind of social gathering slash fund-raiser, especially if there was food serving involved. But since it was at our house, and Mom was in charge, there was no danger of fish sandwiches, and besides, Ginny was in such a good mood from her Forsythe Thanksgiving extravaganza that she actually volunteered to do some of the chores with me. And since it seemed like bad form to be the only Blatchley sister not participating, I found myself dressed up—in Those

Pants this time—freshly braided, and even wearing a little eye shadow that Ginny had helped me put on.

Mom held up a legal pad and starting pacing in the kitchen (which really didn't do much to dispel the whole army-sergeant thing). From her notes, we learned that our battle stations were as followed:

Mom: Obtain and disburse the actual wine and cheese; encourage party guests to pick up a brochure and a donation envelope

Almost-Doctor Andrews: Schmooze with people at the door; wear a tie

Dogs: Stay locked in the tower bedroom so as not to disturb or pee on the guests

Ginny and Plum: Light candles; take out trash; other duties as assigned

Mom had even drawn a diagram of what snacks and what candles went in which first-floor rooms. There was just one slight problem.

"Uh, where am I supposed to put candles?" Ginny came back to the kitchen with a basket of tea lights on her hip. "There's nothing in the living room."

We followed her out and realized it was true: the living room was down to a single love seat. No carpet, no credenza, no coffee table. There was the marble fireplace, but the mantel wasn't exactly wide enough to fit all seventy-two of the tiny candles Mom had bought, especially because we used it as a gallery space for some framed originals from *Five Little Field Mice Make a Friend.* The only thing on the floor was a sleeping Kit Marlowe, and he did not look pleased at the arrival of humans.

Mom looked at Ginny. Ginny looked at Mom. I accidentally dropped one of my rings, because ever since I'd gotten them back I'd been very conscious of their presence around my fingers and taken to twirling them. In the empty room, it sounded like a bomb dropping.

"Furniture," Mom said. "Shit. Shit!"

It seemed that, in all her careful planning for the War and Cheese, our mother had neglected one mundane but crucial element of party planning: having furniture—or, in this case, renting it.

"*Damn* it," Mom said. "Damn it! Pamela gave me the number for the rental people and everything. And I just . . ." She made a mewling sound.

"*Hi dee hi dee hi dee hi,*" Ginny sang into the echo.

"*Ho dee ho dee ho,*" I sang back, in the manner of Jeeves obliging his employer in a round of jazzy singing before a night on the town.

"What are you *doing?*" Mom was wringing her hands. "That isn't helping!"

Ginny and I looked at each other, and I giggled—probably more from nerves than anything else. Mom looked pained, or like she might faint, and there wasn't even a big enough couch for her to do it on.

"This can be the dance floor." Ginny jumped into the middle of the empty floor and scooped Kit Marlowe up into a twirl. Kit yowled, and I burst out laughing, now totally unable to help myself, until I saw the yet-more-stricken look on Mom's face.

"Okay, okay." She waved her hands in the air. "Shut up, everyone. We'll just have to reprioritize a little."

Thus arrived the following emergency addenda to the battle-stations plan:

Almost-Doctor Andrews: Scour house for any moveable furniture and relocate it to the living room

Mom: Avert her eyes and just hope A-D Andrews doesn't scuff or scratch anything; set out the cheese to acclimate to room temperature

Ginny: Guard door to the library so that nobody wanders in and sees that 5142 Haven Lane has a big empty room right on the first floor

Plum: Light candles; take out trash; other duties as assigned

"Oh God, hurry!" Mom darted back and forth from the library to the living room as Almost-Doctor Andrews inched down the stairs, lugging the coffee table from the TV room.

At this sight, Ginny stopped abruptly, holding both dogs by the collars. She then turned to look at me, and I accidentally let a match burn my fingertips.

"Ow!"

Almost-Doctor Andrews stopped. "Something wrong?"

"We don't . . ." I started. "That table is kind of . . . our dad made it."

"Oh," he said. "I'm so sorry. I didn't know."

"It's all right," I said. "Sorry to make you take it up again."

Ginny didn't meet my eyes. But Almost-Doctor Andrews said it was no trouble and took it back up, and with twenty more minutes' lugging had found some end tables, card tables, and a freestanding bathroom pedestal that became presentable with the application of a small tablecloth.

"Plum?" Mom called as she threw down the last of the throw rugs. "I want to have the candles lit by four."

With the dogs now secured in the bedroom, I sidled up to Ginny, who was watching the speed-redecorating from the doorway. "How's it look?"

"Full of stuff," Ginny said. "It's like our own private Potemkin village here."

"A what?"

"Ah," Almost-Doctor Andrews said, smiling. "According to legend, a Russian named Grigory Potemkin used to build false villages to impress Catherine the Great."

Mom folded her arms. She was, of course, wearing all black. "God. It's not funny."

Ginny threw me a look.

"It's a little funny, Mom," I said, as gently as I could. Mom took a longing look at the wine.

Just then, the doorbell rang.

Mom rushed off to the cheese plates in a bustle of black silk. Ginny yelled, "Places, people!" as if we were on a movie set, then thrust herself in front of the library, braced her arms against the doorframe, and growled, "None shall pass."

Which left me, Plum, to answer the door.

From then on, everything was a blur—ladies in wraps, men in ties, hi-how-are-yous, nods, heavy wool piled onto my arms and ferried back to the coat closet behind the stairs, relighting tiny candles, picking up people's crumpled napkins, smiling, smiling, smiling. It was raining, too, which meant that the coats people gave me got gradually more and more soggy. But I bore it gamely, because nothing distracts you from personal turmoil like relighting tiny candles and bundling up big bags of trash.

Speaking of the trash, I wasn't sure what to do with all the bags, since it was raining.

"Just . . . throw them in the basement, or something," Mom told me. She was clutching a little plastic glass of wine, which I had not seen at a level less than nearly full to the brim since the party had begun. Also, judging by the flush in her ordinarily very pale cheeks, it was not her first. "You can take them outside when it stops raining."

I told her I would, and that she was doing great, by the way, and then hustled to the kitchen to throw out the bags. To her credit, Mom was doing a *really* good job of pretending to be normal. I think Mom is actually a way better hostess than she admits, to herself or to anyone else. For one thing, she'd bought about a metric ton of cheese, which was spread over the Potemkin side tables in attractive slices and rounds and creamy little hunks. For another, she was not saying too many things, which is generally a good strategy for someone as easily flustered as she is.

I'd pitched about five bags full of little napkins and toothpicks down to the basement when the doorbell rang for the last time. I remember thinking it was weird that someone was arriving so late, but not enough to truly give me pause.

In the five steps it took me to cross the part of the front hall formerly covered by the antique Oriental runner with the elephant border, I did a quick physical inventory. Clothes (Those Pants, a yellow green boatneck top with no cartoon cat on it, dangly green earrings): normal. Hair (reverse French braid): regular. Makeup (borrowed mostly from Ginny, checked in my reflection in the window door): fine. There was absolutely no reason that my appearance would incur any kind of awkwardness-inducing commentary.

Thus reassured, I swung open the door and found myself face-to-face with Alicia Feingold formerly Kurokawa née Tate.

For a tiny, frozen second, time stood still. The expression *time stood still* had always struck me as, at best, hyperbolic and, at worst, a total impossibility of physics. But I swear, when I saw Alicia Feingold formerly Kurokawa née Tate on our welcome mat, I experienced a moment of pure, atemporal panic.

"Oh," said Tate's mom. "It's you. Hello, you."

Outside, it was now pouring rain, and she was really drippy. I still felt a little frozen.

"May I come in?" she said, after I said nothing.

"Yes!" I said, much too enthusiastically. "Please come in."

She did, after daintily wiping her feet on the doormat, which I realized too late read GO AWAY (obviously as a joke, but still, not the kind of joke you want to be making where the fate of your mother's job hangs upon her ability to be hospitable).

"May I take your coat?" I asked, hopefully politely.

Tate's mom nodded. "Thank you."

She set her purse on the mail table, which was mercifully still there, and shrugged out of her coat. Alicia Feingold formerly Kurokawa née Tate, unlike Mom, seemed to own party clothes that weren't only not black, but were also the right size, which was probably something like a triple extra small. She had on a cocktail dress in some kind of crepe material that went from red to bronze depending on how the light hit it.

I took her coat (which was black) and smiled. Because she hadn't said anything and so probably wouldn't say anything, either she had forgotten my appearance in her kitchen three nights ago or we were both going to pretend it had never happened.

Either way, I was still terrified.

"Well, I'll go hang this up," I mumbled, and hightailed

it to the coat closet. There, in the relative safety of a wall of outerwear, I put the coat on a hook and allowed myself the luxury of a few seconds' recombobulation. (Coat closets are good for that.)

Of all the possible War and Cheese disaster contingencies, the arrival of Tate's mom was the worst because it wasn't even a contingency I had planned for (which I guess meant it wasn't a contingency at all). Worse, no one in my family could *know* it was a disaster, because alerting them would require an explanation of the whole Tate situation, and the last thing that I needed was my mom—or worse, Ginny—teasing me about a boy. (Of course, this was not at all a typical boy-girl situation—more like a series of encounters with escalating levels of personal discomfort—but try explaining that to your older sister.)

With a deep breath, I stepped out of the coat closet and smack into Ginny.

"Dude, Plummy, this is a nightmare," she said under her breath. "These two ladies were whispering about us when they thought Mom wasn't looking. All this stuff about how we got the tiny plastic house of shame because we didn't want to share our inside bathrooms with contractors."

"What?"

"I know, right? We're so not that snooty. Mom even made the meter reader a sandwich that one time." Ginny blew a strand of hair out of her eyes. "Also, I look like an idiot trying to guard the door."

"You're not guarding it right now," I pointed out.

"I left up a sign. I had to pee." She flashed me a smile. "Can you take over for a second?"

I told her that signs never keep anyone out of anywhere but that yes, I would.

As people chatted and ate cheese chunks in the Potemkin village, I stood by the library door in what I hoped was a pose of casual intimidation. Because, as I realized, the only thing worse than trying to talk normally with Tate's mom would be trying to explain to Tate's mom why the crazy Blatchley family had an entirely empty ghost room on their first floor. Therefore, I mentally rewrote my marching orders thusly:

Plum: Ensure that, no matter what, Alicia Feingold formerly Kurokawa née Tate leaves the War and Cheese with no knowledge of the showering incident or the Potemkin village

"There you are."

I nearly jumped out of my skin. Tate's mom had somehow snuck out of the living room with a tiny plate of cheese and was smiling at me.

"Alicia," she said. "I believe we met the other night."

Cripes. "Yup," I said. "I mean, Plum. My name is Plum."

"Plum." She nodded. "So you and Tate are classmates?"

"Um, we're . . . in the same grade?"

"Oh." (This being the literal definition of *classmate*, I can't imagine Tate's mom was impressed.) She gave a little glance over my shoulder. "Is that sign serious?"

I wheeled around to where Ginny had left a sticky note that read, DANGER: DO NOT ENTER: RADIOAC-TIVE. (You see what I mean about her signs not working.)

"Oh, that's just my sister," I said, smiling in what I hoped was an affable manner while crumpling the sticky note into a tiny ball. "Just a joke."

"I see," said Tate's mom. "And . . . is there a reason you're standing in the doorway?"

Tate's mom was clearly a seasoned interrogator. (I guess raising Tate and half raising Benji Feingold would do that to a person.)

"Not exactly," I said.

"Well," Tate's mom said. "I just wanted to thank you."

"Thank me?"

"You don't know how long I've been telling Tate to get someone to help him with his essays. College is coming up—well, I know you know that. And having someone like you . . ."

I must have looked confused, because Alicia's smile widened sympathetically.

"Well, I've read that you're quite bright," she said. "Your father's essay was . . . well, *is*, quite wonderful. He clearly thought very highly of you."

My gaze flew to the ground. "Not me," I said. "My sister."

"Oh," she said, untroubled, probably not even noticing, because, honestly, who cared? "Well, anyway, thanks for agreeing to tutor Tate." She held up a big leather clutch, which she'd held on to after I took her coat. "How much do I owe you?"

"Oh, I . . ."

I was not one to accept money from classmates' mothers without due cause. However, it did seem like we had a ruse to maintain. And, to be honest, I didn't want to get Tate in trouble.

"We paid Benji's math tutor forty dollars an hour," Tate's mom said helpfully. She fished in a big leather wallet. "I only have a fifty, I'm sorry. We can consider it an advance on your next session, how about?"

I almost wanted to ask if she thought I was still worth full price, not being the sister she'd assumed I was.

"Okay," I said, and took the folded-up bill, completely unsure of what to say next. Fortunately, Ginny was clomping down the front stairs from the bathroom at that very moment.

"I'm so sorry," I said to Tate's mom, "but I really need to get the trash."

"You live here?" Tate's mom looked up around the front hall. "This is a beautiful house."

I thought she might have been joking, considering the front hall was sea green and decorated with folk art from our parents' honeymoon, not to mention the fact that the Potemkin-village living room was a hodgepodge of competing styles of furniture. But Tate's mom seemed serious.

"Oh," I said. "Yes. But my mom was the one who deco-rated it. She said it was her mission to make sure none of the walls were boring white."

Too late, I realized that pretty much every room in Tate's house was boring white. But Tate's mom smiled.

"I love it."

"Oh, um, thank you," I said, just as Ginny popped up at my side to take her post again. "This is my sister, Ginny."

"Hello." Ginny gave a polite smile while inching back into position in front of the door. "Wonderful party, isn't it?"

"Ah," Tate's mom said, smiling. "So you're the one with the astrolabe. Pleasure to meet you."

Ginny looked at me, arms half spread in her door-defending position.

"That essay Dad wrote," I said. "'A Treatise on the Astro-labe.'"

"Oh," Ginny said blithely. "I haven't read it, I'm afraid."

Before Tate's mom could answer, Mom slipped out of the living room, and I practically leaped to her side. Another mom, I figured, would be way better at schmoozing with Tate's mom, and way less likely to say something embarrassing.

"*Mom*," I said pointedly. "You remember Mrs., um . . ." I had no idea which last name to use. ". . . Tate's mom."

"Of course!" Mom beamed. "Jennifer!"

There was a long, time-standing-still kind of silence, during which our oblivious mother stood hovering, smiling faintly, and unaware that her laissez-faire attitude toward remembering things had just kneecapped her burgeoning success as a society hostess.

"Well, I . . . think I'll go mingle," Tate's mom said cheerfully. "I'll see you around, Plum."

She slipped back into the living room with a little nod.

"See you around?" Ginny said, but I ignored her.

"Mom!" I cried. "How could you?"

Mom frowned. "How could I what?"

"Jennifer's another one," Ginny explained loudly.

"Shh!" I put a hand on Ginny's mouth. "Keep your voice down!"

Mom went ghost-pale. "Oh my God. I just—" She swiveled her head back to the living room. "*Shit.* Shit! And I bet she's a donor, too."

Ginny pushed me away. "Well, as long she doesn't sign *Jennifer* on the check out of spite, I guess. Right, Mother darling?"

Mom's kohl-rimmed eyes had gone very narrow.

"Don't worry about it," I rushed in. "She won't be spiteful." Probably. "Just tell her you made a mistake."

Ginny squinched her face at me. "What's *your* problem? Who cares if we get all the snobby ladies' names wrong?"

"She's not snobby," I said. Because she wasn't, it turned out.

"You're kidding." Ginny cocked her head at me. "You do

know that's *Benji and Tate*'s mom, right?"

Obviously, I could say nothing.

"Sorry."

Ginny gave her head a little shake. "Is this party over yet?"

I glanced at my phone. "Twenty more minutes."

Ginny sighed. "Fine."

She went back to her post, and Mom went to the kitchen, and I listlessly picked up the candle-lighter thing and relit a dead tea light. Our mother, I hated to admit, had just committed the worst kind of faux pas, i.e., a faux pas that points out that yes, most of the women at these events *were* fairly interchangeable and *did* just need to get their names right on the checks. But what was worse, and what I hated even more to *admit* was worse, is that of all the names to screw up, it had to be Tate's mom's. She'd embarrassed our whole family, and she hadn't even needed the ghost room or our shameful shower situation to do it. I wished, very hard, that somehow my brain would be hit with a selective memory wipe that would make me forget everything after Mom had showed up. That way I could maybe eventually go back over to Tate's house and act like things *were* fine.

In retrospect, though, my powers of forgetting may have worked a little too well.

It started slowly at first. A little buzzy something around my head as I choked down my free-from-the-backyard eggs. A few loopy black dots bobbing in the air above Gizmo's and Doug's doggie beds. And then, the following Saturday, I woke up to the distinct sound of my sister shrieking.

"Aieeee!"

Two seconds later, my bedroom door flung open and a Ginny-shaped blur dove into bed with me.

"What?" I sat up so fast I almost hit my head on the eaves. "What? Is it the dogs?"

"No," Ginny said, quivering in her pajamas. "There's *flies*."

"Ugh." I tried to roll over. "So what? Just ignore them."

"I *can't*, Plum." Ginny thrust a pointy elbow into my ribs as she repositioned herself onto my pillow. "There's literally thousands."

"I sincerely doubt that," I said.

"*Seriously*, Plummy. Go look."

With Ginny at my heels, making retching noises, I reluctantly descended the back stairs. The kitchen was, for lack of a better word, *swarming*. Fat black clumps of flies were clustering on every surface: the blades of the ceiling fan, the corners of the cabinets, even the antlers of the fake moose head. Kit Marlowe, unusually agitated, was scurrying back and forth in front of the Franklin stove, seemingly caught between swatting down the insects and not wanting to expend any effort on anything.

"God*damn* it," Mom said. "What the hell is going on?"

"Mom," I said. "Calm down."

"I will *calm down* when I know why our house is full of all these *freaking* flies."

"She's trying to quit smoking," Ginny said. "Aren't you? Isn't that why you're irritable?"

Mom shot Ginny a withering look. "Yes. I am. If that's all right with you."

"Fine," Ginny said sweetly.

A fly zoomed buzzingly across my field of vision. I shrieked. "Cripes!"

"*I* didn't do it." Ginny folded her arms. "Just so we're clear."

"No one's *blaming* you," I said.

"Well, *someone* should be blamed," Ginny said, swatting futilely in front of her face. "This many flies don't just *show up*. They have to come from *somewhere*."

She looked at Mom for backup, but Mom was too busy tugging up the bottom of the window behind the sink.

"Ginny," she said, panting a little. "Relax."

"You're straining," Ginny said. "The cigarettes have already diminished your VO2 max."

"She's straining because the *window's painted shut,* Ginny," I said.

Mom drummed her fingers along her jaw. "Has everyone been cleaning up their food?" she asked.

"I've been putting eggs in the basket," I said, because there wasn't really space in the fridge for all the eggs our chickens produced, and because Aunt Linda had given us the chicken-shaped countertop basket expressly for that purpose. "Does that count?"

"Eggs don't leave crumbs," Mom said. "I'm worried about crumbs."

"You're thinking of ants," Ginny said, only to yelp and jump out of her chair as a particularly fat one swooped near her head.

"Taking out the trash?"

We all sat there, contemplative in the horrific buzzing silence of a Saturday morning. And a terrible realization crept into my consciousness.

"Um," I said. "I think . . . maybe . . . I know where they came from?"

I led my horrified family to the top of the basement steps.

Below, just visible in light of the bare light bulb that burned by all the coats, was a squishy, rotten pile of trash.

Ginny retched, and it probably wasn't even a fake retch.

"Oh Lord," Mom said. "The basement leaked. All the rain got on the trash."

"Why is there trash in the basement?" Ginny asked.

"It was from the War and Cheese," I said quietly. "Last week. I just forgot."

"Forgot?!" Ginny yelled. I shrunk back and requested softly that they please not murder me.

"No one's going to murder anyone, Plum," Mom said. She had grabbed the previous day's *New York Times* off the kitchen table and had started to wave it around her face. "Except maybe this herd of flies. Or whatever you're supposed to call a bunch of flies."

"*Disgusting* is what," Ginny said, and retched again.

"We could put up flypaper," I suggested meekly. "And I'll go get the trash and throw it away, right now. I'm really, really sorry. I'm terrible."

I didn't realize my sniffling had turned into crying until Mom wrapped her arms around my head. (Mom gives weird hugs.)

"Shh, Plummy, it's fine," she said. "We're not mad."

"Speak for yourself," Ginny said. "*I'm* mad, because this is gross."

Ginny stomped over to the back door, flung it open, and

started windmilling her arms toward the yard.

"Shoo! Get out! Go away, you disgusting bugs!"

Whether any flies actually followed her orders was hard to tell. But Kit Marlowe did.

"Kit!" I cried. "Mom!"

Mom was trying another window. Ginny was busy swatting.

"The gate, the gate!" I cried. "It's not closed!"

There was a scramble for everyone to pull on shoes and outerwear. Kit Marlowe was an avowedly indoor cat. Whatever predatory survival instincts he possessed in his feline DNA were either deeply recessive or overpowered by his desire to avoid any and all aspects of the outside world. He'd gotten out only twice before in his long kitty life, once to the edge of the backyard and once for a terrifying overnight stay in the baseball dugout ten blocks away. The only feasible retrieval strategies were (1) gradually encroaching on him from all sides, or (2) a running tackle.

"Kit!" I yelled down the street, having been the quickest to get my clogs on. "Kitty cat!"

"C'mere, Kit!" Ginny was hot on my trail, sliding through mud and leaf muck in a pair of Mom's loafers. "Here, boy!"

Somewhere, in the direction of Evergreen Lane, I heard the tiny jingling of cat tags.

"This way!" I yelled. "I think!"

We ran down the block, Ginny sliding on the slate

sidewalks and me terrified that I was going to turn an ankle in my dumb clogs, until we arrived at the big house at the corner of Evergreen. My heart sank. But sure enough, as fate would stupidly, unfairly have it, Kit was stalking around in the giant mountain laurel bush behind Tate's house.

"What is he doing *here*?" Ginny scooped her hair out of her eyes, panting a little.

"Doesn't matter," I said quickly. "Let's just catch him."

"Isn't that trespassing?" Ginny said. The mountain laurel bush was actually inside the yard, which meant that we would technically have to cross the threshold of the property to get Kit back.

"It's fine. No one will see us." I very much hoped this would be the case, not only because I was still wearing my pajamas but also because Ginny was there, which multiplied the potential for embarrassment by about 10,000 percent, should anyone come out of the house.

Ginny spread her arms wide, like she was trying to frighten off a mountain lion, and started slowly stalking toward Kit with giant steps. I held my arms out at a much more normal-person angle and followed suit, but from the opposite side. Kit Marlowe, unperturbed, rolled onto his back.

Ginny took a step. I took a step. Kit's tags jingled. We were barely two feet away on each side when someone yelled from the porch.

"Peach?"

Tate was hanging out the back door.

"Kind of early, aren't you?" he said. "I figured you'd come by in the afternoon, or something."

"Grab him!" I yelled, not bothering to explain. Ginny did, and gave me a very peculiar look, which I chose to ignore.

"Get the cat," I told her. "I'm so sorry," I told Tate. "Our cat is . . . he doesn't get out. Kit Marlowe, like the playwright? Um, he hates people. And the outdoors. He is really an indoor cat. He just likes the house. But he ran out the door because . . . well, I guess because he had to escape?"

I was babbling. Tate smiled.

"A break for freedom or something?"

"Something like that." I swiveled my head to the mountain laurel, where Ginny was inches away from an unsuspecting Kit.

"I see. Nice pajamas, by the way."

My face got hot. They *were* nice pajamas, but that is not the point. By now it was almost every other time that I saw Tate, I was dressed somehow strangely. Why he couldn't be there when I looked nice at the War and Cheese, I don't know.

"Thanks," I mumbled. Ginny, meanwhile, had launched herself forward and apprehended our fugitive.

"Bad kitty," she said, as if those words meant anything to Kit Marlowe. "Very bad."

She shook a finger in his face. Tate straightened up. He was also wearing pajamas, which made me even more embarrassed than the fact of my *own* pajamas. I had no idea why.

"Hey, so, my mom said she saw you the other day," he said. "At some wine-and-cheese thing?"

"Oh," I said, as noncommittally as possible. Ginny imperceptibly lowered the volume of her cat scolding.

"Yeah," Tate said. "She said your house is cool."

My house, at that very moment, was swarming with flies.

"It's not," I said quickly. "I mean, it's nothing special. There's nothing to see."

"Oh," Tate said. "Well, anyway, she said it was nice to talk to you."

"Really?"

"Yeah." Tate put his hands in his pajama pockets and nodded again. "Yeah, sure. Uh, are you . . . around later? Like at home?"

"Don't come over," I said, probably too fast. Tate shook his head.

"Oh, yeah, no, I . . . never mind. I just, uh . . . I told my mom you were helping me with English."

"I figured that out," I said.

"Yeah," Tate said. "So maybe . . . can you, actually? Like, she'll pay. And you make all those notes in your books and stuff."

The Senior Tea. I could not believe he remembered. And I could not tell him those were *Ginny's* notes. My heart sank.

"So okay?"

"PLUUUUM!" Ginny bellowed from the sidewalk. "The cat is literally clawing the skin from my body."

She flailed around with a belligerent Kit in her arms.

"I, uh, have to go," I said to Tate. "I'm sorry."

"Okay," Tate said. "Here." He held out his phone. "Give me your number?"

Without pausing to think, I punched it in, and said good-bye again, and jogged back to the sidewalk, and scooped Kit away from Ginny, and together we retreated home.

"What was *that* about?" Ginny said incredulously. "Did I just see you talking to Tate Kurokawa for a nonzero amount of time?"

"I was apologizing," I said. Ginny scoffed.

"Good," she said. "He's loathsome." She stared Kit right in his beady eyes. "Never, ever abandon us again, cat. Understand? You'll leave us *bereft*."

That Monday, it was impossibly cold, and as I bundled my outdoor layers over my indoor layers in the Gregory School vestibule, I contemplated the opportunity before me.

In books, when confronted with the eventualities of abject poverty, young women most often end up shipped to obscure relations, marrying rich, or becoming governesses. We did not have obscure relations, only the cousins in Erie who believed a little too fervently in Jesus, and sending me and Ginny off to live with Aunt Linda and Uncle Phil would probably do very little to solve the problem of our mother's mortgage. Marrying rich sounded noble and selfless and possibly involving elegant dresses with ruffles. Unfortunately, fictional young women are always meeting eligible wealthy bachelors because they're going to balls all the time, and no one in the Blatchleys' immediate social circle gave balls per se. Probably the closest thing I'd ever attended was the Gregory School Senior Tea—or worse, the War and Cheese—and look how those had ended. Rather than a fading annuity from a lapsed estate, we had sporadic event-planning checks and routine social embarrassments.

But I did, now, kind of, have the potential to become a governess. Of sorts. For actual money.

I tied my scarf around my neck with resolve and headed out into the freezing December afternoon.

"Today's the day," Ginny said, when I got into the car. She had on a giant knit hat, and her cheeks looked almost blue in the weak sunlight.

"What day?"

Before Ginny could answer, there was a dreadfully loud rap at the window. Charlotte was crouched by the passenger-side window, waving frantically. Sometimes we gave her a ride home, which Charlotte always promised to reciprocate, or give us gas money, but never seemed to actually remember to. Today she had on a cream-colored sweater under a puffy navy vest, like the kind you'd go duck hunting in.

"Hey, beautiful," Charlotte called through the glass. "Ready to take hold of our futures?"

"Plum, get in the back," Ginny said.

"But—"

"*Go.*" Ginny shoved me, and I tumbled out of the driver's side door and practically *into* Charlotte, who did not look pleased.

"Um, excuse you?" She laughed, then slid herself in and situated her massive tote bag of books at her feet. Ginny revved the engine and backed us out of Jesus Is the Way

Christian Church and onto the street.

"God, it's freezing in here," Charlotte said, rubbing her upper arms.

"Maybe that's because you're not wearing a coat," I pointed out. Ginny glared. Charlotte acted like I hadn't said anything. "Is your heat on?"

"It's broken," Ginny explained. "Sorry, I've been bugging my mom about it forever, but you know how she is."

Charlotte made a little humming sound in the back of her throat, a humming sound I did not care for. "Oh. God, I'm so nervous. Aren't you nervous? I'm nervous. God."

"Yes," Ginny said. "I'm nervous."

"I need a hit of Juul," Charlotte said. "You want?"

"Vape?" I was aghast. This time, Charlotte heard me.

"Not *in the car*," she drawled, then went sickly sweet. "Okay?"

"Vaping is gross," I said. "And it causes lung cancer and emphysema, just so you know. There is scientific proof. Which I know you care very deeply about."

Charlotte set her jaw. "You know what? People who vape are sick of hearing that. Right, Gin?"

"I don't vape," Ginny said.

"You did once."

"You did?" I cried.

"Okay, but *once*," Ginny said. "It was after the SATs. Don't tell Mom."

"Why not?" I said. "She'd probably join you."

"Gin," Charlotte whined, unable to be excluded for the conversation for a full thirty seconds. "My place first?"

"Yeah, for sure," Ginny said. Indignantly, I kicked my backpack farther into place under the seat and pulled out my phone for a distraction. But shockingly, there was a new message, one *not* from Ginny, Mom, or Almost-Doctor Andrews, the only three people who ever texted me.

hey its tate

My chest constricted. Another message pinged.

so my mom actually wants you to tutor me if thats
cool haha

But no, yes, that was right. I was going to be proactive in the pursuit of my dream career—namely, governessing.

Hi, I wrote back. *Okay. I can do that.*

"I'm just, like, I don't even know," Charlotte was saying. "My odds have got to be *so* good, right? I mean my admissions interview went really well, and—"

"Did you wear the blazer?"

"No, it ended up looking too grandma. I did the purple V-neck."

"With the hoop earrings?"

"Yeah," Charlotte said. "Wait. Was that too trashy?"

"Depends on how low you had the V-neck pulled," Ginny said.

"Oh my God," Charlotte moaned. "Fuck."

We had reached the end of Charlotte's street, a line of newish houses constructed in blocky piles of geometry with sand-colored stucco and no charm to them whatsoever. They cost a fortune.

"One second," Charlotte said, clambering out of the car, toward the treasure that awaited her just on the other side of her mail slot.

"Don't open it!" Ginny yelled after her. She spun back to me.

"Plummy."

I snapped my head up from my phone, where the typing dots had come and gone, come and gone almost three times. "Cripes. What?"

"My stomach hurts."

"Why?"

"Because I didn't take advanced calculus." Ginny looked out to where Charlotte was clipping back down her driveway, an envelope in hand. "And I didn't even *do* an alumni interview."

"Nor do you own hoop earrings," I pointed out. Ginny cackled.

"Why do you even want to study science, Gin?"

"Because it makes sense."

"For you? No offense, but I'm not sure it does."

"No, I mean *science* makes sense. There are rights and wrongs. Things are solvable. It's just very . . . tidy. I don't know." Ginny traced a finger around the inside of the steering wheel. "Life's frustratingly ambiguous most of the time. We don't need more people musing about that. We need answers."

We sat in silence for a beat.

"Not to discourage you, Plum," Ginny said suddenly.

"What?"

"You're a muser," she said. "You're going to end up majoring in whatever will let you write in that notebook all the time like Harriet the Spy."

"I am not," I said quickly.

"Got iiiiiiit!"

Charlotte slammed the car door with gusto. "Let's roll, bitches."

Five minutes later we pulled into the driveway at Haven Lane, setting the dogs barking madly. Ginny flung open the car door, followed immediately by Charlotte, followed slightly more slowly by me.

"I think we *could* be roommates," Charlotte was saying, "but my mom says it's good to branch out. And maybe we'll want to live in different dorms, you know?"

Ginny said something I didn't hear, because I was staring at my phone. The typing dots bloomed again at the bottom of the messages. Typing. Typing. Typing. Then, finally:

cool just let me know when your free

Good Lord. No wonder Tate needed an English tutor. He was a grammar moron.

Any evening this week, I wrote back, then wondered if perhaps I should've feigned a fuller calendar for the sake of appearing in-demand as a tutor. But it was too late, because Tate had already replied.

tmw night?

Fine, I wrote back.

k see you then 🍑

Of course. A peach. How droll. I pocketed my phone and stepped through the back door.

The dogs had stopped barking. Ginny already had her coat off, her hair a wild frame of static after her knit hat. She was clutching a piece of paper, looking from whatever was written on it to Charlotte and back again.

Charlotte's face was slack.

"Seriously?" she was saying softly. "What are you even going to *do*, Gin?"

"Char, just—" Ginny said, and then, all at once, Charlotte's expression sharpened into fury.

"No, fuck this," Charlotte said. "*Fuck* this."

She pushed past me with an actual push, catching me right on the shoulder, and the back door slapped behind her. Outside, a noise came—a yell, or a sob, I couldn't tell.

Instantly I knew what had happened.

"Ginny," I said. "Ginny, I'm sorry. You're brilliant; you know that? You're an actual genius."

She looked so pale, practically eerie, with her hair standing up in the air, and I almost told her. I almost told her what Dad had said. But I couldn't. Not quite.

"No," Ginny whispered. "I got in."

"Oh," I said. "Oh. And Charlotte was . . ."

"Wait-listed." Ginny set the letter on the table. We stood in silence for a moment, except for the hissing of the Franklin stove.

"You're just glad I got in somewhere because now you *know* I'm leaving," she said at last.

"No," I said, even though that was partially the truth. "I meant what I said."

"Well, thanks," she said. "I'm glad at least one person thinks so."

She fell forward and buried herself against me, hands folded up between our chests, and started to cry.

I awoke Tuesday morning with a cold feeling in my stomach—dread, perhaps, or just a seeping-in of the actual cold that was penetrating the stone walls of 5142 Haven Lane from every angle. Ginny, somehow, was flung out on the mattress—*my* mattress—next to me.

"Ginny!" I shrieked sleepily, if such a thing is possible, and scared Kit Marlowe from his curled-up place on the headboard. Ginny moaned and nuzzled into a pillow—the good pillow, I noted, which she must have snatched from under my head.

"I was overwhelmed, Plummy," she mumbled. Her hair fell over her eyes, like how we used to comb our hair forward and pretend to be Puddleglum the Marsh-wiggle from Narnia, who, for some reason, we had conflated with Cousin It from the Addams Family.

Downstairs, Mom was reading the *New Yorker* in her robe and sighing into a cup of coffee.

"Don't worry!" She waved the magazine. "I stole it from

work. That's better, right?"

I gave her a look that said, *Not exactly, but I'll take petty theft over wasting money when the cartoons are free online.*

I prepared a single slice of toast, which piqued Gizmo's interest such that he wedged his can-opener nose between my legs and the counter.

"There's coffee," Mom said. "And eggs. The girls are laying like crazy."

"No, thank you," I said. I was jittery enough. My phone had received no new messages, and I had no desire to reach out for confirmation. I would let the question of tutoring hang, waiting for a sign. I would not think about it too much.

Ginny slumped in, and I expected some dramatic proclamation about her feelings, or at least some affected moaning. But she simply poured herself a travel mug of coffee and took two placid bites of a store-brand granola bar.

"It's freezing in here."

"I know." Mom rose. "I asked Almost-Doctor Andrews to split some more logs, but he must've left early for campus. Which, speaking of, I'll be out late for a studio crit, so just order something for dinner." She went to her purse and rummaged. "Shit. Does either of you have any cash?"

"I've got it," I said, thinking of the fifty dollars that I already had and the forty—well, thirty, since I'd been overpaid—dollars that would soon be mine. "I'll take care of it tonight."

"Let's go, Plum." Ginny jammed on her hat and grabbed

her backpack, the trash can swishing as she chucked the rest of her breakfast.

We didn't stop for Charlotte, and so, we got to school early.

The school day passed eerily fast, catapulting toward the afternoon in a string of unremarkable classes and an even less remarkable turkey sandwich I'd made last night and no irksome invitations from Jeremy to play Dungeons and Dragons. My heart was skittering, irritatingly enough, but I commanded my body to calm itself. There was no way I'd be able to focus if I succumbed to apoplexy. For all my scrupulousness in my reading, I had very little idea of the practical realities of governessing. *Jane Eyre* wasn't exactly a how-to manual. (Ginny, when she was little, had insisted that there was a book called *How to Kill a Mockingbird,* which our father had found endlessly amusing. "As if Harper Lee were an avid sportswoman," he'd say. "She and Capote with shotguns behind a duck blind.") And Ginny was right: English wasn't like math, where there was always a formula, always a correct answer. It was subjective, which was both its beauty and its curse. I, being no genius, was not at all confident in my ability to telegraph the intricacies of *Jane Eyre, The Great Gatsby* (our second book of the year), and *Frankenstein* (our third book of the year, although we hadn't finished it yet), and someone who thought *your* was the proper contraction of *you are* might be too far gone. Also, all my clothes were stupid and my sweater looked dumb.

When we got home, Ginny unzipped her coat, then rezipped it immediately.

"Jesus," she said. "Why aren't there more logs?"

"I guess Almost-Doctor Andrews didn't get a chance," I said. Usually he was back by the afternoon, but who knew what mysterious obligations a life of academia entangled him in. Ginny wilted.

"I'll go," I said. A little cardiovascular work splitting logs would surely calm my nerves.

I bundled back up and grabbed the ax from where we left it leaning against the chicken coop. Splitting logs was extremely satisfying: set the log on the stump, hoist the ax, and *thwack*. It made one feel mighty and self-sufficient, like Laura Ingalls Wilder. As I swung and thwacked, I imagined myself making jams, putting up pickled eggs for the winter, sewing us new Christmas dresses out of calico. Laura was always too nice to Mary, if you asked me. If Ginny went blind from fever, I'd let her figure things out on her own. Or I'd describe them for her, maybe, but she would owe me.

Triumphant, logs split, I replaced the ax and carried my bounty to the kitchen, where I dumped the logs in their place beside the stove. All the swinging and thwacking had made me hot.

"There's no food in the fridge," Ginny said. "Except some mustard and two eggs. Also, your phone's been buzzing like crazy."

I scrambled to pick it up.

hey come over whenever

It was obvious who it was from, although I had not yet saved his number as a contact. Too late, I realized I was sweating heavily. I stripped off my scarf, but it didn't seem to do much. Was *whenever* truly *whenever*? Maybe I'd have time to take a shower (something I would never take for granted again).

"I'm going to take a nap," Ginny announced. "Get me tikka masala when you order, okay?"

"Okay." As I was staring at the message, the dots appeared. Then:

actually can you come now theres a sixers game

at 6

Still more dots.

and i know you would hate to miss your boys

I fanned myself in a desperate attempt to lower my body temperature and dug through my backpack for all the requisite books. It was too late to cancel—it'd be rude, and also, I could not pick up tikka masala for Ginny, samosas for me, and palak paneer for Mom, *and* leave a reasonable tip *and* have any actual money left over without Tate's mom's forty dollars. No—thirty dollars since I'd gotten ten extra. So instead, I set out without my coat, thinking the fresh air would naturally freeze away my sweat.

"What happened to your coat?" Tate asked, five minutes later. He was barefoot, again, in sweatpants and a T-shirt that read, TRUST THE PROCESS.

"Nothing happened to it," I said. "It's just at home."

"Okay," Tate said. "Well, come on in."

I did. We stood in his kitchen, silent.

"Uh, I don't have any pizza bagels, or anything," Tate said. "But my mom left this."

He held out the forty dollars. She must have forgotten that she'd advanced me ten. But I wasn't about to ask Tate to make change.

"Thank you," I said, attempting a businesslike tone of voice. "Shall we get started?" That also seemed no-nonsense.

"Sure."

Tate swung onto a barstool at the countertop. There were three stools. Sitting in the third would leave a decorous amount of space between us, and give hopefully a sufficient radius to distance my sweaty self from Tate. But it also would make it hard to reach him. Not that I was reaching *for* him, I mean; just that I might have to write on a piece of paper or something that was near *to* him.

A drop of sweat rolled down my neck. I put my things in front of the third stool.

"You gonna sit that far away?" Tate said.

"Oh, I just . . . I don't know." I moved to the second stool. Why was I always appearing at Tate's house in need of hygienic attention? He was going to think I never bathed.

Tate was resting a forearm on the counter's edge. There was nothing in front of the first stool.

"Where are your books?" I said.

"Oh," Tate said. "Yeah."

He slid back out of the stool and pounded up the stairs, leaving me to stare at the Kurokawa-Feingold kitchen and at the ticking clock above the sink, which had no numbers and, I am guessing, did not play bird calls to mark the hours.

Tate returned and threw down pristine copies of *Jane Eyre, The Great Gatsby,* and *Frankenstein.* The spines had not even been cracked. I was sure that they did not have Benji's notes in the margins, either.

"There ya go," he said, and climbed back onto the stool. "Now what?"

I gave him a look that said, *You tell me.* "What do you need help with? Vocabulary? Reading comprehension?"

"I mean, all of it, kind of." Tate propped an elbow on the counter to lean on and began to fidget with a ballpoint pen with his free hand. "The midterm's coming up, right?"

As if the Gregory School's midterms weren't at the same time every year, just after winter break so that we'd all have a chance to panic properly with our free time. I didn't really intend to study much, but it wasn't like in-class essays were difficult. "Right."

"Yeah," Tate said. "So I'll need help on that, for sure."

The pen clicked against the granite as Tate fidgeted. This was becoming maddeningly unproductive. Then, out of nowhere, I was struck by the line of his neck. What about it, I couldn't say—the way it eased into his T-shirt, the structure of it, just the presence of it. Some boys our age still looked twelve years old, with skinny limbs and round faces. Tate did not.

The silence had gone on too long. I needed to speak, and take governessly charge.

"All right," I said. "Well, how about you write an essay and I can look it over."

"A whole essay? Now?"

"No, just the CliffsNotes," I said. "*Yes,* a whole essay. You only get forty-five minutes for the midterm."

"What, are you going to time me?"

I grabbed my phone and held it aloft.

Tate groaned. "But like an essay on what?"

"Language and theme," I said. "In the books we've been reading." That was the whole bent of honors English—language and theme, language and theme, language and theme. I'd had the advantage of knowing this from Ginny's run-through two years ago, but it was also drilled into us almost every class, which I suppose you'd have to pay attention to know.

Tate sighed, and took out a pencil, and laboriously put it to paper. Then he must have realized that he'd need to look *in* a book to write about it, and so he laid *Frankenstein* flat with one hand and scribbled with the other. I remembered, suddenly, our fifth-grade music teacher, in the recorder unit, when Tate and all the other Loud Fifth-Grade Boys had taken up the alto, had clucked her tongue at their decision. *Your hands won't fit,* she had told him. *I can see the tendons stretching.*

They weren't stretching now. His fingers were as long and fluid as his handwriting was bad. I watched, and looked at my phone for the time, and pretended to reread my own copy.

After twenty-some minutes, Tate put down his pencil.

"I can't," he said.

"What do you mean?" I said. "It's just writing."

"I can't write, though," he said. "It's hard, Peach. Just, like, figuring it out. I need help."

I refused to bristle at the stupid nickname. "What do you mean by help?"

"Like tell me what to say, and I'll say it." He held out the pencil. "Make some notes or whatever."

I stared. "I'm not going to *write your paper for you.* Are you crazy?"

"Sor-ry," Tate said, dragging out the second syllable. "My mom said your dad was a writer, so I thought you did that, too."

The heat came back into my face, and my whole body. I felt flushed all the way to my stomach.

"I don't want to do anything like *this,*" I informed him. "That's plagiarism, in case you didn't know. And if you think

I'd cheat on your behalf, then you're stupider than I thought."

It was, in retrospect, a cruel thing to say.

Tate said nothing. There was a creak and muffled steps upstairs, and a series of thumps brought Benji into the kitchen.

"Whoa," he said. "Did I disturb something?" He laughed, as if he had told a joke.

"Nah," Tate said, leaning back with a nod at me. "Mom said I need tutoring."

"Understatement," Benji said, swiping a banana from the top of the fridge. "For what?"

"English."

Benji guffawed. "Dude, it's English. You're born speaking it. It's like, the easiest subject. How dumb are you?"

Tate was still staring at the ceiling. "Pretty dumb, Benj," he said, a little softly.

Benji snorted through a mouthful of banana. "Dumb-ass."

I continued to say nothing. The stairs creaked as Benji retreated.

"There you go, Peach." Tate tipped forward and leaned over the counter. "You're not the only one who thinks I'm an idiot."

He wasn't meeting my eyes.

"It's whatever," Tate said. "Benji's right. I suck at this, and you can't make me better. No offense. It was just my mom."

"Oh," I said.

"I'll tell her," he said. "I mean, thanks."

"Are you sure?"

"Yeah." Tate got up. "Don't worry. You can keep the money."

He hadn't meant it that way. Or *maybe* he hadn't. But that last sentence stung.

"Fine." My throat hurt to say it. "Good night."

Late December had always been one of my favorite times of year, probably because 5142 Haven Lane was so Dickensian. Its banisters were made for evergreen swag, its steeply sloping roof for snow, and its windowsills for candles—although, as I discovered when digging out the Christmas boxes, about half our fake electric candlesticks had dangerously frayed wires, so I had to ration them to only the front side of the house. Our mother, who was nothing of a cook, was a surprisingly cheerful baker, and, when we arrived home after the last day of school before break, she had foregone her usual afternoon nap to pull out all the canisters of flour and sugar and set herself to mass-producing cookies.

"I could've been an excellent trophy wife," she said, pushing up the sleeves of her peasant blouse and thumping a block of sugar cookie dough onto the countertop. "Staying home and making cookies for the Ladies Auxiliary, or whatever."

"They'd make you cut your hair," Ginny said. "And wear a pastel twinset."

"I'm surprised they aren't making you do that already," I said. "For the silent auction."

"God," Mom said. "Don't remind me."

Flies notwithstanding, the War and Cheese had been such a success for Pamela Wills and her fund-raising efforts that our mother had not only been grossly overpaid but also drafted into planning ArtSong's annual silent auction in just a few short months. Mom had celebrated by taking a nap.

Mom stuck out her tongue, and Ginny cackled. Even *she* was in a good mood. She and Charlotte must have made up, because Charlotte had come over after school with us, and Ginny had plugged her phone into the stereo to blast Handel's *Messiah* and was singing along, although not lyrics that anyone, least of all Handel, had ever heard before. Ginny and Charlotte were at the kitchen table, cutting strips for paper chains—well, Ginny was cutting them, and Charlotte was making occasional half-hearted snips—and I was at the kitchen counter with cocoa and Kit Marlowe on my lap. Kit, perhaps overtaken by the Christmas spirit, had become more and more social, although he'd still stalk away if anyone looked at him for too long.

"Just so we're clear," I said, because it seemed like it needed to be said, "I don't want any presents this year."

"*Christmas just won't be* Christmas *without any presents!*" Ginny gasped. Mom and I laughed.

"You know, I always wanted to try sleeping with a peg on

my nose," Mom said. "But I couldn't quite figure out where to put the peg."

"Please," I said. "*Ginny* is the Amy."

"Oh yeah? And who are you, Meg?"

"I'm Jo."

"*Everyone* thinks they're Jo," Ginny said. "It's like how everyone thinks they're Lizzy and not, like, Mary." She rolled her eyes and glanced at Charlotte for backup.

Charlotte looked blank. "What are you *talking* about?"

"*Little Women?*" Ginny said. "You know, the March sisters."

"No, I don't know," Charlotte said stiffly. "Is everyone *supposed* to know *Little Women?*"

"What? No," Ginny said. "Sorry. We just . . . bring this stuff up sometimes, I guess."

"Mm." Charlotte toyed with a scrap of paper. "Are you almost ready to go?"

"One second." Ginny ran her scissors down one final sheet, slicing out a long red ribbon. "Perfect." She leaped up. "We're going out."

Mom was muscling over the dough with a rolling pin. "Out where?"

"Just to Lily's house," Charlotte said.

"Which one?" I asked.

"Lily *Sweet*," Ginny said. "Relax." She was wearing, I noticed, an actual outfit—black leggings and a big sweater—as opposed to a collage of clothes that did not belong to her. Charlotte had on another of her vests, this one covered in a dust-colored, brushlike fur. The effect was distinctly simian.

"Just don't stay out too late," Mom said.

"We won't," Charlotte said, too nicely. "What time is curfew?"

Ginny looked at Mom. Mom shrugged.

"Two?"

Charlotte, who was stabbing her feet into her boots, gaped. Ginny beamed.

"Works for me."

"All right, then," Mom said. "Gentle go into that good night, or whatever."

"Rage, rage!" Ginny cried, clenching a dramatic fist. Charlotte jerked her gaze up from her phone.

"That's from a poem," I said. Charlotte threw the tiniest glance at Ginny, who went black in the eyes.

"God, Plum, get over yourself," she said. "Do you have to be such a show-off all the time?"

Heat flared in my chest. "But you just—"

"Whatever, Plum!" Ginny threw up her hands. "It was just a dumb joke. Why do you act like everyone *but* you is stupid?"

I gulped, like Ginny had thumped me hard on the back, and looked at Mom. But Mom didn't seem to have heard. Triumphant, Ginny grabbed the keys from the key basket.

"Come on, Char. *Liebe und Küsse, Mutti.*" She ran over

and planted a kiss on each of our mother's cheeks, and then she and Charlotte clip-clopped out the back door, laughing like sleigh bells.

I blew across the surface of my cocoa, sending little chocolate ripples to the other edge of the mug. Kit mewled and leaped to the floor.

I didn't act smarter than everyone else. Did I? I didn't. I *didn't*. Or I did. Maybe I did. Maybe I did, and that in itself was proof of my actual nongenius. No truly smart people make a point of flaunting how smart they are.

"I think you're a Jo, Plum." Mom was picking through the cookie cutters, plucking out only the most non-yuletide shapes: the armadillo, the jack-o'-lantern, the standard poodle. "Maybe Jo by way of Meg. You're less of a brat than Jo. Hey, speaking of nose pegs, maybe after these cookies, we can try out some face masks. I got samples at Sephora." She looked up. "Something wrong?"

"Nothing," I said. I chewed my lip. "What did Dad used to say about people who didn't read?" I knew the answer, but I wanted to hear her say it.

"Oh," Mom said. *"Boring at parties, terrible at crosswords."*

I sipped my cocoa, sending warmth into my whole body. "Right."

"What a snob. Or no, worse." Mom shook her head, her rolling slowing. "An *aspiring* snob. Buck was always such a hypocrite."

"What?"

She said it lovingly, smiling. "Oh, your father *loved* people who didn't read. When we were just kids, we lived above this sports bar in Somerville—which, by the way, was such a shithole; I think I got a fried mouse in with my mozzarella sticks once, but your father never believed me—and he'd go downstairs and drink beer and eat peanuts and talk to the college kids watching the game until two a.m."

"He *did*?"

"Of course," Mom said. "Your father was a huge sports fan. You knew that."

I didn't.

"We had this fight," she went on, "because he went out and bought a jersey for . . . I don't know, whatever team, and I found it when I was doing laundry, and I was *furious*, because we had a rule that neither of us could spend more than twenty dollars without asking the other one first, and so when I found it, I confronted him, and you know what he said? *Oh, I've always had that.* And he had *not* always had it! We'd only been in Boston for two months!"

She paused, theatrically, as if relishing the rare chance to complain about her husband, telling a story she'd thought she'd be telling for the rest of her marriage. I looked into my cocoa.

"Do we still have it?" I asked.

"What, the jersey? Why?"

"Never mind," I said quickly.

"I don't know. You can look for it if you want." Mom became suddenly intent on her work.

I didn't want to. A sports jersey was a pointless reason to open the office. Any reason to open it was pointless, really.

"What was that place *called*?" Mom said. "Bumbler's or Stumbler's or something. Stub's?" The dough was now perfect and sandy smooth, a calm continent of butter and sugar. Mom lifted a cookie cutter, then paused. "God, it looks so nice. Almost a shame to cut a big hole in it."

"*Hark the herald angels si-ing—*"

"No," I mumbled into my pillow.

"*GLO-RY TOOOO THE NEW-BORN KIIIING.*"

I shoved off all the covers to my bed to find Ginny in her pajamas, hands pressed reverently together in front of her chest, a circle of tinsel jammed on her head.

"Merry Christmas, Plum," she said. "We made it."

As is customary, we ate cinnamon rolls from a tube and poured orange juice into champagne flutes (Mom's with actual champagne) and opened the presents I had insisted we not be given.

"I couldn't *not* get my daughters something for Christmas!" Mom tunneled down deeper into the corner of the couch, holding her glass in the air to avoid spills. "It's Scroogey. Grinch-like."

"Oh boy." Ginny dumped a bagful of squeezable packets onto the floor. "Sephora samples. However did you know?"

"Mom." I set the package in my hand down on the coffee

table and shoved away Gizmo and Doug when they immediately trotted over to investigate. "I do not want gifts. I told you."

"I know someone who does." Ginny pulled Kit Marlowe into her lap. "What do *you* want for Christmas, wittle kitty?"

"He wants you to leave him alone," I answered for Kit, and as if on cue, Kit mewled and twisted out of Ginny's grasp and whisked himself away into the empty library, where no sister could touch him.

"*'The real present is being together,'*" Ginny said squeakily. "*'Cozy and happy and warm in our little house-hole.'*"

Five Little Field Mice at Christmastime was among the treaclier volumes, and Ginny's twee rodent voice didn't help things.

Mom looked put out. "Well, what *did* you want, Ginny?"

"Admission to the University of Pennsylvania," Ginny said, mouse voice gone. "Which I've already been granted. So, I don't know. A new pair of ankle boots."

Mom gulped some mimosa.

"Hello?" A man's voice echoed in the front hallway in a perfectly timed interruption.

"In here!" Ginny yelled, so loudly that Mom winced. Almost-Doctor Andrews stuck his head around the corner.

"Hello," he said again, and produced a sugared brown loaf of something from behind his overcoat. "Merry Christmas."

"Oh, Marcus," Mom said. "You didn't have to. I don't even have a gift for you."

"You've given me a month's free rent," he pointed out. "I think that's plenty."

"What?" Ginny swiveled around to our mother. "When did this happen?"

Mom sighed. "Thanksgiving, when you were eating your six kinds of pie. Why don't you just open your present, Plum?"

Ginny narrowed her eyes, first at my bright-colored package, then at me.

"It's fine, Gin. I can take on more tutoring," I said, without thinking.

My sister screwed up her face. "You *tutor*?"

I felt my cheeks get unbecomingly hot. "Off and on," I said, feigning airiness. "Tutoring is like governessing. It's . . . noble."

"Hm." Ginny made a noncommittal noise, neither happy nor particularly inquisitive.

"Why don't I open this?" I said, lifting my package.

"Yes," Mom said faintly, as if I'd just discovered it in the back of a closet. "Go ahead."

I untucked the tape and peeled the paper away from the contents.

If you are a certain type of girl, a girl between the ages of twelve and about seventeen who is introspective and readerly, people are always giving you notebooks. They can't think of any other gift for you: books, you probably have all the ones you want already. Clothes and jewelry, you clearly do not care about, as evidenced by your bluestocking tendencies. Electronics, well, who can keep up with what the kids want these days? And then they wander into a bookstore, and see all those marbled covers and all that gold-edged paper and think, *yes*, that's just the ticket for Plum, the bookish little weirdo. They buy it and wrap it and watch you open it with that barely contained eagerness of a satisfied gift giver: a *notebook*, can you imagine? Paper stacked and bound together, all ready for you to *write in*, since you so love writing—and in such a lovely cover! You smile, as though this is such a novel, thoughtful idea, and move on. Thus is another notebook added to your stack.

But this was not a notebook made to be a gift. This was two golden-yellow cardboard covers, smooth green pages with thin lines, and a wire binding. Nothing at all special. I looked up at Mom.

"I know, I know, it's not fancy," Mom said. "But it's the kind your father swore by. I saw them at the art supply store and picked you up a few."

"But I don't write," I blurted out. I had to say it. I had to insist.

Mom opened her mouth, then closed it. The room went silent, save the faint sounds of caroling. At the door, Kit Marlowe stuck in his tortoiseshell head, eyes flashing, but quickly absconded.

"Oh," Mom said faintly. "Well, *I* feel foolish now."

"Don't!" I cried. My heart was pounding. "I mean, thank

you. I will keep them. I promise."

Mom smiled.

"I love you, Plum. Infinitely."

"My skin itches," Ginny said. Her face was smeared with something cakey and black, a packet torn open on the floor next to her. "Is it supposed to itch?"

"I wouldn't think so," Almost-Doctor Andrews said.

Ginny leaped up, alarmed. "What if I have contact dermatitis? Do you see any swelling?" She clutched the arm of his chair and stuck her face in his face.

"I—"

"I have an idea," I interrupted. "Let's watch Jimmy Stewart." The Blatchley tradition was to refer to movies not by the title but by the name of the starring actor. So *It's a Wonderful Life* became "Jimmy Stewart," while our preferred version of *A Christmas Carol* was—

"I want Mr. C. Scott!" Ginny cried, her contact dermatitis forgotten. Gizmo yipped in agreement.

So we began throwing out wrapping paper and cleaning up dishes and putting cookies on a plate—or *I* did, because Mom had taken to the kitchen couch with Gizmo, and Almost-Doctor Andrews should not be responsible for dishes in his landlady's house, and Ginny was God knows where. I filled the sink with soapy water and pretended I was Sara Crewe pretending she was a prisoner in the Bastille, assuming prisoners in the Bastille were made to scrub cinnamon-roll frosting from a tube off Fiestaware. I was deep into the long-suffering aspect of my reverie when Ginny burst in through the back door.

"I have mail," she breathed, rosy-cheeked from the cold. "Why didn't anyone tell me? It's probably been there for days!"

I barely looked up from the dishes. Mom rolled around to face her.

"Congrats, Meg Ryan. What's it say?"

"It's from *Penn*," Ginny said.

"Did they change their mind?" I said, and both Ginny and Mom shot me a look to indicate that that was not a proper joke to make.

"It's from the financial aid office." A chill settled over the kitchen that had nothing to do with the heat not being on. Truth be told, in all my perseverating over cash flow, I had forgotten that was a thing. Perhaps because it had involved lots of filling out forms, something Ginny had taken to with vigor but which filled me with a mixture of terror at making irreparable mistakes and profound boredom. Or perhaps because I just didn't want to think about the absolute and utter importance of it.

Slowly, Ginny tore the top of the envelope. She unfolded the letter. She read silently. Her face drained.

"What's wrong?" I said. "What happened?"

"No money," Ginny said, surprisingly quiet. "They aren't giving me anything."

"Nothing?" Mom pushed herself to standing.

"Yeah, *after a careful review*, blah blah blah, I get zippo."

"On *Christmas?*" Mom said, incredulous. "That just seems . . . I dunno, *heartless.*"

"It's a heartless world," Ginny said darkly. She sank onto a stool.

"Oh, Ginny." Mom sighed and squeezed Ginny's shoulder. "I had to work to help put myself through college. You know your grandmother—well, I guess you didn't, but point was, we never had anything growing up, and so I worked part-time selling pizza at the Coop—that's what we called the—"

"You can't *do* that anymore, Mother," Ginny said. "You can't pay for college on minimum wage. You need *real money.* Also, not about you, remember?"

Mom didn't say anything.

"Hey," I said. "It's Christmas."

Ginny nodded. She put the letter on the counter.

"Let's just go watch the movie, okay?"

Ginny was staring at the ceiling.

"Fine." She nodded. "Okay."

So we grabbed several blankets and the plate of cookies and tottered upstairs to the TV room for Jimmy Stewart—even Almost-Doctor Andrews, who had found an ancient bottle of glühwein from a German Christmas market and heated up a mugful on the stove. I excused myself to let the dogs out, because they always need to go out, and took the long way upstairs, past the glass office doors.

I hadn't put candles in those windows. Papers were piled up, in the dark, the smooth edges of the desk glowing in the streetlight. My fingers suddenly itched to yank the thin little handle and slip in. Just to look around. Maybe to see that jersey, for the Boston whoevers. Or the notebooks, the ones I now owned pristine copies of.

But of course, I couldn't. Even if they didn't see me, they'd sense it. The doors would creak or the dust would make me sneeze. So I left it there.

Mom barely made it through the opening credits without crying.

"*Moooom*," Ginny moaned. Her face was a little pink, once again, but that could have been the three blankets she'd ensconced herself in.

"I'm sorry," Mom said. "I'm sorry, it's just . . . *God*, this movie. Every goddamn time."

Almost-Doctor Andrews hummed "Buffalo Gals" under his breath.

As we watched, I nibbled my cookies and paid little attention. For some reason, I was thinking of the part in *Harriet the Spy* when Ole Golly tells Harriet that she has to do two things: apologize and lie. I had never been good at either. It was certainly my tragic flaw, second only to my lack of genius. And yet with each bite of each of the seven armadillo cookies I ate, my suspicion that I would have to do both grew.

Jimmy Stewart stepped back off the bridge. The music swelled. Mom swallowed her champagne.

"It's always worth coming back," she said to no one in particular. "Remember that. It's *always worth coming back.*"

The next day, I braided my hair, laced up my snow boots, put on the Amazing Wonder Jacket™, and walked down to Evergreen Street. The gate at Tate's house was closed, and I had to push it open in the snow, which made a horrifying creaking sound that no doubt announced my presence to everyone there. It was officially too late to go back. So I tramped over the snow to the back porch and the back door, which I knocked.

Mercifully, it was Tate who answered. He had on a TGS sweatshirt and green-and-red-plaid pajama pants, and his hair was askew, even though it was already 9:25 a.m.

"I'm sorry to interrupt your, um, whatever it is you were doing," I said, "but I just wanted to come by and tell you I was sorry."

"Sorry?" Tate's eyebrows drew together, cocking his head like he didn't remember how I'd gravely insulted him. "For what?"

I took a deep breath. "I implied," I said, "that you were stupid."

"Oh." Tate shrugged. "I mean, yeah. But if I wasn't, I wouldn't need a tutor, right?"

"Well, I . . . you couldn't *use* a tutor if you were stupid," I said. "Too stupid to learn, that is."

"So you're saying I'm not too stupid to learn," Tate said.

"Yes."

"You got up at seven a.m. just to come over and tell me I'm not too stupid to learn."

"Yes," I said. "And that I'm sorry." Also, it was now 9:27 a.m., but I did not mention that. We both stood there, Tate holding open the storm door and me standing resolute and tall with my hands in my pockets. Behind him, a cheer went up from what had to have been the TV room.

"Watching a game?" I asked politely.

"What do you think?" Tate said. The cold air was turning his cheeks pink.

"I'm sorry. Never mind," I said, just as Tate said, "come in, it's freezing."

So I did.

I pushed off my boots on the mat and set them neatly onto the low cabinet beside the door. The kitchen was stacked with baskets and red ribbons and green swag and dozens of boxes of white candles. There was barely a square inch of counter-top to spare.

"I heard," I said, as a way to make conversation, "that the reason they call it Boxing Day is that it's the day to put the

Christmas things back in boxes."

"Huh?" Tate said, and looked at all the stuff. "Oh. Yeah. We don't really do Christmas."

"You don't?"

"Jewish, remember?" Tate said. "Weren't you at my bar mitzvah?"

"Did you invite me?" I said, rather pointedly.

Tate nodded. "Right, guess not. Well, anyway, yeah, this is all just for my mom's work. She's having a fund-raiser or something."

"Oh," I said. Another burst of TV basketball noise. Tate turned his head back, his neck craning. He'd cut a little V into the front of his sweatshirt collar, through which I could see the little dent at the top of his collarbones.

"Wanna watch?" he said. "Unless you're busy."

"No," I said. "I mean, no, I'm not busy."

I followed him to the TV room, and it occurred to me that I knew where the TV room in Tate Kurokawa's house was: down the first-floor hallway, second door on the right, after the white end table with the lamp and the small bowl of decorative stones. The strangeness of it all was fading into . . . not familiarity, or ease, or anything like that, but a distinct *something*. A ritual, where the steps are always the same but the ending never predictable.

This time, Tate sat on the couch first, flopping in the middle. I wanted a good view, and I didn't want to sit in the chair, so I sat on the couch, too. The TV threw blue light across Tate's face, creating crepuscular shadows over every little angle, even into the V of his sweatshirt and the V at the top of his neck.

"Oh, here." Tate grabbed the remote and jabbed the volume button, and the TV roared with a cheering crowd and squeaking sneakers. "We're up by ten. If you want to follow the game."

"Oh," I said.

"I just picked something random from the DVR," Tate said. "They don't play live games at seven in the morning."

"It's nine thirty-three in the morning," I said.

Tate smiled. "I just mean I can rewind it if you want."

"No, that's okay," I said. "I'd be happy to watch from here."

That was a lie. I didn't really care about the game. Of *course* I didn't care about the game; I had never cared about a game of any sport in my entire life. But here I was. I had apologized, and I had lied.

Tate sat back and threw an arm over the back of the couch. I stayed sitting straight up.

"Don't you have someone better to hang out with?" I blurted out.

Tate blinked. "It's nine thirty-three in the morning."

"Oh," I said. "Right."

He was smiling. I looked at the TV.

"Who are we playing?"

"The LeBrons."

"The what?"

Tate leaned forward so his elbows were on his knees. "I mean, it's the Lakers, but you might as well call them by the only player that matters. Aw, *shit*." He fell backward and rubbed his forehead. "What the hell."

Something occurred to me. "Why don't you play basketball?"

Tate yawned. "You're asking a lot of questions this morning, Peach."

"It's nine thirty-five," I said. "Question time."

Tate smiled. "Yeah, okay. Anyway, basketball's the same season as squash, so I'm already spoken for." He shrugged. "Also, like, look at me."

I had been studiously avoiding doing so. I gave him a quick glance. "What about you?"

"I'm short," he said.

"You're not," I said quickly. "I mean, you're shorter than I am, but I'm pretty tall."

Tate studied me. "Stand up."

I didn't move.

"Come on, stand up."

I stood up. Tate scanned me up and down, and I felt suddenly very aware of the way my belt was bisecting my stomach, and how my stomach curved over the top of my jeans. I wished

I was still wearing the Amazing Wonder Jacket™. Then Tate stood up, so that he was right in front of me.

"Hm." He put a hand on top of his head, and moved it straight out, until he almost hit me in the bridge of my nose. "Yeah, checks out."

He dropped back onto the couch. I followed suit. One of the LeBrons scored another point.

"Hey, how's your sister?" Tate said, out of nowhere.

"She's fine," I said. "Why do you ask?"

Tate shrugged. "Benj said something about Ginny Blatchley being at some party the other day, and then I remembered you had a sister."

No one forgot that I had a sister. It was always the other way around. And Ginny didn't go to parties.

"A party?" I said. I must have looked alarmed, because Tate smiled, which I did not like.

"Chill, Peach. I'm sure it was nothing shady."

"What did he say?"

Tate rubbed his chin. "Just like, he was surprised to see her there, I guess. Her and her friend—"

"Charlotte," I said.

"Yeah." Tate nodded. "That one. She, like, hooked up with one of Benji's friends or something. I dunno."

I cleared my throat. Tate shifted, and I felt an intense need to say something definitive to break the silence.

"Well," I said. "It's always surprising what some people

consider a good time." From his flopped position on the couch, Tate turned his eyes from the game to me for a disconcerting full second and a half.

"Like watching basketball?"

"Sure," I said. "Yes. Exactly."

We watched the rest of the game in silence, save the sounds of the TV. Tate fast-forwarded through the commercials, and I sat and wondered what could have made this so interesting to a man who would rather spend money on books than food. To someone like my father.

Eventually it was over, and Tate jabbed the pause button, freezing an ad for Icy Hot knee patches midframe.

"So there you go," he said.

"It's ten forty-six," I said. I seemed to think that regularly announcing the time was an appropriate way to converse. I wasn't sure what had gotten into me.

"You need to go?" Tate said. "Because we could watch another one, or . . ."

I didn't know what that *or* was supposed to mean. I had to fill it in myself.

"Yes, I should go," I said. "My sister will be wondering where I am."

That may or may not have been true. But Tate nodded. "Yeah. Sure. Well . . . thanks for coming by."

"You're welcome," I said.

"We have that midterm," Tate said. "When's that, like,

the second Monday back?" He stretched his arms above his head.

I nodded. "Yes."

"So I should probably study."

"I'd think so."

"Can you come back?"

Could I? Of course I could. That was, of course, the whole reason I'd needed to apologize. To keep my governessing contract intact. To preserve professional decorum.

"Yes," I said.

"Cool," Tate said. "Tomorrow night?"

"I will see you then," I said crisply.

That night, the temperature plunged, and we indulged in a rare nighttime thermostat boost all the way to sixty degrees. I took two blankets up to the TV room and wrapped myself like a burrito and watched Home and Garden Television and lost track of time until I heard Ginny squeaking up the back stairs. She wandered in, clad in leggings that were black-and-white splotched like a notebook cover, a saffron-colored cotton dress whose sleeves were too long, and hiking socks.

"Oh, Plummy." She fell onto the couch and put her bulky-socked feet in my lap. "I'm tired."

"Were you at a party?" I asked, as mildly as I could.

Ginny flip-flopped a hand in the air. "Of sorts. It was Charlotte's idea."

"I'm shocked."

Ginny snort-laughed. "What, I'm not cool enough to go to parties?"

"No," I said, because it was obvious. "Were you drinking?"

"Plum!" Ginny lobbed a pillow at me, which I did not dodge in time and it glanced off the top of my head. From the windowsill, Kit hissed. "*No*," she said. "I was not. It wasn't even a party qua party, anyway. Just Lily, Lily, Ava, Julia, and Charlotte taking shots of apple-flavored vodka."

"Ew." I had no idea what apple-flavored vodka tasted like, but it could not have tasted like actual apples.

"Yeah. Get this: They were trying to conjugate Spanish verbs, and everyone who messed up had to take a shot. But they kept getting them right, so eventually they just started taking shots."

"That's the most TGS thing I've ever heard," I said.

"*Yo soy, tú eres,*" Ginny agreed.

The TV blasted a commercial for insulation. Ginny wormed her sock-feet farther into the inner edge of the couch, like she always did, either not realizing or not caring that doing so pushed me farther to the edge. She put her hands under her head like a pillow and sighed.

"I don't want to go to college."

"What?"

"I mean, no, I do. I don't know." Ginny flung an arm over her head. "I just wish it were . . . I don't know. I wish I didn't have to *get* something out of it. I wish I didn't have to prove anything."

"You're smart," I said. "You're going to be fine."

"Am I?" she said. "All my friends are smart and accomplished and have the excellent legacy breeding that'll open doors for them everywhere. And I'm *what?*"

I gave her a look that said, *You have been brilliant since you were two years old, and the whole world knows it because there is written proof, Ginny.*

"They should've wait-listed me instead of Charlotte," Ginny went on. "That's the only sensible thing to do."

"She'll get picked for somewhere," I said, which was more charitable than I generally felt toward Charlotte.

"They *should* have picked Charlotte," Ginny said. "She does advanced math and leads the Women in STEM club and really, really *wants* it. I'm just some idiot who wrote a sorta-good essay and has an obscure claim to relevance through my dead father. Oh, *and* I have no money."

She nestled deeper in the couch and turned her head to Home and Garden Television, where a blond woman was clomping her thousand-dollar boots around the ruins of her new fixer-upper, a displeased crinkle in her forehead.

"God," Ginny said. "*That's* what I want."

"You want a pile of boards and a dry-rot problem?" I said. Ginny kicked me with the toe of her foot.

"*No.* I just want a house like that. And a sledgehammer for the walls. You know when you want to kick something down, just to see if you can do it? Like see how far you could punch into a wall?"

"No," I said. "I have no idea what you're talking about."

"Like when you just want to . . . I don't know, be moving all the time, and never having to sit somewhere and *think* so much, and your job is just *doing* things, and you're actually *useful* to people in some actual, concrete way. You know what I mean?"

I didn't, not really.

"No, Ginny."

"Well, it's what I want." She turned back toward the screen. "Sometimes. It's what I think about wanting. A physical *thing* to do. Day in, day out."

I hugged my knees to my chest. "You'd be bored out of your skull, Ginny."

"Maybe," she said. "But I'd be free."

The following afternoon, I arrived at Tate's house to find him already at the countertop, his books piled together in a small clearing of holiday paraphernalia. That day he was wearing some kind of loose gray jogging pants and a sweatshirt with a big red-and-blue *P* on it. It was as though, when at home, he never wore anything that could not be comfortably slept in. I, of course, had outfitted myself to look as professional as possible, meaning in a pair of corduroys that did not have worn patches on the knees and a garnet-colored cable-knit sweater that I thought set off the color of my braid nicely.

My mom, he mouthed as he got up to open the back door. He jerked his head over his shoulder just as his mother rushed in, shoulder pressing her phone to her ear.

"I *know*," she was saying. "Well, what am I supposed to do? It's"—she shook her wristwatch into place—"four thirty. I can't just—"

"Mom, do you have any cash?" Tate interrupted, and nodded at me. "She's here."

I felt a small clench in my stomach, embarrassed that technically, yes, I was paid to do this—an employee, or a subcontractor of sorts, a hired gun. But forty dollars two times a week was $320 a month, and that was not nothing.

His mom widened her eyes at him, smiled apologetically at me, and tucked her head back into her phone.

"I have to call you back. See what you can do, okay?" She set down her phone and pulled over a big black purse from under a floppy red bow. She was wearing a dark green dress with long sleeves and, curiously, only one pearl earring.

"Here you go," she said, handing me the forty dollars. "I'm sorry everything's so . . ." She waved her hands around.

"Thank you," I said, then added politely, "I think you're missing an earring."

She put a hand to her ear. "Oh. You're right. Thank you." She shook her head. "I'm sorry for interrupting. Just a last-minute fund-raiser crisis, as usual!" She laughed a laugh of very little mirth.

"What, like you ran out of those little quiches?" Tate said.

"Very funny." His mom had picked up her phone again. "No. The jazz quartet we hired for the historical society holiday party got stuck in New York, so now I have an empty piano and no music." She smiled grimly. "You don't happen to be a classically trained pianist, do you, dear?"

My heart fluttered. "No, but . . . well, I know one."

Tate's mom stopped bustling. "You do?"

"Our tenant," I said. "He lives in the carriage house. He's a pianist. A doctor of music. Well, almost. But he's been playing all month—holiday things." I breathed out.

"Really?" Tate's mom said. "You mean he's just down the street? Oh, that'd be— We can pay him, of course. And he wouldn't be too busy to play in, well"—she glanced at her watch again—"more or less two hours?"

"I would honestly be surprised," I said. "I could give you his number, if you want."

I took out my phone, and Tate's mom tapped Almost-Doctor Andrews's number into hers.

"Thank you, dear. Calling him right now." She grabbed a box of bows and clicked back down the hallway.

Tate swiveled back to me. "Well, I got out the books."

"A good start," I said. "Have you read them?"

"Sure," Tate said.

"So you feel in command of the material ahead of the midterm."

"Sure," Tate said again. He was silent a moment. "Man, I wish this were fourth grade again."

My heart plunged to my stomach. He didn't remember—did he? Surely reading my stupid, infantile notebook aloud on the playground was one in a long, unrecorded succession of mundane cruelties he'd committed that year.

"What do you mean?" I said, with commendable steadiness.

"Those tests were just like, *Why did the mouse start riding the motorcycle?*" He pushed his hair out of his eyes. "Easy stuff."

"Reading comprehension."

"Yeah," Tate said. "Here's the thing. You want to know what I can't do?"

"Okay. Sure."

"I can't . . . you know when we sit down to write the essays, and we're supposed to say something about the book's themes, or whatever, and use quotes from the book?"

"Yes," I said. "That's how writing an essay works."

"Yeah, well, I don't get it. It's a story. It's just about stuff that happens. So what am I supposed to write?"

To be honest, I didn't know. I didn't know how to answer Tate specifically, but I also really had no idea how to answer that question, period. Writing, it turns out, is frustratingly difficult to justify with words.

"You'll figure it out," I said. "I mean, you might not know until you're through writing it, but it's important that you just start."

"Yeah, but I don't know *how* to start."

"No one ever knows how to start," I said. "Maybe start with the words."

Tate looked blank.

"I mean, don't focus so much on the events of the story as on how the author chooses to write about it."

"Uh-huh." Tate pressed his lips together, nodding slowly. I didn't seem to be getting through.

"Symbolism," I said. "Linguistic devices."

"Yeah, see, what are those?" Tate said. "Peach, you're talking like you're talking to a teacher. I need this stuff dumbed down."

An idea nipped at the back of my mind, urgently enough that I neglected to be annoyed at the nickname.

"Okay." I folded my hands on the counter. "Try this. Tell me a story."

"What, like make one up?"

"No, no," I said. "A story about something that happened to you. Recently. For example, tell me what you did last night."

Tate's eyebrows went up. "Okay." He exhaled and shifted forward in his seat. "Last night. Well, I basically dicked around for a couple of hours watching TV, then I nuked some tacos, then remembered my mom had been busting my ass about laundry, so I threw some stuff in the wash and passed out on the couch."

"Now tell it like you would tell it to your mom."

Tate glanced back at the hallway. "Seriously?"

"Just try it."

"Okay." He tipped his head to the side. "Last night I watched a little sports, had dinner, and did my laundry. I went to bed at around midnight. What's your point, Peach?"

"You changed what you said," I said. "Even though the

203

same things happened. You used different words."

"Yeah, duh," Tate said. "I'm not going to say *busting my ass* in front of my mom."

"Why not?"

"Because she'd bust my ass about it."

He smiled, and I smiled.

"Meaning it would sound more disrespectful," I said.

"Yeah."

"So the words you use change the effect of the story," I said. "Even if the same things happen. The way you present things . . . it tells as much about the story as the story does. It tells you how to understand it. Or who it's supposed to be for."

Tate drummed a pencil on the table. "Yeah. Yeah, I guess. So I'm supposed to look at every individual word and figure out what it all means. But not, like, *mean* means, but what it, like . . . implies."

"That's it," I said. "More or less."

"Huh," Tate said—not a confused *huh,* necessarily. He rubbed the back of his neck and set his hand back on the counter, those broad hands, with long fingers. This was the sort of thing you began to notice when you spent a lot of time in close quarters with Tate Kurokawa.

I cast around for a tangible example. "Maybe it's that . . . words are like beads. They have to be together to mean something. And the kind of bead you pick matters. String together a bunch of pearls and it looks one way, or a bunch of rocks and it looks another way."

"Or a bunch of Froot Loops," Tate said. "And then you can eat it."

"I . . . guess so," I said. "I mean, you're not wrong." He wasn't misunderstanding the metaphor, at least.

"I'm not wrong," Tate repeated. He nodded. "Yeah, I like that. Beads. Did you just make that up?"

Now I stared intently at the counter. "Yes."

"Cool," Tate said. "Yeah. It's stuff like that. I just don't get how people get that. Like you just come up with this stuff to say about the book and you don't even have to try."

"Well . . ." I almost said *It's obvious*, but retracted, seeing as that would not be the most sensitive governessing strategy. "It just sort of . . . comes to you, I guess. Good writing is . . . extrasensory," I said. "No, supernatural. Or maybe it's more paranormal. It's hard to find the right word."

"You're telling me."

"I mean . . ." My neck felt hot under my sweater. "Just . . . when you read, you see things without seeing. You sense them without sensing that you're sensing them. It doesn't tell you *what* to feel but maybe just *how* to feel. If that makes sense."

Tate smirked, then went straight-faced, and looked right in my eyes.

"Peach, you're like, a genius."

My stomach flipped. "I'm not."

"Seems like it to me," Tate said. "This shit's crazy."

"It isn't," I said. "It's just how it works. I'm not making it up. Here." I smoothed out a notebook page. "Pick a sentence you like and write it here. Then we can talk about why it's good."

"I don't like any sentences," Tate said. "That's the core problem here."

"Well, pick one you hate, then," I said. "And we can figure out why it sucks."

"We can?"

"Sure," I said. "You're allowed to say a book isn't good. You just have to prove it."

Convinced—or at least intrigued—Tate set to flipping through pages, and over the next forty-five minutes we conducted multiple, actual instances of close reading, which proved surprisingly productive despite my need to remind Tate what the word *adverb* meant.

"So that's it," Tate said. "Huh."

"Not . . . exactly," I said. "There's more to it than just talking about words. Maybe try writing an essay before next time?"

"Yeah," he said. "Tuesday the . . . whatever it is?"

"Yes," I said. "And then we can talk about it."

Tate agreed, and I departed.

The whole thing made me quite proud, proud that I had actually taught something. It is a bone-deep, satisfying feeling, when you have articulated something so instinctual, so interwoven to your own daily operation, that you cannot help but be pleased with your own insight. You have to know things to teach them, I think. Even if you don't fully understand them until you're through with them.

Too soon, it became New Year's Eve. The end of winter break, which I had no plans to celebrate beyond an evening with Mom and the dogs and a bottle of champagne—for her, not for me or the dogs—to watch Dick Clark (which Mom insisted on calling the New Year's Eve program even though Dick Clark was long dead and replaced by some male personality with highlighted hair I did not care to know the name of). Ginny, meanwhile, had some plans that involved a spangly shirt and Charlotte. At the moment, they were crammed together by the mirror over the kitchen counter (since the kitchen was the only warm room in the house), attacking their faces with makeup. I was huddled on the kitchen couch, with a swiftly cooling mug of tea and *Frankenstein*, reading and incidentally visually eavesdropping over the top of the pages.

"Ugh," Charlotte said. "My service is crapping out." She held her phone aloft as if it were the torch and she were the Statue of Liberty.

"You have to go by the window," Ginny said. "The walls are too thick."

"Ugh," Charlotte said again, but tromped over to the sink and leaned over, phone proffered toward the glass. A tinny *ding* signaled her success. "Thank God. Gin, look."

Charlotte swept back over to Ginny, who read the screen and shrugged, her tank top throwing pinpricks of light like a disco ball.

"Oh, come *on*," Charlotte groaned.

"I just don't care," Ginny said. "Is it okay if I don't care?"

Charlotte stuck her phone back in her pocket. "Maybe you'd be less uptight if you *did* smoke."

"Eh." Ginny squashed her eyelashes upward in a gruesome-looking silver curler. "Remember two years ago when they found all those seniors with weed on the Spanish trip and told their colleges?"

Charlotte stood up straighter.

"I don't think you should be kicked out for smoking weed," she said, her voice clear and definitive as if she were delivering an oral presentation. "Everyone smokes."

Ginny rolled her eyes and kept swiping makeup. Charlotte picked up one of the borderline-stale chocolate chip cookies left over from Christmas and chewed. Then she made a face, stomped on the trash can pedal, and dropped it in. Then she turned to me.

"Do you want to come, Plum?"

"Me?" I said.

"Yeah, you!" Charlotte smiled. "To Benji's. I think some kids from your class are going to be there. You wouldn't be alone. It'll be fun."

"Plum hates the kids in her class," Ginny said, clicking her makeup case shut. "Right?"

I thought of bagel-smelling Jeremy Beard and his Dungeons and Dragons. Then, of all people, I thought of Tate.

"I . . . yes," I agreed.

"And I for one can't blame her."

Charlotte's face briefly flashed its bad-smell expression. "I mean, I think they're fine."

"You want to smoke weed with a bunch of sixteen-year-olds, be my guest." Ginny flounced over to the couch and threw her arms around my neck.

"Save me, Plummy," she whispered. "This is going to be an ordeal."

"*Tonight, tonight, there's a party tonight!*" I said, in my Field Mousiest voice. Ginny tried not to crack up.

"*And they all had scones and little sausages on sticks,*" she squeaked back.

I giggled, very softly.

"Text me if you get bored."

"*Absolument.*"

Mom fell asleep by nine, as was her wont, and I switched the TV to the local public broadcast, which was cannily showing a marathon of costume dramas for those, like me, who had no particular investment in the pageantry of modern New Year's Eve–ism. I wondered what it would be like to live in the past, and tried to imagine Ginny and her friends pulling on gloves and stuffing feathers in their hair to attend a ball, where there would be sherry to drink and pianos to play and gentlemen to woo. It seemed as much a waste of time as it did now. I decided I would have been the one hiding in the library with a copy of *Ivanhoe*.

At about 11:58, Kit Marlowe stalked in, the usual fiendish gleam in his eyes. He regarded me coolly but did not immediately turn his tail and stalk back out. I folded my arms above my many layers of blanket.

"Well," I said. "Are you going to be friendly or not?"

On the table, my phone buzzed. I picked it up, figuring it was some all-caps missive from Ginny, desperate to recount something stupid at her party.

But it was not.

It was from Tate.

    happy new years

I put down my phone. There was, of course, no response I could give. Was there?

Kit Marlowe mewl-growled, then grudgingly rubbed his back against the edge of the sofa and lifted his chin. I scratched it.

"See," I said. "Maybe this is the year you'll stop being so stuck-up."

He hissed, but for once, did not run away.

School recommenced, and with it, a flurry of nervous activity. At the Gregory School, college application was a personal, private process, so, naturally, a massive blue SENIOR COLLEGE CHOICES bulletin board dominated the biggest wall in the front hall. It was bigger than the rotating display of uninspired student projects from Foundation of Art; it was even bigger than the oil portrait of Amos Coffin Gregory, our illustrious muttonchopped founder, whose small brass plaque neglected to mention that said illustrious founder did not himself attend college, probably so as not to diminish his illustriousness. The COLLEGE CHOICES bulletin board was—ostensibly—a mechanism for congratulation, with all attendant good intentions, but it more often served as an immediately arresting selling point for affluent young couples touring the campus in search of a suitably prestigious kindergarten for their children, or—more often—as a social leaderboard. As soon as anyone made a final commitment to matriculate somewhere, the name of his or her chosen alma mater to be was immediately affixed beneath their school photo. Photos could not change, of course, but upon our January 2 return, the beaming smiles of those lucky few with a secure future seemed to beam brighter than the rest.

Absent a definitive financial-aid decision, Ginny's photo remained unlabeled. So, of course, did Charlotte's; one of the Lilys had been plucked for Stanford (her mother was an alumna), and Ava Kestenbaum was bound for Brown. The rest were all still fair game, still on the market, and a restlessness overtook the hallways that even those of us not yet at the age of college majority could sense. It vibrated in the air, a palpable anxiety comingling with the universal dread of midterms coming the following week.

There was, however, a new development in the college courtship process, as we learned that evening.

"Interviews," Ginny declared.

"Interviews?" Mom said. We were around our ersatz kitchen table, eating noodles Jefferson. Noodles Jefferson is the only dish that Ginny can cook, which she had adapted from a book of our childhood called the *Kidz Can Cook Anything Cookbook*, where almost every recipe began, ironically, with "find an adult to handle the knife and/or boil the water." Kidz, it would seem, could not, in fact, cook anything. The dish consists of pasta with cheese and nothing else, which was convenient, seeing as that was what we had in the pantry: pasta, cheese, and nothing else.

"Yes," Ginny said. "Well, not, like *formal* interviews. But you know. Ava and Lily were talking about it today. You just meet with someone your father knows who's an alumnus or a trustee or whatever and they ever so coincidentally help bump you to the front of the line. For admissions, financial aid, a good dorm room, whatever. So that's what I need. But at this point I'm sure their dance cards are all full."

I twirled more noodles Jefferson onto my fork. What it lacked in nutrition, it made up for in tasting appealingly like something a four-year-old would eat.

"I couldn't ever do interviews," Mom said. "I break out in panic splotches. It's why I use that goat's milk lotion. But you"—she indicated Ginny with her glass—"should absolutely do one. Learn the skill soon. Any job worth paying involves an interview. Do you know how I got my first teaching job?"

Ginny hissed out an exhale and looked at the ceiling. "You ran into the—"

"I *ran into the director at an art show,*" Mom said, "and ended up smoking hashish in his apartment with a group of alternative circus performers from French Canada. And do you think any of those people ended up with a paying job with dental benefits?"

Ginny and I exchanged a look.

"No," we said at the same time.

"And do you know why?"

"Because they never got into the University of Pennsylvania

with adequate financial aid," Ginny said.

"And probably smoked too much hashish," I said, although I did not know exactly what hashish was. Ginny glared at me.

"I mean, it might have worked out anyway," I offered. "They do about a dozen shows a week in Vegas."

Mom swallowed a mouthful and shook her head, earrings smacking her in the neck. "Not Cirque du Soleil. The other ones."

"I don't think there *are* other ones," I said.

"There were," Mom insisted. "Or there were until they had that incident with the trapeze."

"That's what's going to happen to me," Ginny said. "I'm going to end up in an off-brand French-Canadian circus troupe risking my literal neck for no health insurance. *Cripes.*" She dropped her fork into the middle of her noodles Jefferson. "And we've been eating pasta for *eons* because no one has gone to the market. I see you found time to go to the liquor store, though."

Mom drank more wine.

"Here." I pulled out an envelope with all my tutoring earnings, which I had been keeping on my person at all times. "I have some grocery money. We can go after school tomorrow."

"Oh, Plum." Mom pulled the end of my braid so she could kiss me on the cheek, which left a tawny smudge where her free-sample lipstick had grazed it. "You're an absolute angel." She stood up. "All right. I had two critiques in studio today and *then* I had to solicit donations for this silent auction all afternoon, and I have to lie down or I'll faint."

"Fainting *is* lying down," Ginny said. "And what about my interview?"

Mom lifted her arms and sagged dramatically. "Ginny, my darling dove, do I look like someone who can scare up a University of Pennsylvania graduate on short notice?"

Given that our mother was wearing a Philadelphia Folk Fest T-shirt over ballooning purple pants that cinched at the ankle, the answer was both implied and obvious.

"I see where you get your fashion sense from," I said, as Mom retreated upstairs, with Gizmo clicking after.

Ginny wasn't paying attention. She was twisting her napkin, which was actually a paper towel, into a tight coil, and staring hard at the table, as if she expected it to rearrange into our father's face like in a Disney movie and whisper some words of wisdom.

"I *have* to get an interview, Plum." Wisps of paper frothed out between her fingers. "I have to. I have to."

"You will," I said.

"*No*," she said. "I *won't*. They're all gone, and the only ones left are left for people who *know* someone. And I don't know anyone. I don't know *an-y-one*." She dropped the napkin and slammed her palms against the table. "Ugh!"

"Ginny," I said. "Calm down."

"I *can't*." She jumped out of her chair. "This is the rest of my *life*, Plum. I've already screwed it up enough by not having any *money*. I'm not going to make it worse. I *can't*."

"The money isn't your fault," I said. But Ginny had started pacing.

"It's hopeless. I'm hopeless. I can't do this."

"Ginny," I said, as patiently as I could stand. "You're being hysterical."

"Hysterical?" Ginny whirled on me. "What do you mean, hysterical?"

"You're not making any sense," I said. "You're freaking yourself out."

"You mean I'm crazy," Ginny said.

"I didn't say that," I said.

"No," Ginny said. "But you've been thinking it. You've been thinking I'm crazy and annoying and that you just can't *wait* to get rid of me."

"I *haven't*," I said, even as the guilty recognition that I *had* wormed down into my stomach.

"Well, congratulations!" Ginny threw her hands into the air. "How's it feel to be right?"

Her eyes shone, and her chin was juddering up and down. I sat stock-still in my chair, not sure how to move. Ginny hugged her arms around her chest like she was trying to warm herself up—which she could have been, given how cold it was in the kitchen.

"Everyone's going to go somewhere," she said. "Everyone

but me. I don't even know what's going to happen to me."

"Ginny . . ." I got up, not sure what to do. "Why don't you sit down?"

Ginny threw me a wild-eyed glance and stalked past me and to the couch. She lay upside down, so that her ankles were on the backrest and her hair streamed down onto the floor.

"Take a deep breath," I said.

"I can't," Ginny said. Her face was bone white. "I can't. I can't. I can't."

She screwed up her eyes and wailed.

"Ginny," I said softly. "You're scaring me."

"*I'm* scaring me, Plum." Ginny opened her eyes. "What's wrong with me? Am I going crazy?" She rolled her legs over and down, so that she was lying properly on the couch. With her hair loose over the pillows, there was something Pre-Raphaelite about her again, like Ophelia tossing dead bouquets to the wind, or Persephone graying away in the underworld. She was beautiful as ever, but hollow.

"God. I want to throw up. I want to *throw. Up.*" She covered her face in her hands, and when she pulled them back, there were tears on her cheeks.

"We're going to have to move, Plummy. We're never going to be able to stay. Even if I leave, you and Mom will have to go somewhere else. And it's my fault. It's my fault for having to go to college."

"Okay," I said. "One thing at a time. You're catastrophizing."

"No. No, I'm not." Ginny breathed out hard, and sat up. "Quit being *useless*, Plum. I *need* that interview. And unless you're actually going to *help* me, I don't want to hear anything you have to say."

She stalked out, leaving nothing but me, Doug, and a tableful of rapidly cooling noodles Jefferson.

So I was the one who cleaned the kitchen. And once I had cleaned, I wandered.

The fact is, 5142 Haven Lane is not just anywhere. It is not a polished, asbestos-free, renovated-kitchen playground of a house. It is an existence.

I walked, and I touched something in every room: a banister, a doorjamb, a nonfunctional switch plate with a button like a flattened pearl that used to ring a servant's bell, a framed painting of the Five Little Field Mice twirling around a tiny maypole. At the edge of the library door, I heard a floorboard creak and peered through the doorframe to see Mom, draped in a shawl and her hair loose, running her hand up and down the edge of one of the bookcases. That was it—just rubbing it like it was a genie lamp.

I knew from touching it many times before that the wood was strangely soft, that it had been so finely sanded and expertly stained that there were no splinters or bubbles of finish, all seamless and mitered and exact and strong. It existed and was useful in a way that other things in our house were not. It was something we needed.

I followed Kit up the stairs, up to the second floor, repeating that thought with every floor creak. On the landing, the sconces gleamed into the glass of the office doors, bouncing back, so all I could see was empty shine. Opposite the glass, the muffled sounds of Ginny's TV show bled through the walls.

Kit jingled upstairs, and so I followed, and padded into Ginny's empty bedroom, where Kit had situated himself on the windowsill to peer out at his domain.

I lay on Ginny's bed and stared up.

The sky part of the mural was doing the worst. A water stain like a spilled mug of coffee bloomed in one corner, and the paint was flaking off in sapphire-colored shreds, revealing what had to have been lead paint underneath. I breathed in deeply, probably lowering my IQ with every inhale, and turned onto my side, facing the dent where Ginny's shoe had left a hole in the tiny mural universe. Her bedroom was sloughing itself to bits, and whether we sold the house tomorrow or died in our beds and turned it over at an estate auction, it would get painted over or disintegrate on its own or otherwise get lost.

I hated thinking like that—or, really, I hated feeling like that. The feelings coursing through me were so stupid and useless I just wanted to burn them and sweep them out of myself like ashes. I wanted solidness and sense even as I saw things pulling themselves into pieces.

And yet, even then, some part of me was peering at the corner of everything, wanting to see what would come next. I could not help it. I have a reader's tendencies.

 FOUR

Long have I known a glory in it all
But never knew I this;
Here such a passion is
As stretcheth me apart . . .
—Edna St. Vincent Millay

The following day—Tuesday—I was due back at Tate's. And Tate was late. More than late, he was not there.

I stood on the back porch for almost fifteen minutes, holding my books, wrapped in the ancient wool coat of Patience Mortimer's that I had finally swapped out for the Amazing Wonder Jacket™. It was a green plaid and smelled equally of lavender perfume and mothballs.

I pulled out my phone, debating a text message; maybe he was upstairs, or somewhere else too far to hear the doorbell. But on my phone was Tate's most recent message to me.

happy new years

He had somehow, incorrectly, combined *Happy New Year* with *New Year's Eve,* and neglected the apostrophe to boot. It would take either a miracle or a traditional TGS parent intervention for him to earn above a C on this midterm.

And, furthermore, why had he even sent the message? Probably, since the party had evidently been here, he was high or drunk. Perhaps he meant to send it to someone else, someone he recently texted or someone else whose name began with a *P*. Perhaps it was a prank to tease me into responding—which only made me gladder that I had not.

However, I was still on the porch, and cold. I rang the doorbell one more time, and this time, got an answer when Benji loped in, looking confused.

"Hello?" he said, pulling open the back door.

"Hello," I said. "Is Tate home?"

Benji looked back over his shoulder. He had stubble on his face, which I supposed was to be expected for a boy who was at least seventeen. Still, it gave him a distinctly rough-around-the-edges look that clashed with his salmon-colored button-down shirt.

"Dunno. I guess you can come in."

I did, decorously removing my shoes and hanging the mothy coat as far from the rest of the Feingold-Kurokawa outerwear as possible.

"So are you his girlfriend, or something?"

"No," I said quickly. "I'm his tutor. For English. We've met before. Plum. Plum Blatchley."

"Oh, yeah, right." Benji nodded and grabbed a green plastic water bottle from the countertop. "You're the sister."

I stood up straight. "I'm Ginny's sister, yeah. Yes."

"She's hot shit, right?"

I didn't know what he meant. "I . . ."

"Isn't she in, like, everywhere?" Benji swigged from his

water bottle. "That's what her friends have been saying. Just refusing to commit until she knows who's going to give her the most money."

My mouth fell open, and I quickly snapped it shut.

Someone clomped at the back steps. Tate, coming in through the back door, shedding a jacket, pulling socked feet out of boots, dumping a lumpy bag of some type of sports equipment on the floor. Tate, and Stevie, and Tommy.

Tate stopped, and Stevie and Tommy slammed into him like he was a doorstop.

"Yo, what the hell?" Stevie said.

"Hey," he said. "Peach."

Under the coat he was wearing a white collared shirt with the TGS crest over the heart, white mesh shorts, white socks, white sneakers, white everything. Stevie had plastic goggles dangling from a strap around his neck, and Tommy was swinging three plastic Wawa bags.

Instantly I was in fourth grade again, cowering, burning up, stomach clenching, hating that I'd ever thought to put anything down in writing. Even if they didn't remember—they didn't, of course—I did. The muscle memory was there.

"I have squash until five," Tate explained.

"Of course," I said.

"I let her in," Benji yelled, retreating up the stairs. "You left her on the porch to freeze like an asshole."

"Thanks." Tate nodded at him. "Sorry, Peach. Well, uh, I

guess I can . . ." His hair was sticking in every direction, and his face was still red. Even the small space of throat between his opened collar button was a little red.

"'Sup, girl?" Tommy, all six foot million of limbs and elbows, threw himself onto a barstool.

Stevie put his hands on the counter and leaned in, grinning. "You and T, huh?" He bobbed his head up and down. "I can see it. Yeah. The freaky stuff."

"Hey, guys." Tate had his hands in his pockets. "I should probably . . ." He looked at me. "I forgot. My mom's paying her to tutor me."

There it was again: the clench in my stomach. Tommy, oblivious, burped.

"Yeah," Stevie said. "All right." He grabbed his plastic Wawa bag and shouldered his pack of athletic equipment. "Come on, Tom, let's bounce."

Tommy slunk to standing and gave Tate a salute. "Later."

"Bye," Stevie said, and jerked his head upward in my direction. "Spank Tate hard for me."

Tate smacked his hands to his sides. "What the fuck, Steve?"

Stevie shrank. "*Sorry*," he said. "Jesus."

They slammed the door and lumbered away.

Tate rubbed the back of his neck. He was, I had to notice, the shortest of the three. Four, if you counted me.

"Sorry," he said again. He exhaled. "Shit."

"It's all right," I said. "I wouldn't expect any less."

"Yeah." Tate folded his arms. "I . . . uh, I mean, I have my stuff, but . . . I usually take a shower, is all. After practice," he finished. "Can you give me, like, five minutes? You can wait in the TV room, if you want."

"Okay," I said, and gathered my books.

The TV was off, and even though I knew how to turn it on, I decided that wouldn't be polite. Other people's remote controls were always a festival of hieroglyphics, and the last thing I needed was to accidentally blast something indecently loud so that Tate came running out of the bathroom to make sure I hadn't broken anything.

So I sat, and listened to the rushing sound of the pipes.

I imagined again this scene two hundred years in the past. Tate and Tommy and Stevie in shirtsleeves and cravats, freshly in from . . . something equestrian, I supposed, or a foxhunt. I wondered if women back then still found them unbearable. At least there used to be conventions, the kind of manners that would prevent men of good upbringing from saying things like "the freaky stuff."

My thoughts were brought to an abrupt stop by the banging of a kitchen cabinet. Ten seconds later, Tate reappeared, hair damp and in the same big *P* T-shirt as the other day, carrying a plate with a paper-wrapped sandwich and a half gallon of Wawa iced tea.

"I have an extra pretzel," Tate said, lifting the bag around his elbow. "In case you're hungry."

"No, thank you," I said reflexively. "Maybe we should just get started."

"Yeah. Let me just eat this." Tate sat and started to unwrap his sandwich. He smelled like men's body wash, probably one of those scents that are supposed to drive women crazy like in a commercial, and it amused me to think of Tate buying something labeled for men even though he was only sixteen. In fact, more likely, since he *was* sixteen, it was his mother buying it. She could have gotten something unscented, or with a neutral soap smell, but instead it was the babe-magnet fragrance. *Here*, she would think, *I will select this so that my son Tate can continue to get girls.*

Not that Alicia Feingold would think like that. She was probably just trying to think of the best way to rid her teenage son of the typical smells of teenage boys. And not, of course, to imply that it was a bad smell. Tate's, or the body wash's.

"Hey, sorry, I forgot about them," Tate said, chewing. "Being back at school just threw me off."

"It's all right," I said.

"They should be jealous," Tate said. "I'm going to ace this thing, and they're going to fail like assholes. Hey, maybe once I pass, you can expand your services. Get a whole cabin industry going."

"Frankly," I said, "I do not want to spend more time with them."

"Yeah," Tate said.

"And it's cottage industry, not cabin."

"Yeah." He swallowed.

"How was your New Year's Eve?" I asked abruptly. I couldn't say where the question came from, but there it was. Tate shrugged.

"It was fine. Benj had some people over. Saw your sister."

"Ah," I said.

"How was yours?" Tate asked.

"It was fine," I said. "Just fine."

He hadn't mentioned the text message. It must have been an accident.

"Do you have your essay?"

Tate wiped his hands on his sweatpants and dug in his backpack for a piece of paper. "Yeah. Here you go."

I smoothed out the essay and looked it over, marking with a pencil as I went. It was poorly punctuated, and he misspelled a lot of things, or used the nominal form when he should've used participial, or just swapped in homophones. But his observations matched his quotes, more or less.

"This is getting better," I said, when I'd finished.

"Yeah?"

"Yes," I said. "You actually made a point and backed it up."

Tate licked his lips, nodding, and smiled. "All right."

"But your conclusion is vague," I said. "You can't just end

by saying, 'Brontë uses her language to highlight important themes in the novel.' You have to say how the writer did it, and why it matters."

"Can I ask a dumb question?"

"Can you ask any other kind?" I said, without thinking. But Tate smiled.

"What *is* a theme?"

"It's . . ." I chewed my lip. "It's what a book is about—I mean, not the story, but the ideas behind it, if that makes sense? Something . . . abstract? Abstract but specific. A theme is . . . basically the point of writing the whole story. What you're giving to the reader. Why the story's worth reading."

"It was worth reading to pass English," Tate said. "Is that a theme?"

I opened my mouth to protest, but Tate shook his head. "No, I . . . I think I get it. Ish."

"Okay," I said. "So that's why you can't just say that she's using language to highlight themes. Because that's what *all* good novels do. The specifics of this book are what's worth analyzing."

"Maybe this is a *bad* novel," Tate said.

I gave him a look.

"Yeah, all right. I know it's good because they made us read it." He took the paper back and looked at it. "You have nice handwriting, Peach."

I felt myself flush. "Thank you."

"Does that come with being smart?" Tate looked up at me. "Or does it come with being a girl?"

"I don't know," I said. "I've always written that way."

"So it just comes with being you."

"I . . . yes."

"Damn. Well, good thing I have lots of other redeeming qualities." Tate folded the paper and, to my utter surprise, smacked it against my knee. "Right?"

The paper was light, as paper is, but I still felt like I could feel the touch of it all the way down to my skin.

"You're very good at sports," I said. "From what I hear."

Tate smiled. "Yeah." He slammed his notebook shut. "Well, I'm done. You wanna watch something? Your boys are on at six."

"No, thanks," I said.

"You have to go, or . . ."

"No, I just . . . am going to go."

"Oh," Tate said. He didn't stand up. His arm was over the back of the couch, the crook of his elbow slightly bent. "You sure? Doesn't have to be basketball. We get, like, every channel."

"No, thanks." I stood up. "I feel bad enough that I kept you from your friends earlier."

"Mm." Tate nodded. "They're just . . ." He glanced back into the kitchen. "You know how it is. Friends are jerks sometimes."

"I don't have any friends who are jerks," I said. Implication being, of course, *I don't have any friends, period.* But Tate knew that.

"You have me," Tate said.

I blinked.

"I'm not your friend," I said. "I'm your tutor."

I piled my books and proceeded to the kitchen, where Tate grabbed for something and held it out to me as I reoutfitted myself with boots.

"All yours." It was a white envelope with *Plum* written on it. "Don't spend it all in one place, tutor."

Inside the envelope was a business card, a buff-colored note card with *Alicia Feingold* written in gold script at the top edge, and five twenty-dollar bills—this week's worth of pay, plus either an advance or a bonus.

Dear Plum, it read. *Thank you so much again for your help finding us Mr. Andrews. And thank you for helping Tate—I know it isn't easy work. :) Be in touch if I can ever help you with anything.*

The business card listed her name, email address, and job title.

Alumni Relations, University of Pennsylvania.

"I can't get out of bed," Ginny declared the following morning. Except, given that she was *in* bed, in her room, I had to go all the way upstairs to hear her declare it. And judging by her tone of voice, she'd been declaring it vociferously at length until someone came to attend to her.

"Are you sick?" I said.

"I don't know," Ginny said. "Maybe. Yes. I'm not getting out."

"But it's a school day," I said. "Don't you have a midterm?"

She rolled over.

"How am I supposed to get to school?" I cried.

She pulled the covers over her head.

The bus not only got me to TGS earlier than usual, but it also provided a good chance to get a head start on the second-semester English reading. The English department always managed to wedge a little poetry into every year, sneaking it in between the novel unit and the Shakespeare unit like a pill coated in spreadable meat. I was not fooled, and I loathed it. Poetry was always about death or sex, and although I had not experienced either, I just didn't see how much there could possibly be to say about it.

Of course I didn't *need* to start on second-semester work before we'd even taken the midterm, but after learning all of first semester twice over in order to governess, I needed something fresh, something new. Not that my copy of *The Selected Poetry of Edna St. Vincent Millay* was new, of course, but I was surprised to find that I didn't loathe it. For one thing, Edna St. Vincent Millay was such an elegant name (unlike, say, Patience Mortimer Blatchley, which sounds as elegant as a cinder block hitting a driveway). For another, Edna St. Vincent Millay was one of several woman poets we would be studying in second semester and was, so far, the only one who used exclamation points.

Oh world, I cannot hold thee close enough!
Thy winds, thy wide grey skies!

Deep penciled-in troughs dug underneath those lines. They were rapturous. I didn't need to know what Edna St. Vincent Millay actually looked like to picture her: a wide hat, a lace collar, a skirt whipping in the wind as she strode through a field of heather and flax, throwing her arms out to embrace the everything around her. I couldn't even remember the last time I'd *seen* a field, but in those words, Edna St. Vincent Millay made me *feel* it.

The bus lurched, and then it was time.

I had, of course, gone to school without my sister before in my life. But now it felt especially strange, as though, without her shadow to stand in, I was suddenly in bright daylight, intensely visible in a way I had never been before. In the crush of the cafeteria, I found myself looking to the customary space of the High-Strung Smart Girls before remembering she wasn't there. It was just long enough for them to see me and wave me over.

"Where's Ginny?"

"Is everything okay?"

"Is she sick or something?"

Lily and Lily and Ava and Julia leaned in, politely, smiling at me but eyebrows drawn in concern, carrot sticks abandoned on their table.

Charlotte waited until last. "What's going on?" she said evenly. "I've been messaging her all morning."

"She's sick," I said.

"And she doesn't have her phone?"

"She might be asleep," Julia put in.

"Oh, right." Charlotte considered. "There's a midterm today," she said slowly.

"So?" Lily G. said. "She'll make it up."

"True." Charlotte laughed, her eyes still on me. "I was going to say that she's really screwing herself over but . . . well, you know your sister, right, Plum? She's probably going to wake up at eleven and watch *House Hunters* all day and still come in and ace the fucking thing." She smiled, and it wasn't a fake smile, although it wasn't really a happy smile, either.

"Is it the stomach flu?" Ava asked, blinking her giant eyes.

"I think so," I lied.

Charlotte winced. "Ugh. The worst. I had that and it sucked."

Julia frowned. "You did?"

Charlotte had started stirring her yogurt, staring straight down. "I missed three days of school."

"Tell Ginny I hope she feels better," Lily S. said.

"Same." Charlotte jerked her gaze up from her yogurt. "Thanks, Plum."

Her tone was definitive; I knew my cue to exit. I left the High-Strung Smart Girls and their insulated lunch bags and wove past the Sporty Senior Boys and their paper bags of off-campus fast food and slipped past the Loud Sophomore Boys, none of whom noticed me and none of whom could be expected to.

I ate my sandwich in the school bookstore, and while I did, the school secretary stopped in to give me information about a makeup exam for Ginny. Jeremy Beard didn't even look up from Dungeons and Dragons.

If I had stomach flu, I had to wonder, would anyone bother with any of this? Even if I missed three days?

I took the bus home when the day ended and heated up

some noodles Jefferson, waiting out the last few minutes before I was obliged to take Ginny her things. I was always obliged to Ginny, somehow. I would be Ginny Blatchley's sister forever, even once she left the TGS universe and was no longer my lodestar. I would always have to be less, just a little less in the way that needing context makes you meaningless, that needing to be possessed to give you shape makes you formless on your own. I couldn't claim myself. I would never know what it meant to be Plum. Just Plum.

I had sat on the floor next to the cardboard box of our mother's books. I set down my last mouthful of noodles Jefferson and lifted out a copy of *Five Little Field Mice by the Seaside.*

There had been a time in my life when these stories were as integral a part of our bedtime routine as brushing our teeth. Ginny always preferred *Five Little Field Mice Have a Birthday,* but my favorite was always this one—or "beach book" as I'd called it before I knew about titles. I loved that the field mice, who ordinarily went around in nothing but their fur, donned bathing suits when they went swimming. Mom had drawn them in little old-fashioned bathing costumes, onesies with navy and white stripes, their mousey mouths open with delight as they splashed.

I turned pages back and forth. How many other kids got this as a bedtime story? Enough that Pamela Wills knew about it. Which meant that even Tommy Wills-Wyatt had had these books. And probably other kids at TGS, and definitely other kids elsewhere. If Mom had died, too, this would've been her legacy: mice in bathing costumes. Which felt embarrassing to think, at first, but when I poked at the thought, I found I couldn't hold on to it. I loved those little mice. So many of us loved this small thing she'd made.

I finished eating. Ginny wasn't watching Home and Garden Television or watching *Amadeus* or even watching TV at all. Her bedroom door was closed, and only the faintest strains of something orchestral were seeping out. I raised my fist to knock, then thought better of it. Then I went downstairs and grabbed *Five Little Field Mice Have a Birthday* and a sticky note, which I then left leaning against the baseboard right outside her room.

> *Everyone says get better (including me). Hi dee hi dee*
> *hi, sir.*
> —*Jeeves (Plum)*

When I went back up after dinner, the book was gone.

Ginny got better, if she'd even been sick, thanks to a hefty dose of some probably expired prescription cold medicine Mom gave her, and received special dispensation to take her midterm the following day. Mom pointed out that we didn't need to be sick to take sick days, the school builds them into the academic year, and I said no, that was snow days, and Ginny said shut up both of us, she was fine and had only briefly lost her grip on reality. Mom asked if it was about the interview, and Ginny did not answer.

I knew what I had to do. I retrieved Alicia Feingold formerly Kurokawa née Tate's business card and sent an email. Then I arrived at Tate's house at the prearranged time, prepared to dispense with pleasantries.

"We have two days until the midterm," I said, as soon as he opened the door. "Are you ready?"

"Man, you never waste time, do you?" Tate said.

"I waste plenty of time," I said. "Just not on this."

"Sure," he said. "Why don't you come in?"

I padded in, slipping off my boots in the customary way, putting them between the mud-flaked soccer cleats and the cracked galoshes just like I always did.

We sat at the counter. Tate presented me with a rewritten essay. I made him tell me in detail about the varying linguistic styles of Brontë, Fitzgerald, and Shelley. I drilled him on the themes of each novel. I had him write six mock thesis statements for every foreseeable essay prompt that might be there.

"You are *determined*, Peach." Tate rolled his neck around. "You know you still get paid if I fail, right?"

I refused to let myself blush. "This is not about the money."

It was about networking gracefully and creating a good impression upon my employer, i.e., Tate's mother. It was about securing my sister's future, securing *all of our* futures. And that was, in turn, eventually, I supposed, about the money.

But it also wasn't about that at all. I'd tricked myself into investing a grander nobility into this plan than was justified. And I wasn't even making that much money.

"Yeah," Tate agreed. "It's just about getting my mom to chill out."

I couldn't disagree. Instead, I lied. "I think you're making good progress. You should be proud."

"Thanks," Tate said. "I don't care about grades."

I shouldn't have been surprised. "Well, of course *you* don't. But your mom does."

"Yeah, I guess," Tate said. "Mostly she wants me to not screw around."

"Screw around?"

"Not like *screw around with girls*," Tate said.

"Did I say that?"

Tate blinked. "No."

"This doesn't count," I said quickly. "Having me over."

"I know," Tate said. "I mean, you *were* over here that one time, but we saved it with the tutoring stuff."

He looked up at me, and widened his eyes.

"Jeez, Peach, you look like you're gonna murder me."

"I'm sorry," I said, rearranging my face as best I could without seeing it. "It's just . . . well, that was different."

"Do you remember why you even came over here the first time?"

"Vaguely," I demurred.

"Yeah, so, I can't just be like, *she was coming over to take a shower*," Tate said. "It would not look good."

"Well . . ." I pursed my lips. "Well, *that* sort of . . . thing is obviously not an issue here."

"Obviously?" Tate said, and put a hand to his heart. "Ouch. You're saying I'm not hot?"

He smiled a smile that hit me in the stomach. My sweater was too hot. I felt desperate to crack a window.

"It has nothing to do with you," I said. "I just . . . I don't."

It practically goes without saying that no one would *not* find Tate Kurokawa attractive—physically, of course, and assuming they were of the sexual orientation to do so. And although I did not know much, if anything, about sex firsthand, I did know that attraction had to be mutually expressed in order for anything satisfactory to occur. And plenty of people would not find me, Plum Blatchley, attractive.

Ouch, indeed.

"Mhm," Tate said. He threw his arm over the back of the barstool. He was always doing that, like some kind of nervous tic. But it didn't make him seem nervous; it made him seem only ever more relaxed. "You never answered my text, by the way."

"What?"

"I told you happy New Year. You didn't want to say it back?"

"I thought it was an accident," I said. "I assumed you'd been drinking."

"Nah." Tate stared at me. It was so quiet in here, without the TV on in the other room, without anyone home. "Peach, you don't like me very much, do you?"

"When did I say that?"

"You didn't. I can just, like, tell." He leaned forward. "Is it 'cause my friends are dicks?"

I said nothing.

"Is it 'cause *I'm* a dick?"

"It's neither of those," I said.

"But you still think we're dicks."

"No," I said. "Well, maybe. They are."

"No shit," Tate said. "I'd say they're good guys if you get

244

to know them, but . . ." He shrugged. "That might not be true. For any of us."

He looked at me, just sideways this time.

"I don't think it is," I said. "We're just different. You're . . ."

Tate held still.

"You're experienced," I finished, and immediately regretted it. Only someone with a true dearth of experience would use something as obtuse as *experienced* to describe what I meant.

Tate grinned, but not in a way that made my skin crawl. "What, like with girls?"

"Yes," I said. "Isn't that what we've been talking about?"

"Yeah," he said slowly. "I'll say. It's all been an experience."

"So I don't know if you respect them. Us. Girls. Women." I sat up straighter. "That's all. That's why I don't . . . I can't . . ."

Tate nodded. "Peach, you are too good for me."

He must have been inching over, maybe unintentionally. I hadn't realized it; I had stopped thinking so much when we sat next to each other, it had become so natural. Tate was alarmingly close and yet I was not alarmed, not until I looked over and registered his closeness, how near he was and the warm foreign-familiar smell of his skin and the cotton and his shirt collar.

I want to kiss Tate Kurokawa on the neck.

The thought jarred me. I wanted to jump back from it, or bury it in a lead casket, or drop it into the widest ocean and let it sink forever. But no sooner had I thought that than I thought it again, and picked it back up in my mind like something precious and impossible not to touch.

"That isn't true," I said softly. And in that moment I was ready, I would do it, if he only acted like I knew boys like him would act, I would do the foolish thing and let him have me.

But he didn't. Of course he didn't. He stood up and gathered his books.

"You deserve the kind of guy who respects you, Peach." His hair fell in his face as he spoke. "Don't settle for us assholes."

Alicia Feingold formerly Kurokawa née Tate was a quick emailer. I was in the backyard, splitting logs for the stove because no one had bothered and the kitchen counters were like blocks of ice that would freeze your skin dead and gray as soon as you touched them, when Ginny came bounding out of the house, revived.

"Guess *what*?" she said.

"What?"

"I have it. An interview." She beamed. "Did you know that Benji Feingold's mom works at Penn? She reached out and said she heard I was applying. And if I wanted she could get me a supplemental interview with someone. And maybe that could boost my chances of getting some aid."

A log dropped off the stump with a *thud*.

"Cripes," I said. "Congratulations."

The interview was set for that Saturday afternoon, which meant that that Saturday *morning* had to be scrubbed free of obligations so that we could all submit to Ginny's extensive toilette. Mom reminded Ginny that she had a whole stock of single-serving makeup packets to avail herself of. Almost-Doctor Andrews made spinach omelets. The dogs were secured in the TV room, lest they commit any last-minute mischief. I was called upon to braid her hair.

"I look good, Plum," Ginny said, tilting her head to and fro in the kitchen mirror. "Or I think I do."

"Hold still." Her hair was clean and slippery and not easily subjugated, and the stool she was sitting on made her almost too tall for me to reach the crown of her head.

"What do you think I should say? About my accomplishments, I mean. Do you think she'll ask about accomplishments? Or will it be more specific to their rigorous course of study?"

Concentrating as I was on the six crisscrossing segments of her hair, I did not have time to formulate a response before Ginny plunged on.

"She's going to ask why I want to go to Penn. I need to know why I'm going. I need a good answer. What should I say?"

"If you answer honestly, you're just going to end up saying, 'My mother is determined that I get a real job and not become some kind of failed artist.'"

"I can't say *that*," Ginny said, aghast. "It'd be like going to a job interview and saying you want the position so you can garner a paycheck."

"But that's why people *get* jobs," I said. "And go to college, I suppose, to get there in the first place."

"Capitalism," Ginny said darkly. She closed her eyes and breathed in a robust breath. "It's exhausting, this whole courtship process. You have to look respectable and give the proper answers and never actually act like yourself. And yet the whole purpose of the process is to *show who you really are.* But they don't actually *care* who you really are. They just care that you're a few points better than everyone else on some invisible scale." She opened one eye. "How can I lie to them about becoming a scientist? Is just generic *science* good enough or do you think they'll want to know about specific research interests? Maybe it's better to be interested in a lot of things, right? Should I seem more focused? Do I look like I haven't slept? Because I haven't." Ginny shook out her hand. "I'm trembling, Plummy. I have a distinctly waxen pallor in my cheek."

"It's just the caffeine," I said.

"I'm sunken. I'm ashen. I have some unspecified wasting disease, like I'm in an opera."

"Which opera?"

"I don't know. Any of them." Ginny sucked in her cheeks.

"They're always getting wasting diseases in operas," said Almost-Doctor Andrews from the soap-filled sink. I rolled my eyes.

"If I died of a wasting disease," Ginny thought out loud, "I would never have to go to college."

"Do you *want* to have a wasting disease?"

Ginny paused.

"I don't know," she said at last.

"Well, you'd be *dead*," I said. "And you have to get regular TB shots to go back to TGS, so you're likely not dying of one anyway."

Ginny smiled weakly.

"I'm sorry, Plum. You're being an agreeable lady's abigail and I'm being imperious." Ginny smoothed out the top of her skirt—which was my skirt, I realized, a knee-length blue pleat from a sixth-grade Sailor Moon costume I had never fully constructed. Of course it would still fit her.

"Perhaps Madame would like a bracing glass of brandy?" I said drily, darting the final strands of hair into a tail. I rolled the elastic off my wrist. "Or a calming dose of laudanum?"

"No!" Ginny cried. "Not *laudanum*!"

"It'll put you right."

"It'll be the end of me! She's trying to murder me, do you hear?"

"I . . ." Almost-Doctor Andrews rinsed the final dish. "Isn't laudanum some kind of poison?"

"Yes," I said. "Well, it's actually a sedative—"

"But we kept reading about it in this one book when we were kids, and I was terrified I was going to take some by mistake," Ginny said. "I think I thought it was sold in drugstores or something, maybe in those gummy vitamins."

"So for a while you could scare her just by saying *lauda-num*," I said.

"It's my number one fear," Ginny said.

"Laudanum," Almost-Doctor Andrews repeated.

"Yes," we both said.

"And Salieri's manservant," I added. "Don't forget him."

"Plum!" Ginny shrieked. "No!"

"Salieri?" Almost-Doctor Andrews said. "Like the Italian composer?"

"It's *Amadeus*," I said. "The movie. There's just this one manservant that Salieri has, and he comes back and says—"

"*'That lady is here again, sir,'*" Ginny interjected.

"Right," I said. "And he's just . . . I don't know. The way he says it?" I looked at Ginny. "Why is this even so funny?"

Ginny couldn't stifle her giggles. "'That lady'"—she snorted—"'is *here* again, sir.'"

Almost-Doctor Andrews smiled, the kind of smile you give to Gizmo when he's trying to eat a glob of spreadable meat stuck on top of his own nose: kind, amused, faintly impressed at the intensity of the endeavor.

"You girls are too much," he said. "Makes me wish I hadn't been an only child."

Dishes clean of omelet, he retreated back to the carriage house, and Ginny turned herself back to the mirror.

"What else do you need?" I asked. "Lead powder for your face? Tighter corset strings? Or can I go now?"

Ginny cinched her hands around her waist as if she were actually considering.

"Do I look okay? And do I sound okay, or do I sound dumb? This is going to go fine, right?"

My patience was wearing thin. The dogs needed to be walked, the fish given their flakes, Kit Marlowe cajoled into gumming down some wet food. "Why are you asking *me* all these questions?"

Ginny frowned. "Because you're my sister, duh."

"Well, I don't know anything," I said.

"Plum, you're certifiably brilliant."

"Ginny, stop," I said.

"It's true!" She reached backward and up to squeeze me, awkwardly, on the shoulder. "I need every ounce of insight you can muster."

"I don't *know* anything," I said. "I have no insight."

"Oh, Plummy." Ginny rose, eyes on her reflection, and smacked herself once in the cheeks. "You really ought to learn to read between the lines."

I spent the afternoon watching Home and Garden Television. Ginny came back around six o'clock, whirled through the door, stormed up the stairs, and slammed a door.

Mom was at the kitchen table, hand-lettering invitations for the silent auction. Almost-Doctor Andrews was baking focaccia in our oven, since it had a wider door than the one in his kitchenette. He looked at her, and she looked at me.

"Was that good?" she asked.

The strains of the Duruflé *Requiem* seeped through the ceiling. Ginny must have had it on at several thousand decibels to penetrate this far through the house.

"Honestly?" I said. "I don't even know."

The night before the English midterm I sat on the kitchen bookshelf and stared into my books. I wouldn't even have particularly *thought* of it as *the night before the English midterm* except that I was thinking about Tate. Not thinking about him qua thinking about him; thinking about him taking the midterm. If he failed, I had failed as a governess. But if he passed—and passed well—I would have no reason to return. I would have to pack my metaphorical bags and set sail for India with St. John. It was a frustrating line of work indeed, where your professional success was contingent on an idiot sixteen-year-old boy not spelling *Gatsby* incorrectly. And it was frustrating, I realized, when your entire entrée into said profession was based on handwritten notes that you hadn't even made.

The memory made me glum. I half-heartedly thought about themes, underlining a verb or two, and made it about seven pages before my thoughts drifted. I was, I realized, in a distractible state, spurred by my unwelcome and intrusive thought at Tate's house. If things were not otherwise, one could say I was infatuated.

Of course I had thought about potential romantic partners, in the abstract. The right boy for me—a theoretical boy—would be one who read books, and could talk knowledgeably about art, and perhaps left poetry in my backpack. I imagined him in sweater-vests. He would not be loud. He would not be experienced—well, more so than I was, but not by much; just enough to evince some virility. Tate was simply not the right kind of person to inspire those thoughts. We matched nowhere.

The tip of my pencil made loops in the margins of the book, loops that somehow morphed into hearts halfway through. Then, because it just came out of me, I added a line from Edna St. Vincent Millay:

My soul is all but out of me.

I wasn't quite sure what that meant, but I loved the sound of it, relished writing the words on the page. When I was little, I had pictured souls as rectangular, pink, and wobbly, like a sparkling, ethereal Jell-O brick that plugged into your chest. When I had told Ginny this, probably after Sunday school, she'd laughed and told me that souls were wisps of smoke, and I had just assumed that, of course, Ginny must know the truth. She was older; she knew everything back then.

I read the line again. Maybe Edna St. Vincent Millay did actually write about death.

"Plum?"

Mom had wandered in, a slim bundled package under her arms and circles under her eyes. Kit, sensing the presence of the only human he liked, mewed and wove between her ankles. I snapped my book shut.

"There you are." She rubbed her eyes. "I'm exhausted. I've been working my fingers to the bone for this silent auction."

"Yeah." I didn't bother to ask what aspect of party planning could cause that kind of injury.

"Can I enlist your help with the rest of the stuff? Just some favors and name cards and . . . I forget what else. You know."

"Sure," I said.

"Ginny, too," Mom said. "But . . . God. Is she all right?"

"I don't know," I said.

"I tried to ask about the interview, and she just said, 'Ugh, Mother,'" Mom said. Kit had submitted to being stroked on the back. "And she keeps playing Libera Me over and over again."

"Sounds about right," I said.

"Did she say anything to you?"

"Of course not," I said. "I'm sure it went fine. It's Ginny."

Mom straightened and set down her package. "Want to be depressed?"

I did not, but Mom tugged something out of the package anyway. "Look at this." A big rectangle of a picture book, with five cartoony, flat-colored mice dancing on the front of it. They were wearing—I shudder to remember—*sunglasses*.

"Oh," I said. It actually hurt my heart to see them.

"I know." Mom stuffed it back in its envelope. "This is what they've done for the twenty-fifth anniversary. Twenty-fifth! Jesus Christ, I'm old."

"You're not old! You're"—I had to think about it—"forty-seven."

"That's old enough." Mom shook her head. "Don't waste your life, Plummy. Listen to your old mother."

"I'm trying," I said.

The kitchen got quiet, except for the rumbling purrs of Kit under the table. Mom sank into a chair and pulled him to her lap.

"Or don't. I don't know. You don't have to listen to me." She sighed. "I just want what's best for you two. I'm not trying to be a helicopter mom. I know I'm not *perfect*, but at least grant that I don't do that."

"You don't," I said. "You could push worse."

"I don't know what I'm doing, you know. I'm just a lady who had babies and could never sell a painting."

"I know, Mom."

"You two are the only successful things I've ever made," she said, more softly. "I want you to do better than I did."

"You're doing fine. We're doing fine."

Mom looked back toward the staircase.

"Well, be nice to Ginny," she said. "One day I'll be dead

and you'll be all each other has left."

"Mom!"

"It's true," Mom said. "So don't be so ready to get rid of her."

I exhaled hard through my nose. Kit decided he had had enough of being petted and yowled out of Mom's hands.

"Anyway." Mom lifted her arms and let them slap against her sides. "She's sleeping in your room. Just so you know."

The midterm passed without incident, so far as I could tell. Tate never spoke with me at school, and that day, and the week that followed, as with all days and weeks, he didn't. I did not expect anything from him and would continue not to. Besides, there was an overwhelming amount of activity at home as the silent auction drew nearer. Mom was in and out constantly, panicking about petits fours, and our kitchen had become a repository of crates of expensive champagne, rented tablecloths, and stacks and stacks of invitations. On Saturday, Ginny and I found ourselves conscripted to tying maroon ribbons around tiny bags of chocolates intended as silent-auction party favors. I was pouring the chocolates into the bag, and Ginny was tying, and also sulking. We kept silent, mostly, except for the muffled sound of the jazz coming out of the radio from behind a heap of napkins.

"Charlotte found out I had an interview," Ginny said abruptly.

I frowned and poured. "You didn't tell her?"

Ginny shrugged. "It seemed . . . vaguely imprudent. I don't know. I didn't want to jinx anything." She cut more ribbon. "It was after the informational meeting for the TGS Women's Alumni Association, which they all want us to join when we're educated and employed so that we'll give money back to the school. Which is such a racket, by the way, because we already *pay* to go here. They're probably just grooming us so we'll send *our* children to TGS down the road."

"Procreation," I said. "The ultimate pyramid scheme."

Ginny cackled, which was the first time I'd seen her laugh in a long time. "Oh, yes, I wouldn't *dream* of sending Branderly and Saturnalia anywhere else! Can you imagine what inferior education would do to their college chances?"

I giggled and allowed myself one piece of candy to eat. Ginny composed herself.

"So Charlotte's all *Benji's mom is an interviewer for Penn?* And I'm like, how am I supposed to know that? And she says that Benji told her that his mom told him that I had an interview."

"Is that bad?"

"I honestly don't know," Ginny said. "But it isn't making Charlotte happy."

The radio thrummed up another tune.

"Hi dee hi dee hi dee hi," Ginny said listlessly.

"Hi dee hi dee hi dee hi, sir," I repeated, in a stiff, Jeeves-ish accent. Ginny actually smiled.

"That *sir* at the end of the line throws it off," Ginny said, in her poshest Wooster voice. "Though it's the proper feudal spirit and all."

I handed her a filled bag. She tied. I handed her another; she tied.

"Sometimes I think these fund-raisers do nothing but raise money for the next fund-raiser," Ginny said.

"Agreed," I said. "The party-favor budget alone must be enormous."

Ginny laughed again. "Wait, what is that from?"

"It's not *from* anything," I said. "I just made it up. You never think I can actually think of funny things to say on my own."

"I do, too," Ginny said. "I just really thought it was from something." She spun the scissors around her finger, watching the blades arc through the air.

"I think Charlotte hates me," she said, after a while.

"Really?"

Ginny rolled her eyes. "Well, don't sound so *surprised*. Cripes."

"Sorry," I said. "I just . . ." I crinkled the bag in my fingertips. "She didn't ask how you were, when you were sick."

Ginny twirled the scissors again. "Yeah."

"Why are you even friends with her?"

Ginny set the scissors down. "We *do* have fun together. I know it doesn't look like it, but we do." She chewed on her lip. "I guess it's like . . . we have so much in common on paper.

We have the same goals. We're the same *kind* of person. So it's easy to talk to her."

"It is?"

Ginny sat still. Then she made a sound like a deep, purring wail.

"I *hate* this!"

She slammed her palms on the table. I didn't move.

"I *hate* this," she said again. "I just want to be done."

"Done with what?" I said softly.

"Done with *everything*," she said. "I don't know."

She raked her fingers through her loose hair, and gnawed on a fingernail. The brief coziness of before had ebbed away, leaving the kitchen feeling cold and unsteady.

At my elbow, my phone buzzed—an unusual occurrence, for someone with no extrafamilial friends. I picked it up, and Ginny rose from the table as if it had been some kind of secret sign.

"I'm not feeling well again," she announced. "I'm going to lie down."

"Okay," I said. I scooped all the completed bags and the remaining candy and put it into a giant Tupperware container, for which there was no space on top of the fridge thanks to the stacks of yet-to-be-filled auction baskets. I stashed it in the oven instead, which was a decidedly dog-proof storage place, and since we barely used the oven *as* an oven, it was essentially a heavy-duty bonus cabinet, and therefore the perfect place to store something like the party favors.

Having thus packed everything away, I looked at my phone.

hey

i got a B

It was from Tate.

Congratulations, I typed back. *I'm happy for you.*

The dots popped up under my text.

thanks, came the reply. Then more dots.

your boys are on

first quarter. against the warriors

I held my phone in both hands, close to my chest. This was a statement, but one I was meant to respond to; why send it, otherwise? I tiptoed upstairs and peered into the den. The sound was on, but soft, and Ginny was not visible above the waterline of the couch.

My sister is using our TV, I wrote. Another statement, nothing further.

The dots reappeared, moving left to right like a thought working its way through the mind of the little gray bubble.

you know were to find me

I plunged my phone into my pocket.

"I'm going out, Ginny," I called into the den. Silence.

"I'm going *out*," I called again.

"*Okay*," Ginny said back. "Congratulations."

That was dispensation enough. I changed into a black sweater and took Mom's red scarf and locked the door on my way out.

This time I didn't even have to knock. Tate was waiting in the kitchen.

"My mom's upstairs," he said in a low voice. "But she's asleep, or about to be. So just come in."

I hesitated only a moment. If I was sneaking in, I was sneaking in. There would be no plausible reason for an English tutor to be in the living room at 9:07 p.m. on a Saturday night.

"You that desperate to see the game, huh?" Tate half whispered as we crossed the kitchen. The white cabinets and tiles and everything looked blue, except where the microwave buttons shone green. It was all very still.

"I had nothing better to do," I said, only realizing after I said it that that made me sound a little pathetic.

"That's 'cause there's nothing better *to* do." Tate pushed open the living room door and swept out an arm. "Come on in."

I did. I knew Tate's TV room well by now, almost to the

point of being comfortable in it. I sat on the couch, my back leaned all the way into the back, my foot tucked under my leg.

"We benched our good starter," Tate explained, pointing at the screen as he sat. "The idea is that if he doesn't play, then we'll lose and get a better pick in the draft. And we left some space in the salary cap to take over bad contracts and stuff, so we could end up with, like, the next LeBron. If we're lucky."

On TV, the announcers picked up their pace. The shoe-squeaks intensified.

"We were 116–92 against the Warriors last time, which was *pretty* good," Tate was saying, "but we're trying to—"

"Is Benji worried about college?" I blurted out. Tate looked away from the TV.

"Huh?"

"College," I said. "Is he worried about it?"

Tate had probably just wanted to watch basketball. I was disrupting everything.

"I don't think so," Tate said. "I mean, maybe. He's probably just going to end up where his dad went. Why?"

"My sister," I said. "She's . . . very upset about it."

"Ah," Tate said. "Yeah. I don't think guys care as much. Or maybe just Benji doesn't."

"You mean *you* don't worry about it," I said.

"I don't even think about it," Tate said. "And if I do, I just start watching sports until it goes away."

Maybe that was all Ginny was doing, except with Home and Garden Television instead of sports. It would go away soon, then. It usually did, with Ginny. It usually did.

"I think that's why they invented sports," Tate went on. "The opposite of school."

"The opposite of books," I said.

"There are books about sports," Tate said. "You can like both."

"*You* don't," I pointed out.

"Books are growing on me." Tate fiddled with the remote. "Now that I know how to read them. And I bet you like sports a little more now that you know how they work."

"My dad loved sports," I said. "I just found that out recently."

Tate's expression didn't change. "All guys love sports."

"Not all," I said. I couldn't, for example, picture Almost-Doctor Andrews watching a game of anything.

"Nah, we all do," Tate said. "It's just genetic."

"That's reductionist."

Tate angled a glance at me.

"You can't let me get away with anything, can you?"

"No," I said, almost proudly. Tate nodded and looked back at the screen.

"What was his favorite team? Your dad?"

"The Boston one," I said. "I think. That's where he and my mom lived for a long time."

"Celtics. Huh." Tate tipped his head. "Or—God, not the Patriots. I hope he didn't teach you to like them?"

"No," I said. "I was only six when he died."

"Oh," Tate said. "I'm sorry."

"It's okay," I said. "It was almost ten years ago."

"Do you miss him?" Tate asked.

"Of course I *miss* him," I cried. "What kind of a question is that?"

"The kind you ask? I dunno."

"Nobody asks that," I told him.

"They don't?"

"Nobody asks *me* that."

"Oh."

Maybe that *was* the kind of question you asked. And maybe I was supposed to have more of an answer. But when your father dies when you are that little, you don't miss a whole person so much as you miss parts: an arm scooping you out of the ocean, hands hoisting you up to shoulders, a leg in blue jeans that you can grab for attention.

Of all the people who missed my father, I realized, I was the one who'd known him the least.

Tate flopped forward. "You know you make it really hard to talk to you, right?"

The words hit me hard, and I felt myself sag back into the couch. "What?"

"You're just, like . . . matter-of-fact, I guess. You always have something to say. It's hard to keep up."

I folded my arms. "I'm sorry," I said softly.

"Don't be sorry. It's just how you are."

I did not like the sound of that. The actual *sound* was ordinary, conversational—Tate's voice was hardly harsh. I just didn't like knowing that. Or realizing it, I suppose. I knew my own character and shouldn't have been surprised.

But with Tate, I didn't want it to be true.

"Then I'm sorry you have to suffer through it," I said.

Tate smiled. "Do I look like I'm suffering?"

He didn't. "No."

"You know, Peach, I could be watching this game with Tommy or Stevie." He laced his fingers together between his knees. "Or by myself."

The thought of kissing him came back. It came back and I couldn't even make an effort to banish it. I wanted it like I wanted to run my fingers over it like a smooth stone, turning it and turning it and savoring it forever.

"So why don't you?" I asked.

"Maybe I want someone who's hard to talk to."

On top of the couch cushion, Tate touched my hand.

I didn't move, too stunned. Or perhaps I moved a little, subtly stiffened, because Tate pulled back, easily as if it'd been an accident.

"So I'm thinking we're going to tie up by the end of the second quarter, and then they'll bench our second-best guy, too, that one, the one with the ball right now?"

I nodded. That was it, that one bright little moment, and I would have to seal it in my mind forever. That was all I was ever going to get.

"Yeah, so he's good. Not the best, right? But good. But they'll wanna sit him out. And then they'll full-court it until—"

"You're talking fast," I said.

"Am I?" Tate said. "Yeah. I guess."

I looked at his lips, his eyelashes, the edge of his nose. I could look at him, and he wouldn't know why. Sometimes people just look.

"Nervous habit," he said.

"Are you nervous?" I asked.

"Nah," he said. "Are you?"

I shook my head.

"Okay. Good."

Tate pressed the mute button on the remote. Then he came closer, easing his arm over the top of the couch. And then I just knew.

I don't know who moved first. Tate's face was pressed against mine and his lips were pushing gently at my mouth, and my entire body was fizzy and tremulous.

I kissed back.

I didn't know how—I didn't know physically how to do it; I didn't know how it was happening; I didn't know anything. He put his hand back over my hand and eased closer to me, and I could feel the collar of his shirt brushing my neck as he leaned in and over me. His lips were a little dry; I didn't care. I was alone in the dark and I was kissing Tate Kurokawa. I was kissing Tate, and no one knew where I was.

I wanted to do it forever.

"Oh," I said.

Tate smiled. "*Oh* what?"

"Just . . ." No words were coming. "Just oh."

I could not say any of what I was thinking, that for all the things I had done and made and read and fixed and lived through, that kissing someone—kissing Tate—made everything unfold in color and sound, like a bursting-out music box.

Long have I known a glory in it all . . . Here such a passion is as stretcheth me apart.

It was like finally coming to life, when you realized how much of the world there really was.

"Was that . . ." Tate blinked. He breathed out. "Oh."

"*Oh* what?" I said—almost daring to flirt.

"You've never kissed a guy before," Tate said.

My heart squeezed. There were girls who did this, I realized. There were girls who just went to boys' houses and shimmied their way onto couches and laid themselves out. And there were boys like Tate who would do that, do anything they could get away with. It was shallow; I knew that. It was hurtful. It was the hallway at TGS and everyone staring. And yet I envied those girls' their bravery. They did not know how to be embarrassed. Or maybe they just knew it wasn't actually embarrassing at all.

"Hey," Tate said, unbearably soft. "Peach. I didn't mean to—"

"No!" I said. "It's fine. Don't worry about it. Just forget it."

Tate pressed his lips together. He sat back and looked at me. There was a strand loosening from my braid, I could feel it.

"Do you want to do it again?"

"You're *asking* me?"

"Well . . . yeah," Tate said. "It can't hurt to be sure, right?"

Behind us, in another universe, a key tumbled in the kitchen lock. Tate rose off the couch, all his ease forgotten, and stuck his head into the hall doorway.

On the porch, someone hooted. The door squeaked.

"Benj," Tate said, looking back at me. "I guess he was out. Hang on."

Tate went out, and there were voices—Benji, Tate, some other Sporty Senior Boys I couldn't and didn't care enough to distinguish, shoes thudding off on the floor, fridge opening, closing, footsteps up the stairs, then silence.

When Tate came back in I had already stood up.

"No," I said, before he could say anything. "I shouldn't be out this late anyway."

"Okay." Tate nodded. "Do you need me to walk you home?"

It was something he'd never asked before. I shook my head. "No, thanks. I want to be alone."

Evergreen Street was a bluish dark, with only pieces of moonlight scattered on the slate sidewalks. How many times had I walked these three blocks? In the past months? In my life? Yet now I wanted to see everything: the ivy on the walls, the stop sign slightly askew, the gleaming SUVs parked three deep on the endless curve of someone's driveway, the few, far stars. I wanted every part of it registered and saved, this moment locked up as tightly and vividly as I could make it. I wanted to fling my arms like Edna St. Vincent Millay must have done in her field and hold every little piece of God's world.

When I got home, the kitchen was alive.

"Plum!" Mom cried, as soon as the door swung shut behind me. "Where were you?"

All the lights were on, and the stereo was pumping out Beethoven's Ninth at full volume. Mom had a jelly jar in her hand, the dogs were barking and turning in excited circles, and Almost-Doctor Andrews was even there, pouring a fizzing bottle of wine into a teacup.

My heart literally throbbed, thinking back to where I'd been not ten minutes ago. But before I could answer, Ginny burst forth from the kitchen table.

"PLUM!" she bellowed. "Look!"

She flashed something in my face so fast that I couldn't tell what it was.

"I can't," I said, "unless you slow down."

"It's her financial aid," Almost-Doctor Andrews explained. "Champagne? Er"—he darted a look at Mom—"can she have some?"

Mom shrugged. "Sure. That's what they do in Europe."

"No, thank you," I said to Almost-Doctor Andrews. Everything was all too much. I couldn't overload it with imitation champagne from California.

The strings crescendoed, and Ginny started singing along in made-up German. Mom laughed. Doug yipped with glee and Gizmo nosed around the floor for errant food. And I smiled—I grinned, because my sister was happy and our house was lit up and I had tucked up in my mind the most glorious secret I'd ever had.

"I got it," Ginny said. "I got it. I got it. I got it."

She waved the letter in the air like a little flag. Almost-Doctor Andrews and Mom clinked glasses. The music ended, and Almost-Doctor Andrews turned down the volume before the next movement launched. Ginny sank onto the kitchen couch, dazed-looking and flushed.

"Finally," she said, draping the letter over her heart. "Everything is going to be okay."

Monday dawned crisp and strikingly clear, cold enough to dry up that kind of mid-winter melting mugginess that made you sweat in your rain boots when the TGS radiators came on full blast. If optimism were a morning, it would be this one.

In the Jesus Is the Way parking lot, Ginny immediately bustled off to relay her good news. I walked along with measured step, knowing who else was, if not on campus, fast approaching it in Benji Feingold's Range Rover. It was a funny thing, having kissed someone; suddenly you felt as though there was this halo around them, this radiance to their presence that wasn't there before and might never go away. Your senses attuned to the possibility of their arrival; you felt it in your body—not in a visceral, churning way, but in a light shimmer on the surface of your skin. But no sooner did the thought cross my mind than I rebuked myself for my good mood. There was nothing in my life experience to suggest that I would ever get anything more than the things that had already happened. Investing hopes in future good fortune was a waste.

And yet, there, at the lunch break—there he was.

We wouldn't say hello, I knew that much. We wouldn't make eye contact, even. Even if Tate wanted to, I wouldn't. I didn't want Stevie and Tommy and all the other Loud Sophomore Boys encroaching on this, not even as a joke, not even though they would never in a thousand ages suspect that their friend Tate, their fellow broad-shouldered squash player, would ever have deigned to kiss someone as plain and unassuming as Patience Mortimer Blatchley on the mouth. This was much more than secret fourth-grade poems in a notebook. Very much more.

So at the picnic tables, I kept walking, briskly. Briskly and right into a tree root.

I catapulted forward, the weight of my backpack heaving over my shoulders and pulling me even faster toward the ground. I flung out my hands, and my palms burned as they scraped against the asphalt. From behind me, I heard some *oooohs* and *that's gotta hurts*. I got to my feet, attempting briskness, and shook off my hands.

Stupid, of course, to be distracted by my own limerence. The shimmer had evaporated, replaced by literal pain. I turned the corner as quickly as I could and examined my palms, which upon inspection had been grated raw by the ground. They stung, too.

Fortunately, the school nurse was just inside the next building, across from the lower school science room, at the tail end of the boa constrictor skeleton in its long glass box.

"Oh dear." The nurse clucked her tongue at my raw hands. "Let me get you some gauze."

She busied herself in a cabinet. She was wearing a beige ribbed turtleneck, which could only mean that today was the day that the fifth graders were learning about childbirth. When Ginny was eleven, she had come home from school one day wide-eyed, and recounted with horror what they had learned in health class.

"And then after all the birth-canal stuff, she pulled her turtleneck *over her head*," Ginny recounted breathlessly, "and pushed it back out and said, 'There, I was just born.'"

A pause, for dramatic effect.

"Ew," I said.

"I know," Ginny said. "And next week they're going to give us"—she shuddered—"*tampons.*"

I remembered my chest filling with part relief and part utter panic at knowing exactly what excruciation lay in store, and a wordless wave of gratitude that I had Ginny to tell me these things ahead of time. How people without older sisters survived fifth-grade health class, I did not know.

"I'm so sorry, Patience"—the nurse had never bothered to learn what I was actually called—"I'll have to go to the supply closet. Two seconds. I know you have to get to class."

She disappeared down the hall, and I sat on one of the plastic chairs and stared idly around, palms still stinging.

The nurse's office had a private bathroom, which was primarily a place to throw up, and a series of cots hidden away behind a paper curtain. Behind the paper curtain, on the end of one of the cots, a pair of shoes was sticking out. I recognized them; they were *my* shoes, my purple flats with the rhinestones on the toes that I had not noticed disappear that morning.

"Ginny?"

I pushed back the paper curtain a little. My sister was lying back, her hands folded over her stomach, engulfed in one of mom's oversize sweatshirts.

"What are you doing here?" I said. "Are you okay?"

"Sort of." Ginny's voice wavered. She sounded hoarse.

"Are you throwing up?"

"No."

I stood there. She lay there.

I looked back toward the nurse's now-empty desk. "Did you see the turtleneck?"

Ginny didn't cackle. She didn't even smile. "Oh. Yeah."

She pursed her lips.

"I just had to lie down," she went on. "I needed something for my cold."

I, unlike Ginny, knew the difference between hypochondria and actual illness. This did not look like the former. But Ginny didn't have a cold, either.

"Are you going to go to class?" I asked.

Ginny put her hands over her face.

"I left my backpack," she said, from behind her fingers. "Under the stairs."

"I'll get it," I said, because she didn't even have to ask. When you are a younger sister and your older sister makes a statement like that to you, you know she's actually asking for a favor. But now I didn't mind.

The nurse returned and patched me up, and with my taped-over palms I strode across campus in the three remaining minutes of the lunch period.

Under the math building stairs, on the bench of the alcove where Ginny would have ordinarily been sitting with her friends, I saw it, the saggy navy blue with *VEB* embroidered on it. Ginny'd had the same one since the third grade, but they never really went out of style.

I squeezed behind one of the tables and picked it up without talking to any of the High-Strung Smart Girls, because I never had anything to say to them anyway. But their heads all tilted up, in almost unison, like a flock of sparrows.

"Excuse me," I said, as if I needed their permission. "I'm just getting Ginny's bag for her."

"Hmph." Charlotte said. She got up from the other table, shouldering her gargantuan tote bag, which swelled out with the corners of various books poking in every direction. "I'm sure you're very happy for your sister."

There was nothing happy about her tone, not even a

manufactured happiness. I gave her a look that said—well, it did not say enough.

"I'm sure you're very happy for your *best friend*," I replied.

Charlotte did not reply. She brushed past me, one of the corners in her tote bag hitting me square in the shoulder.

When I went back to the nurse's office, Ginny was pretending to be asleep. I was five minutes late to math.

"Here," the nurse said. "Let me write you a note."

"But I'm not sick," I said. What I meant was: *but* Ginny's *not sick*.

I took the note anyway.

For dinner that night, Mom and I microwaved baked potatoes.

"These look terrible," Mom said, poking one with a fork.

"The only point of these is to put butter and salt on them," I said. I felt a deep-seated need to be cheerful, to parcel out the feeling of the other night for as long as I could.

"Yeah," Mom said.

"So they're delicious no matter what."

Yet each of my attempts to force out the cheerfulness made it lose shape. I wasn't trying hard enough. I was not behaving the way a girl who'd had something magical happen.

"They're just potatoes, Plum. Let's not lose our heads."

Gizmo trotted in, a paper towel stuffed into his collar. He plopped his head onto my lap, which was unsavory given that his face was wet and one of the toilet seats somewhere was surely open. I pulled out the paper towel.

DINNER'S READY! xo Mom

A Gizmo-gram return to sender. I crumpled it into a ball.

"The school called," Mom said. "Ginny's on academic probation."

"What?" I said.

"Someone accused her of cheating. On the makeup midterm."

"That's patently ridiculous." I put down my fork. "Who told them that?"

"They didn't say," Mom said. "Honor system. It's anonymous."

The honor system at TGS was as anonymous as its college process was personal and private.

"So it was Charlotte."

The butter spilled onto Mom's plate. Neither of us was going to eat our potato, I knew.

"Can't any of us get a break?" Mom said. "Just one goddamn break."

She swooped up from the table, taking her wineglass with her and leaving no one but me to clean everything up.

It turned out that the oven had not been the right place to store the party favors.

At first, everything that Saturday was normal, if impossibly busy. 5142 Haven Lane became a hive of activity, singularly focused on preparing every last precious detail of the silent auction. Mom was up at 6:00 a.m. ironing tablecloths. I fed the chickens and fed the dogs and fed Kit Marlowe and even fed the fish, who honestly were the most neglected of the Blatchley menagerie, and then began the hours-long process of printing out tiny cards with aliases on them. Ordinarily, silent auctions used something straightforward, like playing cards, to anonymize the bidders, but Mom in her infinite tendency to overdo things had decided it would be much more on-brand to use the names of famous impressionist artists. This put our printer under considerable strain, and I spent almost two hours gently force-feeding it sheets of perforated place cards in #017 pebble gray.

It was dull work, the kind that made me vaguely wish I had

some kind of hand-occupying hobby like knitting or needle-work. However, while I was feeding the pebble-gray perforated card sheets into the printer, I got a text message.

you get home okay?

i mean i guess you did haha

i just never asked is all

I wanted to reply, more than anything, more than I wanted to admit. I clenched my hand tightly around my phone, pressing into the gauze over my scrapes, and waited another two perforated sheets' worth of time.

Yes, I typed back. *Thanks for inviting me.*

The read-receipt check mark appeared. Then the dots. My chest contracted against my will. Whoever had invented this technology had the rare distinction of creating with it an entirely novel human neurosis. The sadist.

i would have done it sooner if i'd known, came Tate's answer.

you should watch games more often

Maybe, I responded. *I don't pay that much attention.*

you around tonight

?

Was I?

From the floor, Kit Marlowe mewled, his fluffy belly turned up and his tail curling one way and the other.

"You shameless exhibitionist," I told him. "Since when are you so friendly?"

Kit gave a coy meow. I stuffed another sheet in the printer and went back to my phone.

I wrote back truthfully. *I think I have a family thing.*

ok, Tate responded.

That was it. That was it until we'd packed up the baskets and shook out the ironed tablecloths and triple-checked the number of tiny candles and lined up the decanters like clear glass soldiers at attention. Then I received one last message.

well let me know

And then we smelled it.

Ginny had sorted about four baskets before she took a break to make toast, and since toast was food, neither Mom nor I nor Almost-Doctor Andrews thought to discourage her, even though it was really outside of Almost-Doctor Andrews's jurisdiction as a tenant. It wasn't until Mom returned to the kitchen after wrapping herself in her formal blacks for the silent auction that anyone realized anything was wrong.

"What's that *smell?*" Mom put a bell-shaped sleeve over her nose and mouth, coughing. "Plum?"

"Huh?"

I was certainly not wasting time rereading a single text message. I was, in fact, de-perforating the place cards and stacking them in alphabetical order, and had made it as far as *Cézanne.*

"Oh no," Mom said. Gizmo and Doug were up, tails wagging, since clearly either Something Was Wrong or There Might Be Food.

"Cézanne is a postimpressionist," came Ginny's sharp voice. She had drifted in, wearing another one of Mom's gigantic Ferrars College sweatshirts, the one with sleeves so long they concealed her hands entirely. "What's that *smell*?"

Ginny jogged to the oven and yanked it open. There, in its gaping, metallic maw, lay a mess of melted chocolate, singed ribbon, and cellophane that had gone brown and crispy at the edges. A plume of carcinogenic odor wafted through the room.

"What the hell, Plum?" Ginny yelled. "What's wrong with you?"

"What do you mean, what the hell?" I said.

"*You* put them there," Ginny said.

"I was going to take them *out*," I said. "I just forgot. Besides, it's *your* fault for not looking in the oven before you turned it on."

"Why would I look?" Ginny said. "We never *use* it. And why did you even put them there in the first place?"

I looked at Mom, helpless to defend myself, unable to explain. Mom pushed her headband further up her forehead.

"Girls, don't. Not now."

"But, *Mom*," Ginny said. "Plum ruined—"

"I did not!" I cried. "And I don't see *you* helping. You're just lying around being *useless*."

"*Girls.*" Mom's voice was steely and tight as piano wire. "I don't need this right now. I need to get this to the living room, and I need you to be dressed, and I need everything tonight to not be *hopelessly fucked-up* the way it usually is. So act like adults for once, okay?"

Mom never talked like this.

Ginny wavered. "But—"

"No. You think you're going to get through college with an attitude like this, Ginny? Because I'll put up with your bullshit, but only because I'm your mother. You can't be like this in the real world. Don't push it."

"Seriously," I muttered. "I hope you weren't like that in your interview."

Ginny huffed, hard, but her eyes looked weak and watery.

"Oh, so now all of a sudden you *care* about my future?" She crossed her arms. "*Now* you want to know how my interview went?"

"I *asked*!" I yelled. "You think I don't care? I care a *lot* about that stupid interview."

Ginny scoffed. I was actually trembling.

"I'm the whole reason you *got* that interview, Ginny," I said. "*I* talked to Alicia Feingold for you. She owed me a favor, and I told her to talk to you."

Ginny's face fell.

"What?" She practically bellowed it.

"Yeah," I said. "So I *do* care. You're welcome."

"I can't *believe* you, Plum," Ginny yelled. "You didn't think I could do it on my own? You thought I was that stupid?"

"I did *not*," I said. "I can't believe you would think that."

"Don't, Plum," Mom said. "She's being hysterical. Don't engage."

"But she . . ." Ginny could barely form a sentence. "Plum ruined everything!"

"Ginny, you can either help, or you can leave. I'm not dealing with histrionics right now." Mom looked at the clock, swore, and grabbed her keys. "I'm going."

Ginny's eyes filled with tears.

"Mama," she said. Her voice sounded stuck in her throat. "Wait."

"I *can't* wait, Ginny," Mom said. "Now I have to go to the florist's and get new favors. Just cool it with the hysterics."

"I'm not hysterical," Ginny said, even as she was crying harder. She swabbed at her face with the end of a sweatshirt sleeve.

"Uh, actually, you *are*," I said. "Get a grip."

Ginny fixed me with a look, then melted to the floor.

"Oh, for Christ's sake," Mom said. "Virginia, you are eighteen years old. You can't fall to pieces like this over nothing."

"It's *not* nothing," Ginny sobbed. "It's the *f-future*. And neither of you t-trust me. It's *my* whole future."

I looked at the mangled mess of plastic. And then I had had enough.

"It is not," I said. "You just can't stand for there to be a crisis that doesn't have *you* at the center of it."

If Ginny's tragic flaw was her reactivity, mine was my own spite. It was just too easy to be mean when you really wanted to be, even to your sister. No—especially to your sister. I could hurt her more than anyone else, more than Mom, more than Charlotte, more than the entire University of Pennsylvania. It was a true and essential ability, and, in that particular moment, I relished it.

"You don't do *anything* useful. Ever. All you do is lie around and cry like the crazy person you are."

Ginny cried harder.

"I'm going," Mom said. "I'm already late. Ginny, you're just going to have to deal with this. I don't know what to tell you anymore."

She slammed the door, and when she did, Ginny made a strangled noise and pushed herself to standing. She stood very still for a moment, then dashed up the stairs.

"Good riddance!" I yelled after her.

I stood alone in the kitchen a moment, wishing I had somewhere else to go, until I remembered that I did.

Actually, I'm free now if you want

The dots were there barely five seconds.

front row seat. all yours

He was waiting at the back door.

"Hi," I said.

"Hi," Tate said.

Immediately I did not know what to do. I'd never allowed my imagination to go this far forward into the future. And even if I had, I would have conjured absolutely nothing. I barely knew how to reciprocate, let alone initiate, anything romantic.

But there was Tate, in his striped rugby shirt, the collar hanging crooked, the sleeves rolled up to his elbows, and I thought: *I know you. Maybe not the way other people know you, maybe not the way you want people to know you, but I know that at least once, maybe even twice, you have seen fit to kiss a girl like me.*

And looking at him, I wondered if he thought that about me, too.

He opened the screen door. I came in. The kitchen was quiet.

"TV room?" he said.

I nodded.

We went in. I sat down. Then he sat, too. The light from the table lamp was shining up and down in warm swaths against the red walls. Tate was wearing shorts. His knee was touching mine.

"I'm sorry about your hands," he said.

"What?"

"Your hands," he said again, and nodded at where I'd folded them in my lap. "I should have come to help you, or something. When you tripped."

What could I say?

I kissed him.

It is hard to be kissed back by someone like Tate Kurokawa and not feel at least a little bit beautiful. It is hard to be kissed like that and not think about almost nothing, and not be swallowed up. I felt glorious. There was truly no other word for it.

Tate kissed me on the lips and on the corner of my mouth and then on my neck and then on the lips again and then we were lying farther on the couch and my hand found its way to his hair and I was trying so hard to notice it all, to save it all up in perfect detail so that I could have it forever.

There are not many perfect moments—that much, you know. And maybe this wasn't one of them. Maybe I wasn't actually beautiful. Maybe I didn't actually know Tate, and maybe there was nothing true or tender about the way he kissed me because I simply didn't know any better. All I knew is that when I left, it was like I'd left my heart in the palm of his hand.

It was late when I got back. Late, and quiet. But all the lights were on.

I creaked in the back door.

"Hello?"

The kitchen was the same mess as before. But no dogs came barking. And for some reason, Almost-Doctor Andrews was sitting at the counter.

"Plum." He got up, too quickly. "There you are."

"I'm sorry," I said. "I was—"

He looked so pale.

"I don't know how to tell you this," he said. "I'm so sorry."

 *FIVE*

For the sake of a single verse,
one must see many cities, men, and things.
—Rainer Maria Rilke

I can't even begin to explain what this was like.
But I will try.

It wasn't serious. It wasn't life-threatening. She was going to be fine. That's what I remember being told, over and over. Almost-Doctor Andrews whisked me to the hospital in his tiny, impeccably clean Honda. I took tiny breaths the whole time: at the counter, up the elevator, down the hall, to the doorway. Everything telescoped; everything felt far away, like it had happened long ago.

She had drowned, Almost-Doctor Andrews explained. Almost. She had almost drowned. She had almost drowned in a bathtub in a bathroom with a locked door and only the dogs wouldn't stop barking, so he slammed into the bathroom shoulder-first and found her. You don't think of people drowning in bathtubs, but you only need a few inches of water to drown, everyone knows that, and you aren't supposed to take that kind of cough medicine when you're not sick, even if you *are* sick, you're supposed to be careful, because it makes you so sleepy, and yes that's the *point*, that might be why, but you still aren't supposed to, you can't keep your head up, you could hurt yourself, you could get hurt.

There was a question and it vibrated between us, but I couldn't ask it, not of poor Almost-Doctor Andrews at the wheel looking drawn and unshaven, the first time I'd seen him that way, and I wouldn't ask it, I vowed that I would never ask that question for the rest of my life, I would never, never, never.

But I still wanted to know, in my sick ugly way. I wanted to know if she'd done it on purpose.

The hospital, terrible in the same ways that all hospitals are terrible, anodyne and sterile. We sat and waited. I put my mittened hands between my knees and preoccupied myself with the smallest pieces of my surroundings, the digestible parts. I couldn't think about anything bigger or I would burst open like a dam. So I noticed the cushions of the waiting couch, the gray-brown color of cat food. The Exit sign that flickered. The refrigerated hum of the water fountain as it cooled water you just knew was tooth-chilling and tasted like lead. The nurse in lollipop scrubs behind her scratched-up pane of glass—maybe bulletproof. You never knew. You never knew who might try to throw a punch or come into a hospital with a gun. You never ever knew.

"Plum."

I looked up. Mom, still in her black party clothes, washed-out and green-skinned in the ugly hospital light. She grabbed me by the shoulders and slammed me to her chest.

"Mom."

"She's okay." Mom pushed me away. "It wasn't serious. She's going to be fine."

"I'll get some coffee," Almost-Doctor Andrews said, even though no one had asked. That was just what you did in hospitals, if you were a good person: you got the others coffee. He disappeared through the double doors.

"She's going to be fine," Mom repeated. "She aspirated water. She did lose consciousness. But it was less than three minutes. No reason to believe"—her voice caught—"brain damage. Or anything like that. They're monitoring her body temperature. Giving her oxygen."

Then, out of doctor's words to repeat, she sank into a chair.

"Oh, God. I wasn't there."

I hadn't been there, either.

"I'm sorry," I said in a tiny voice.

Mom didn't say anything. Almost-Doctor Andrews came back with two white plastic cups. She buried her face in her hands as he set them down.

"Iris," he said gently. "Something to drink?"

"We should've done something," she said from behind her hands. "We knew she was all . . . messed up. I don't know." She looked up. "Where were you, Plum? Why didn't anyone . . ."

She started crying.

"We should've *done* something," she said, and looked at me with big, wet eyes, and for some reason I found myself thinking of the nurse in her scrubs, her studious inattention, her focus professionally trained elsewhere, and yet she had to notice. There was no way she wouldn't notice. People notice things like this. A crazy family. A bad mother. A sister, motionless. *I was moved to tears*, we say. But I had gone stiff and cold. There was no way to cry now. There was only being still and stiller, as if I could stop my own heart.

A doctor appeared. Details were given—I barely listened. We were summoned to a green curtain with a bed behind. She looked sunken, and not in a beautiful way. There was nothing actually beautiful about seeing my sister this sick. It was ugly and it hurt.

I ran away.

It is natural to think about your parents dying—they are older, it stands to reason. They don't always make it past your own childhood. Grandparents, too, never exist outside a state of oldness, fragility; maybe they're already gone by the time you arrive. But as I lay in bed that night, and thought of my sister sleeping, hopefully peacefully, I realized an obvious truth, that barring some terrible dual accident, one day one of us would have to live without the other. It was senseless—there was no *world* without my sister. No gravity. But one day, if I was lucky, I would be there to hold Ginny's hand—or her mine, and—

Or it would be a phone call, across the country, across the world, from her husband or mine, a hospice nurse, a caretaker—

Or it could be in a hospital bed, young.

And yet how much of my life had I spent wishing her out of my life? Wishing finally to be alone?

I did not deserve a sister.

The next day I locked myself under the stairs.

I was almost too big for it, but not quite. It turned out that you could make yourself very small if you needed to, if you didn't mind being uncomfortable. And I didn't mind. I wanted it. I needed the eaves digging into my shins and the bruise on my head from climbing in the first time.

I didn't want to go anywhere else, do anything, or see anyone. And no one would notice I was gone—not Mom, who was in her studio, not Almost-Doctor Andrews, who was practicing, and not Ginny. Not Ginny in her bedroom. The door was closed for a reason.

It was warm under the stairs, with its familiar musty-wood smell. The door pulled shut with the same crooked nail as always. There was nothing to see or do. It was private and, in the way of true privacy, calm—but not an easy calm; the kind of calm that is forcibly quiet, the calm of a beachfront after a tornado. I don't know how long I sat there.

A scratching sound came at the door.

"Go away," I said, to whoever it was. My throat felt thick.

More scratching. I closed my eyes and put my head against my knees and tried to ignore it.

"Stop it!" I flung open the door so hard it banged against the staircase. "Stop it, you idiot!"

Kit Marlowe shrank, his eyes bright and wide, and I felt a flash of guilt. He was just a cat. This wasn't his fault.

"Kit, wait," I said, but it was too late. I was alone. I was talking to no one.

And yet, in the middle of all this, I was still made to go to school.

The aim of school was allegedly receiving an education, an aim I respected. The academic environment, though, I found I could not understand. People had managed to internalize everything from mathematics to irregular Latin verbs for centuries without the aid of formal schooling. Those of us with enough discipline to become autodidacts would have fared perfectly well given enough books and peace and quiet. Forcing us into classrooms with our peers, insisting on standard hours, measuring everyone by grade point averages and standardized scores and my-dad-knows-someone and you-can't-put-*my*-daughter-in-remedial-math was inefficient at best. Besides, if we were only there to learn, why did we have to go to Senior Teas and perform in *Oklahoma!* and eventually attend end-of-the-year picnics?

I was turning all this over in my mind when the school secretary stopped me not two steps within the Gregory School's threshold.

"Plum. Your mother called—your sister's absent?"

"She's sick," I said, the simplest-sounding answer.

"Oh dear." She clucked sympathetically, but it was a man-ufactured cluck, with too much of a dart around the eyes to be genuine. "What's the matter?"

"It's her head," I said, trying not to sound hoarse. This was me, equivocating.

"Oh," she said. "Migraines?"

"Something like that," I said. "I have to get to class."

I wished for a larger student body, where the social spec-trum was wide enough to swallow up individual incidents without system-wide disturbance. But this was the Gregory School, and if something had happened to 1/80th of the senior class—*especially* around college time—there was no way the other 79/80ths were going to ignore it.

So every day, the seniors at the senior table stared at me as I snuck through the front hall: Shiny-Hair Party Girls darting eyelinered glances at Sporty Senior Boys; High-Strung Smart Girls looking up from their advanced biology textbooks. Some might have been pitying, others just evalu-ating, scouring me for any evidence. I wasn't used to being visible, let alone parsed and picked apart, and so I hurried onward.

Every day, I took my lunch into the bookshop and ate, unremarked upon by the Weird Sweatshirt Kids.

And every day, when I walked to my fourth-period class, I passed by the Loud Sophomore Boys at their picnic table. I did not even look in Tate's direction.

And then, because I could not help it, I paused before the COLLEGE CHOICES bulletin board on my way to math.

It was just over two weeks into this routine when I noticed it. Someone had written over Ginny's name.

VIRGINIA BLATCHLEY—CRAZY BITCH!!

My stomach twisted. The words were in black ballpoint, scribbled bumpily over the cork beneath the colored paper. Before I knew what I was doing, I ripped the piece of paper from under her picture and stuffed it in my pocket.

The High-Strung Smart Girls were clustered in their usual place under the math building staircase. Some had binders of loose-leaf open, some were tapping at their phones. Charlotte Forsythe was sitting in a chair facing the rest of the lounge area, and when she saw me coming—and she certainly saw me coming—she started laughing even harder at whatever Ava or Lily was saying to her.

"Hey, Plum," she said, tipping her head to the side as I approached. "How's it going?"

I took out the piece of paper and opened it on the table. "Someone did this."

Charlotte's eyes darted downward, then back up at me. Her smile hadn't fully faded away.

"So?"

"So . . ." I looked at the other girls, but they'd all fallen silent, lips pressed tight and eyes wide. "So why would some-one do that?"

Charlotte glanced sideways at the others. "I don't know. You tell me."

"Tell you what?" My voice came out tiny and afraid.

"Plum, we aren't stupid. Ginny isn't really having migraines." She leaned in closer. "Is she okay? You can talk to us, if you need to."

For a moment, I wavered. I almost did. But then my mind clicked firmly into place.

"You did it," I said. "You told them she was cheating."

"I can't talk about that," Charlotte said, calm as ever. "It's the honor system."

"But you *did*," I said. "And you know Ginny would never cheat."

"Then how'd she get such a good score when she was out sick the day before?" Charlotte said. "Come on, Plum. We all know she was desperate. It's okay. I know things are hard."

She reached out to touch my arm, but I jerked it away.

"I can't believe you," I said, my voice rising without my meaning it to. "You had no proof."

"Well, I mean, look, the way things are now . . ." Charlotte puckered her eyebrows. "Ginny just needs all the help she can get."

"What are you talking about?"

"Plum." Charlotte lowered her voice. "She tried to kill herself."

"What?" I cried. "That's not— Who told you that?"

"So it *is* true," Charlotte said. "God, I actually can't believe it."

It took a moment to sink in. She had tricked me.

People were staring. People thumping down the stairs from second-floor math rooms, people loafing on the couches in the first-floor common area outside the computer lab, people eating mini-pizzas and drinking illicit Frappuccinos. All the High-Strung Smart Girls. Everyone was waiting for me to melt or shrink down or scurry away.

Propriety would've dictated that I not make a scene. That I be polite and brush this under the rug, keep a stiff upper lip. But I couldn't. I quite simply had nothing to lose.

"Shut up, Charlotte," I said. "You've spent the past four months trying to destroy everything Ginny's working for. And you know what? You *still* couldn't stop her. Did you ever think that the reason she got in and you didn't is because she's *smarter* than you? Sure, maybe she didn't get financial aid, and she had to figure that out somehow, but guess what? Our dad is *dead*. We *don't* have tons of money. So she did everything she could. And the only way you could actually stop her was by *lying*."

I sucked in a breath. "Second of all, my sister is *not* psycho. She's a good person. You know how I know? Because even though you're the kind of person who makes fun of her and gossips behind her back and accuses her of *cheating* and writes stuff like this over her name"—I held up the paper— "she still calls you her friend."

Charlotte's tan had gone a spoiled-milk color. She crossed her arms under her breasts, badly faking an air of nonchalance.

"Honey, you don't have *any* friends," she said, sweet as aspartame. "So, no offense, but how would *you* know?"

"I have Ginny," I said, and for the first time in my life it didn't feel like a failure to admit that my sister was my friend, my only real friend. It felt true. It was true. My voice rose in my throat. "You're a manipulative bitch, Charlotte."

The last words came out so loud and clear I swore I could've heard them echo.

I was suspended. Patience Mortimer Blatchley—suspended! You cannot call someone a manipulative bitch in the middle of the math building at TGS and not expect to get in trouble; I got in trouble. No one ever bothered to read the entirety of the student manual at TGS, myself included, but I was not surprised to discover that my behavior was a suspendible offense. I was, frankly, proud—although I tried not to appear so when the principal and the vice principal and the school psychologist were summoned to an informal disciplinary hearing to decide the terms of my punishment.

The verdict was three days of suspension and a follow-up counseling session with Dr. Kaplan. At TGS, there was no such thing as a "bad kid"; there were merely students with behavioral problems stemming from unaddressed emotional issues, the emotional nature of said issues increasing in proportion to the family's contribution to the school's annual giving fund. I didn't think it would help my case to explain that perhaps Charlotte Forsythe was the one who could use counseling, but then again, "being a bitch" is likely not an entry in the *DSM-V.*

The suspension I didn't mind. The true punishment was calling home.

Mom sounded like I'd woken her up, which I might have. "Plum?"

"Hello," I said. "It's Plum."

"I know," she said. "My only other daughter is upstairs. What's going on?"

"I've been suspended," I said. "There was an incident."

"What?" Just like that, Mom was awake. "Did you get in a fight?"

"We don't have fights," I reminded her. "We have incidents."

"So what was the incident?"

"Calling Charlotte Forsythe a manipulative bitch."

"*Plum.*" Mom sighed. "Well, I guess it's well deserved."

"I know," I said. "But I've never gotten in trouble before."

"No," Mom said. "I meant what you said to Charlotte."

"Oh." I paused to suppress a smile so the school secretary would not think I was making light of my infraction. "Thanks."

"I'll come get you."

"Thanks."

Everyone stared as I left, and I did not even remember to shrink.

It was even better when I told the story a second time. Almost-Doctor Andrews, who was home at midday in the way that only part-time academics seem to be able to, made me a cup of Earl Grey and listened with no small amount of interest from a kitchen stool.

"My goodness," he said, when I had finished. "Could you go back in time to my junior high years? Because I knew a few people at the Topeka School for the Performing Arts who could use a dressing-down."

I blushed into my tea. "I didn't know you were from Topeka," I said politely. "What made you come here?"

"School." Almost-Doctor Andrews stirred his mug. "Twenty-two years down, two to go. Ish."

"*Twenty-two years?*" I said. "But you'd have to have been playing since you were . . . six?" I guessed.

He held up four fingers, half grimacing.

"Wow," I said. "Like in *Amadeus*."

Almost-Doctor Andrews laughed. "Oh God, no. My

teacher had a saying: *prodigies aren't born; they're built.* Not that I was a prodigy, or anything. I'd rather die than rewatch my audition tapes."

"But you still started young," I said.

"Well, yes," he said. "That's really the only way to do it right, isn't it?"

A few moments of silence passed.

"So what does Ginny think?"

I lifted my head. "About what?"

"Your suspension."

"Oh, she . . ." I glanced at the back stairs. "I think she's asleep."

"I see," Almost-Doctor Andrews said. "Well. You might want to tell her. At some point."

I wanted to ask him what he thought I should say, how he would propose I broach this topic with my sister who had almost died for reasons that were squarely my fault. But he was too tactful to press, and I was too humiliated with myself to pursue the topic, and we each made our polite excuses and retreated in opposite directions.

That evening I made scrambled eggs, half for Mom to take up on a tray and half for me to not eat much of. I slept with Gizmo and Doug on either side of me and Mozart's *Lacrimosa* playing softly.

The next day was Ginny's birthday. March 2, as it falls every year, and I didn't even realize it until 10:00 a.m.— long after Mom had left for campus, a full hour after Gizmo and Doug's first real walk of the day, several minutes after remembering the chickens needed to be fed.

It is the sort of thing one could have forgiven me for forgetting, except at that point I was not willing to be forgiven for anything. Ordinarily birthdays were a production—cakes (box mix or supermarket with the super-sugary roses), candles in creative formations, whatever streamers and balloons we could scrape out of the junk drawer. As of that day, which was gray but mild, Ginny and I had not spoken in over a week.

I remembered, nevertheless, when I returned to the house, dusting chicken feed from my hands, and spied a small package on the back porch, which I realized was from Almost-Doctor Andrews and which contained, despite its plain white exterior, a birthday present for my sister.

Inside, Kit hissed as I crossed the threshold. I scowled at him, and he, chastened, padded off at a clip. I set down the package, then picked it up, and then I followed Kit, all the way to Ginny's room. The door was closed, and Kit sat, his cat's bulk spreading out fuzzily in front of the door, and mewled.

I knocked only very lightly.

"Whoizzit?"

"Kit Marlowe," I said, for some reason.

A muffled sound, like pillows and blankets.

"Does Kit Marlowe have a dead mouse for me?"

I looked down at his little marble-eyes.

"No," I said. "Just a present."

"All right," came her voice. "C'min."

I pushed open the door.

"Plummy?" Ginny, hair spread on her pillows, frowned at me from bed. "What are you doing home?"

"Happy birthday," I said. "I'm suspended." The words blurted out before I could stop them, and then, I burst into sobs. "I'm sorry. I'm sorry. I'm sorry I'm sorry I'm sorry."

Ginny coughed. "What for?"

"I just . . ." I was hysterical. My breath was jerking up my throat. "Everything. Everything. Ginny, I'm sorry."

"Wait. Wait." Ginny blinked from her mass of pillows, pushing aside the Five Little Field Mice book she'd evidently been reading. "You're *what*?"

"Suspended," I said, drawing a shaky breath. "I . . . I

told Charlotte Forsythe she was a bitch in front of the entire math building lounge area."

"You *what?*" Ginny sat up in bed. "You didn't."

I looked at my sock-covered feet. "I did."

Ginny cackled. "Oh my God." She fell back onto her pillows and scissored her legs under the sheets. "Oh my *God*. Yes! Ahahaha."

I didn't know at all what to make of this reaction. "You're not mad?"

Ginny flopped her head to one side. "Cripes, Plum. She did have it coming. I just never thought it'd be *you* to say it."

"Desperate times." I looked back up. "I mean . . . you're welcome. I think."

"Mm." Ginny stilled. She narrowed her eyes at the package in my hands. "What is it?"

"I don't know. I think it's from Almost-Doctor Andrews." I handed it over. Ginny surveyed, pulled off the red string tying it shut, and uncovered a very fine, very fancy bar of chocolate.

"Oh," she said. "Oh. That was kind of him."

She turned it over a few times.

"Want some?"

I shook my head.

"How are you feeling?" I asked.

"Breathing air," Ginny said. "Can't complain."

The one time she was actually sick, and she understated it

entirely. I found myself almost wishing she *would* be hysterical, rail against her condition, cry out in frustration, anything.

The edge of the Five Little Field Mice book peeked from under her comforter.

"I see you're doing your usual reading," I said, untucking it.

"Ha. Yes. It has changed very little these past thousand readings," Ginny said. I leaned against the end of her mattress, paging.

"'Five little field mice lived in a hole, warm and dry. Today, it was somebody's birthday,'" I read softly.

"More like, *today someone relinquishes her youth*," Ginny said. "Eighteen is too old, Plum. I should go burn my toys on the altar of Artemis."

I put down the book. "What do you mean, too old? You can't even legally drink."

"Too old to do anything," Ginny said. "An eleven-year-old aces the SATs? Fantastic. An eighteen-year-old? So what. Eighteen is the age of unremarkability."

"Well, not all of us were child geniuses, okay?"

Ginny shrank back into her pillows.

"You know what, Plum?" she said in a small voice. "Every English teacher I've ever had has brought that essay up to me. They even teach it in the creative nonfiction seminar for seniors. Everyone knows what they think I am, and I don't know how not to disappoint them. It's like . . . I just keep working and working and working and eventually I want someone to say, *Okay, Ginny, you know what? That's enough. You get a break.*"

I had never thought of that.

"Do you know what I wrote my college essay about?" she went on.

"I have no idea," I said flatly. "Marie Curie."

"No," she said. "You."

"What?"

"*Yes,*" Ginny said. "Well, I mean, you, and a lot of other things. *Amadeus,* the Brontës, the nature of youthful genius, blah blah blah. I came to some kind of conclusion. You know how it is. It's hard to say in any other words except the ones I said it in. I borrowed some lines from Rainer Maria Rilke—"

"Who?"

"The German poet?" Ginny said. "I thought you studied him sophomore year. Have you even been *reading* those books?"

I folded my arms. "It's a little bit *hard,*" I retorted, "given that they're buried in your stupid notes."

Ginny looked wounded. "Well, I'm sorry. I only put them there for you."

"For your information," I said, "I can make my *own* notes."

Ginny shook her head. "No, no, no. I mean I put them there to say hi. I thought it'd be fun, if you got my books later. To send you a message from the past. I knew you'd obviously know everything about the *language*." She threw her hands in the air. "See, that's what I'm saying! I mean, look, college essays are supposed to be a place to brag, right? But it was *devilishly* hard to write about how supposedly brilliant *I* am when Dad already exhausted that topic for me. And I was thinking like . . . well, I was thinking that you never got someone to write about how brilliant you are. And that I wasn't even the best person to write about you, that it should've been Dad, but I was the only one left, so . . . so I wrote it. So there."

I was silent a long moment.

"You didn't have to," I said.

"Plum." She fixed me with a stare. "I did, too. For one thing, you're hilarious."

"I am?"

"Yes!" Ginny rolled her eyes, like I was being intentionally obtuse. "First of all, you're so funny that half the time I think your jokes are from somewhere else because they're so good. And you have that way of just . . . not saying anything for the longest time and then swooping in to say one devastatingly clever thing. You have to be smart to do that. You have to notice stuff. And you're responsible, you keep everything organized in your head, and you're patient, just like your name implies."

"I suppose so," I said. "Yeah."

Ginny looked like she might start crying but didn't let it

faze her. "And I know I'm exhausting and dramatic and waste just . . . *oodles* of my limited human energy on things like being convinced I'm dying and crying and pacing up and down the stairs. You have the good sense not to do that, on top of everything else you already do."

She flung her arms around my neck. I let her hug me, and then, when she wouldn't let go, I tried to hit her with the Five Little Field Mice, but she shrieked and rolled away.

"No!" She pressed a hand to her temple. "Killed by the thing I loved the most! How dreadfully poetic!"

"The thing you love the most is Five Little Field Mice?" I regarded the book in my hand. Ginny nodded heartily.

"After Mom, the dogs, the house, and to a certain extent Kit Marlowe, absolutely," she said. "Well, and you, of course. You will always be the thing I love the most." She paused a beat. "So please don't kill me."

And for the first time in perhaps my entire life, I will tell you truly, I did not want to.

"Fine," I said, and sat on the edge of the mattress. Ginny moved over, giving me space.

"Read to me?"

"Sure."

I went back to the books. There were her underlined passages, of course, but frustratingly—well, no, really, *obviously*—those were the passages I would've underlined anyway. In the back matter, the part I'd admittedly never read, I found them:

HELLO PLUMMY it's me! Do you like Jane Eyre so far?

Plum is it just me or is Helen, like, kind of annoying?

Sooooo sleepy can class be over?

Sorry but literally WHO WOULD BE FOOLED BY MR. ROCHESTER'S FORTUNE-TELLER DISGUISE!!!!! Am I wrong????

omg Charlotte keeps pronouncing it "Saint John" and I'm dying inside

themes: self-sufficiency, religion??, feminism, don't put your wife in the attic

Did you see that the Brontës wrote weird fan fiction when they were kids? CELEBRITIES THEY'RE JUST LIKE US. I mean they are literally like us, Plum, except you're basically Charlotte and Emily combined and I'm Anne with a touch of Branwell.

I don't understand the religious parts at all, but by the time you read this book I will be almost in college or dropped out of school or dead or something, so here's hoping I made it, okay?

You, of course, will be fine fine fine.

B ut even then, I was not done reading unexpected messages.

That afternoon was dozy and pleasant in the way that only a weekday with no school can be. Ginny slept, and I spent an hour or two reading Rilke, who was, in fact, next on the syllabus, and which Ginny had underlined scrupulously, along with many smiley faces and random phrases in French.

"Plum?" Almost-Doctor Andrews called up the back stairs.

Our mail had been delivered to him, again. There was little hope of this ever changing, no matter how many times we assured the mail carrier that Gizmo and Doug were incurably friendly, especially if you gave them a biscuit.

I took the stack of envelopes with a thank-you. Junk. Junk. A white-enveloped reminder to purchase tickets to the TGS graduation luncheon—quaint. Something about health insurance, for Mom. A letter to me.

I never got mail. I ripped it open.

Dear Plum,
I realize I never actually call you by your real name and
maybe thats rude of me. Do you ever go by Patience? You
probably have a lot of it to tutor me. Ha ha ha
   Anyway I just wanted to say that I hope your doing
okay because I heard some stuff was going on with your
sister. I thought about texting you but that seemed weird
and you seem like the kind of person who would appreciate
a letter. Even if its in terrible handwriting.
   Also if there was anything I did to you then I'm sorry.
I hope we talk again soon
   sincerely
   Tate
   PS. Sorry this is so badly written. Its not my tutors
fault

I read it seven times in a row. Then I picked up my phone
before I lost my nerve.

Thank you for your letter. Everything is okay.

I put it down, upside down, as if I were unconcerned with
receiving a response. It hummed on the counter ten seconds
later.

   no problem
   i heard you got suspended???

Yes, I wrote back. *If you can believe it.*

whoa

damn peach

watch out

A pause, for the dots. This time I didn't put my phone down.

so your just home now

Yes

can i come over?

I thought about it. I really did. But something about being not only the kind of girl who would kiss Tate Kurokawa, but also the kind of girl who would call Charlotte Forsythe a bitch in a crowded math building lounge area, and the kind of girl who might actually be, in some way, in some people's eyes, a little brilliant, made me inclined to say yes.

Sure

Ten minutes later, just as I was hastily finishing rebraiding my hair, there was a knock at the door. Not the door we actually go in and out of, which is the kitchen door, but the front door. I sprinted from the kitchen to the front hallway and yanked it open.

"Hi," I said.

"Hi," Tate said. I had forgotten just how good it was to see him up close.

"Thanks for the letter," I said, before I forgot to be polite. "Do you want to come in?"

Tate stepped inside.

"So this is your house," Tate said.

"Yes," I said, a bit defensively. "It's not in the best shape, I'll admit. But it is us."

"I like it," he said. "Is the polar bear real?"

I stared at him. "What do you think?"

"Yeah." He rubbed his chin. "I guess they're usually bigger than that."

"Do you want to sit down?" I asked, before remembering we didn't have couches. "We can go to the kitchen."

"Okay."

I led the way, through the dark of the dining room and out into the chaos that was our kitchen.

"Whoa," Tate said.

"Yes," I said. "It's us."

He sat on Gizmo's couch, where Gizmo already was, and gave his ears a scratch. Tate had the uncanny ability to look at ease no matter his surroundings. It was infuriating, but also, I realized something I admired about him. Something that made me like him. One of a few things.

"So . . . ," he started. "Were you actually mad at me?"

"Mad?" I said. "Why?"

"Because you weren't talking to me." He patted Gizmo's head. "I mean, I guess we haven't actually talked that much. But I got the sense that you were, like, avoiding me."

"Well," I said. "Things got . . . complicated. Here.

And . . ." I didn't know how to say what I felt. "And I never figured you'd actually care if we didn't speak."

"What? Why not?"

"Because . . ." I let out a breath. "You probably don't even remember."

"I can barely remember what I had for lunch," Tate said. "So yeah, probably."

"When we were kids, you, and Stevie, and Tommy . . . that time you took my notebook in fourth grade. You all laughed at me *so much*. I guess I have a hard time thinking that you're not just setting me up to make fun of me again. It seems like something you would do."

"Oh," Tate said. He looked at his shoes. Then up again. "It does?"

"It does. Or it did. I don't know." I tucked hair behind my ear.

"You still think about that, huh?"

"Yes," I said tightly. "I do. I don't suppose *you* do."

"Not really," Tate said. "I mean, now that you mention it, yeah. But not as much as you did. Do." He rubbed his forehead. "Look, Peach, we were idiots back then. I mean, the other guys still are. And I probably am, too. But, okay, now that I'm thinking about it, you know what I *actually* remember thinking back then?"

I shook my head.

"I was like, *Wow, this girl is smart.*"

"Really?"

"Yeah. Like your writing and stuff. And the fact that you were someone who just wrote for fun. And I remember thinking my friends were kind of assholes."

"Even then?"

"It's not like it's hard to notice," Tate said.

That was a fair point.

"I'm not trying to be like, *Oh, they just peer pressured me,* because I'm sure I was being an asshole, too. I can't deny that stuff. I don't know. It was dumb. I probably can't say it didn't mean anything without sounding like I'm full of shit, right?"

"No," I said truthfully.

"Yeah, well . . . that's kind of it, right? I'm an asshole. So the idea that someone like you would actually want to spend time with me . . . I don't know. It kinda blew my mind."

"Someone like me?" I said. "What do you mean?"

"Someone smart," he said. "Someone interesting. I dunno. I think it might be kinda better to hook up with someone like that than someone . . . I dunno."

My cheeks went hot. "I'll have to take your word for it."

Tate looked at the ground.

I wanted to believe him. In fact, I think I did believe him. "No," I said. "No. It's just . . ." I hugged my arms to myself. "I mean, me? Seriously? Look at me."

Tate lifted his shoulders. "Sure. What do you mean?"

"I mean . . . look at me." I had to get this across. I couldn't believe it wasn't landing. "Look at you."

"Maybe I didn't tell them for the same reason you didn't. I knew they, like, wouldn't get it. And you didn't tell any of your friends, did you?"

"You mean my sister," I said.

"Sure."

I stood silent a moment.

"No," I said. "I didn't. But that was different. I thought I'd . . . I don't know. Jinx it or something."

"Yeah," Tate said. "Same."

He looked at the couch next to him.

"Do you want to stop standing up?"

"You mean sit down?" I said.

"Sure."

I sat down, with my hands tucked between my knees. Tate leaned forward.

"So . . . now what?"

I felt wildly out of control. My mind could hardly seize on a single idea long enough to articulate it into thought.

My soul is all but out of me.

"This is going to sound stupid," I said.

"From you?" Tate said. "Bullshit."

I smiled. "Okay. Do you remember that poem we read in English class?"

"The one about the fly buzzing?"

"No," I said. "Not a death poem. The one about holding the world close enough."

"Oh, yeah," Tate said. "That one was okay."

"What did you think it was about?"

"I dunno," he said. "The woods?" He widened his eyes. "Wait, no. That's too easy. I guess it's about . . ." He squinted. "Being alive, maybe. Is that too dumb an answer?"

"No," I said. "No, I think that's exactly what it's about."

"Why do you ask?" Tate said. "Are you stealth-tutoring me?"

"No," I said again. I took a quick breath. "It made me think of you. The poem. I'm not fully sure why. But it did."

"Yeah?" Tate's whole face brightened. "No kidding."

"I'm not kidding," I said. "'Oh world, I cannot hold thee close enough.'"

"Oh. Damn."

Then he laughed, and for the barest second my heart fell.

"No one has ever said that hooking up with me made them recite poetry."

"Oh," I said.

"It's awesome," he said.

I smiled again. Tate smiled, too.

"So, like, are we *ever* going to have a conversation that doesn't involve English class?"

"Are we ever going to have a conversation that doesn't involve basketball?"

Tate's smile broke into a grin. "Yeah, but, like, that's different. Basketball is, like, the heartbeat of our city."

"A metaphor."

"Damn, Peach. Did you just take the game and English it?"

I shrugged.

"You're good," he said.

"I try."

He sat forward even more, craning his neck to the dining room door, then toward the back door.

"What are you doing?" I asked.

"Checking to see if anyone's here," he said. "Is anyone here?"

"No."

"Good."

He turned his head and kissed me, right in the middle of the kitchen, and, I have to tell you, every part of it was glorious.

Oh world, I thought. *Oh, world, oh, world, oh, world.*

From the windowsill, Kit gave a lusty *mrowl*.

That night, it thundered over 5142 Haven Lane. I woke with a start at a crack of lightning, though I couldn't tell what time it was since the electricity had already skittered out in terror. All I could tell was that the sky was black, the house was dark, and the air was cool and fresh.

I turned over, and onto Doug, but the thunder was too loud, or I was too awake now. So I rose and pushed off my sheets and padded downstairs, to the landing, down to the first floor, to the front porch overlooking the garden.

"Hey."

I jumped. Ginny was already there, stretched on the chaise with the striped cushions.

"Wanna sit?"

There was a picture of the two of us on that chaise, in our matching bathing suits, eating ice cream from plastic cups using those little wooden paddles. We would not both fit there together now; there was no way. But Ginny patted the space next to her, and when I got in close to her, it was not as uncomfortable as I had thought.

She dropped her head onto my shoulder. Wind whipped over us, pushing her hair practically between my eyelids. There is a way you get to be familiar with the smells of people you are around, or maybe it is simply being sisters that does it. In either case, Ginny's hair smelled like pineapple shampoo, a little too strong, so specific I could practically see the crusting bottle in her bathtub.

"It's cool to be out here," she said. "It feels magical. You can experience the storm without actually being in it."

"Who says *experience the storm*?" I said. "As in, 'experience the storm on one of our exclusive tours. Call today and reserve your tickets'?"

Ginny cackled. "I would ask you what that's from, but this time, I am going to assume you made it up yourself."

"I did."

Outside the frame of the porch pillars, the wind was ripping through branches, the yew tree dropping sticky red buds onto the flagstones. A distant flash lit up a swath of clouds. Ginny tucked her arms up into her sleeves.

"Can I tell you a secret, Plum?" She was staring straight ahead. "Drowning is terrifying."

Thunder cracked.

"I'm sure," I said slowly.

"I know what you want to ask," she went on. "And I can't even tell you. I don't think it was on purpose, and if I don't think it was on purpose then it probably wasn't. But I also didn't *not* do it. I don't know if that makes sense. I just wanted to be nowhere. I wanted to stop having to make choices." She drew in a breath. "The doctors asked, Mom asked, the health insurance people even asked so they'd know how to bill it properly when they send me to a psychiatrist. But I honestly don't know. Isn't that fucked-up?"

I looked at my sister. My sister who was so much like me it hurt not to understand something about her, even something she couldn't understand herself.

"Well, don't fall all over yourself to help me out, Plummy," she said drily.

"I'm sorry." My mouth felt sandy. "You're going to a psychiatrist?"

"I think so."

"Aren't you scared?"

"Plum, I'm scared of everything." Ginny pulled her arms farther into her sleeves. "I can hardly see how a specialized doctor would be any better or worse than the rest of it."

"Yeah."

"Yes, well, so there." Ginny lifted her chin. "One day I will be untroublèd."

There were tears going down her cheeks.

"I'm just tired of being freaked out all the time," she whispered. "I'm tired of it. I'm *sick* of it."

I couldn't get to her hand, so I reached out and squeezed her foot. "I know."

The rain kept on, and the wind swept so hard it felt like a physical *thing* pressing over us, rattling the windowpanes. My mind went to Tate, and that afternoon, and for once I did not try to seal it away for safekeeping. Actually, I found I wanted to tell Ginny.

"I have a secret, too," I said.

Ginny tipped her head. "Oh?"

"Yes. And to be honest, it has been tearing me up inside. But you can't laugh."

"Okay," Ginny said, and laughed, like I knew she would. "Did you do something else bad at school? Oh my God, did you smoke a cigarette? Has Mom led you down the path of iniquity? *Are your lungs already black?*" She grabbed my chin and forced my jaws apart.

"Ginny!" I shoved her off.

"I'm just saying," she said mildly. "Remember in health class when they showed us the healthy lung and the smoking lung? And how the smoking lung was all shrively like popcorn you leave in the microwave too long?"

"I'm not smoking," I said. "It's something else."

"*What?*"

I told her.

"Tate Kurokawa?!" Ginny crowed. "No *way.*"

I buried my face in my knees. I had made a grave misjudgment.

"Plum!"

"He's very nice," I said into my pajama pants. "In my defense. Once you get to know him."

"Why didn't you tell me?"

333

I moved my head so my chin was on top of my knees. "I don't know. I thought you'd judge me."

"What? Why?"

"Because you judge *everything*," I said.

Ginny considered. "Fair. But you do that just as much as I do. So if you found some reason to deem him acceptable, I could come around on it."

"You would not have."

"He is very attractive," Ginny said.

"I know," I said, at the risk of sounding immodest. "I really like kissing him."

Ginny narrowed her eyes and bit her lip, thinking. "Yes. It all makes perfect sense." She tapped the side of her nose. "He's your Gilbert Blythe."

"He's going to rescue me from under a bridge?"

"He's *annoying*," Ginny said, "but handsome, and with many redeeming qualities, and he will buy you a dress with puffed sleeves."

She lay back on the chaise.

"I'm happy for you, Plum," she said, after a moment. "I think this is the first thing I've been happy about in weeks."

I tucked my legs up under myself. "Good."

The wind gusted mightily. From upstairs, there came a tremendous *bang*, and a tinkling sound like glass breaking. Then dogs barking. Ginny and I looked at each other, then leaped to our feet and scrambled inside, lighting up Ginny's phone as a flashlight.

Upstairs, on the landing, Mom crouched on the Oriental rug. The doors to the office had cracked apart and blown open, and every pane had split and shattered.

"Don't come closer," Mom warned, waving a hand. She was futilely pushing her sagging pajama sleeves up to her elbows and picking up fragments. "You'll cut yourself open."

"*Mother!*" Ginny said. "You can't just . . . *handle* those! Cripes. Are you even wearing shoes?"

Mom squinted against our phone flashlight. "I'm not stupid, Ginny." She stuck out a foot, slippered in one of those foam mesh shoes with the rhinestone flowers on top.

"Those aren't enough," Ginny said.

"Maybe I should get the vacuum," I offered. From inside Mom's bedroom door, Gizmo and Doug sent up yips of distress.

"No, you're right." Mom straightened up. "I can't see anything."

She looked at the doors.

"I guess I should've . . ." She folded her arms. "Christ. It's a mess in there."

"Maybe because you've never cleaned it. Or even gone in there," Ginny said.

Mom glared. "I don't see you offering to help."

"I didn't know I was allowed!"

"You're not not allowed," Mom said.

"Then why don't we ever go in there?" I asked.

Mom stared at both of us. Then, gingerly, she stepped

past the glass and over the threshold.

Within it smelled old—not musty, but dignified, if such a smell is possible. Organized it was not—naturally. It was still dark—Ginny uselessly yanked a lamp's pull cord—but my eyes were adjusting enough to see. There was something more than careless about the way the study was stacked with papers, books, manila folders, expanding files. It was some kind of conscious disorganization, less neglect and more intentional jumble. In the corner was what looked like a wooden stool, pale, with no finish, which Ginny sprang toward.

"Dusty," she said. "Gross."

"What did you expect?" I said.

She ignored me and picked it up, surveying.

"I'm going to put finish on it. It needs it."

"What? How would *you* know?"

"I don't. But I could figure it out. I've watched an awful lot of Home and Garden Television." She set the stool back down. "Yes, actually, I think that's brilliant. I would like to know how to do something practical with my hands. It seems . . . fulfilling."

"Weren't you the one afraid of becoming a coal miner?" I said.

Ginny tossed her head. "That was a long time ago, Plum."

It had been seven months. But, also, it had been a long time.

I turned my attention to the desk, where, beneath a stack

of receipts and invoices and God knows what else, a bright corner of paper peeked out. I pushed away the other layers and immediately recognized it. In careful, preschool letters, the top read PLUM's MAGAZINE FOR KIDS, with each S turned charmingly backward. Inside there was a notional amount of content—scribbled humanoid circles, something that was probably a cat, a sun with angular rays spiking out in all directions. But it was the back cover that was most striking.

The lettering wasn't our mother's—she wrote in a script-print hybrid with lots of flourish. This was tighter, more straightforward, but certainly adult.

Children of every age and reading level will appreciate this fine work of magazine journalism by a brilliant new talent in the media world. List price $2.00.

You simply couldn't know how finding that made me feel—or maybe you could. I held it to my heart.

Lightning flashed, and I saw Mom looking away from a bookcase.

"It gets such good light in here," Mom said. "It's a shame we don't . . ."

"You should have it," I said. "Make it an art studio."

Mom gaped.

"I don't—"

"We don't mind. Right, Gin?"

Ginny looked up from *Beginner's Woodworking*. "Absolutely not. In fact, I think it's a fine idea."

Mom pursed her lips, arms folded. "We'll see."

Thunder rolled, more distant now.

"*Finally.*" Ginny slammed her book shut. "This has been the longest storm of my life."

 SIX

You are indeed the finest comic writer of the present age.
—Jane Austen, in a letter to her sister

And yet there still remained the issue of Ginny's probation, and my own suspension. An explanation had to be made, and, perhaps not coincidentally, the explanation fell to me. Because, yes, I had been explaining everything, this whole time, in notebooks, furtively, secretly—ashamedly, even, at times, given my own inescapable naïveté.

But I could not have resisted writing it, and then I became glad of it.

There was, of course, no smoking gun, and no previous record of academic dishonesty, and, when pressed, Charlotte prevaricated. My written account attested a plausible timeline of innocence, and so Ginny was absolved; what became of Charlotte I could not tell you.

You may have surmised the end effect of this story. However unintentionally humorous and stupidly youthful-sounding my account—

But Ginny told me that there is no way I am ever unintentionally funny; it is simply that I'm so good at it that it comes like a reflex. And it should also be remembered, as one can read in the back matter of their books, that Charlotte Brontë and her sisters began writing fantasy stories when they were children. Jane Austen wrote two novels when she was twelve, and also a whole host of letters to her sisters. Mary Shelley was nineteen when she wrote *Frankenstein*. And Edna St. Vincent Millay was only twenty when she won her first poetry prize.

I am only fifteen now, it is true. And one day I will be eighteen, and twenty-five, and thirty-five, and fifty, and hopefully older, and hopefully at *least* that old, and I will think of these days as foolish or inconsequential or only invested with meaning with the benefit of hindsight.

But I will also not see them as I do now. They will not be raw, fresh, stinging, bloomingly warm as this afternoon when I sit on the windowsill with Kit Marlowe over my feet. I will forget the smell of his fur, the lead paint peeling just so, like an opening mouth, the unabashed clanging of the fat wind chimes that hang beneath me in the garden. So perhaps it is in fact in my best interest to write now, and encapsulate something.

Rilke, as we learned in subsequent classes on poetry, didn't think writing young would produce anything. But he was also never a fifteen-year-old girl. He had not been Patience Mortimer Blatchley living through a year that did have, for the record, an awful lot of unexpected meetings and illnesses and long nights of love (although maybe not in the embarrassing sense of *love* he probably meant, judging by his other poems).

I had not set out to do a literary project, to make anyone laugh, or to exonerate myself from charges of name-calling, or to testify to my own sister's innocence in matters of academic integrity, but at this point in the story, that is what happened. And now, having recovered this account, and being inclined to continue it, and feeling that in retrospect I have gained both a keener sense of my own project and the realization that, indeed, some parts of the story of this year were in fact ridiculously funny, especially the parts with the porta potty and the flies and anything involving our mother trying to plan a party, and if there's any point to this story at all it's just that things were all right, then bad, then terrible, and now they are better.

My sister and I are happy, for the most part, and alive, and we miss our father terribly. That is what I wanted to say, I suppose. That is all I have ever wanted you to know.

 EPILOGUE

"Summer is coming, summer is coming
I know it, I know it, I know it.
Light again, leaf again, life again, love again."
Yes, my wild little Poet. . . .

Summer is coming, is coming, my dear
And all of the winters are hidden.
—Alfred, Lord Tennyson

R eader, she graduated.

There was a resolutely festival air to the Gregory School graduation, as is traditional. Tasteful nosegays (white) for the girls; small boutonnieres (also white) for the boys; an anodyne valediction from some democratically elected representative of the senior class who also happened to have lobbied her peers for the four weeks leading to the ceremony; a reception of chicken-salad sandwiches and something sure to be gluten-free.

Two by two they came down the center aisle of the Gregory School's Ecumenical Chapel and Meditation Space, white dresses and suits. And when it came her turn, Ginny marched straight ahead, eyes trained on the giant frosted window above the altar that had long ago replaced the cross, almost outpacing poor, diminutive Nick Cartwright at her alphabetically ordered side.

Her hair was wound into one of my finest braids, a thick four-stranded plait over one shoulder and a tinier one arcing above her brow like a coronet. Small white blossoms wove through her hair, peeking out like little stars. The dress, it must be noted, was new—a graduation gift from Almost-Doctor Andrews.

He sat on my left, Mom on my right, clutching my hand. If anyone wondered what Iris Mortimer-Blatchley was doing with a much younger man who was certainly not her husband, they were polite enough to wait until out of earshot to remark on it.

"Look at her go," Mom whispered.

When they gave out diplomas, we cheered at Ginny's name, even though the printed program requested we kindly wait for the end of the distribution.

And then the mad crush of everyone's parents looking for their child while the children were all looking for their friends and the teachers were just trying to get out of the way and on to the lawn, where the tent of refreshments was waiting.

Ginny, trapped behind a wall of slow-moving grandparents, bugged her eyes at me.

"I'll wait," I called over her. She made a face, then hitched up her skirt and climbed over the first two pews.

"Ginny!"

"What are they going to do, expel me?" She rolled her eyes and tugged at my hand. "Come on!"

We threaded our way to a side door and burst out, where the brick-walled buildings and the freshly replanted impatiens looked as Ginny let go of my hand and, with a whoop, threw her nosegay into the air. It landed with a splat on the bricks of the school commons, splattering petals everywhere.

"Ginny!" Mom was calling from just outside the chapel. "What are you *doing*?"

"I don't know," Ginny called back. "It just seemed like the thing to do. The girl who catches it will be the next to get in early admission."

"You could have saved it," I said.

"And do what? Hang it upside down and dry it?" Ginny said. "Put it in my hope chest?" She shook her head. "No. I don't care. I don't want it."

She did, however, go back to scrape it off the bricks.

"What a lovely braid." A gray-haired woman in a dress printed with tulips in almost radioactive shades of pink and green caught Ginny's elbow.

"Thank you," Ginny said. "My sister did it."

The woman smiled, revealing the smallest smudge of lipstick on her teeth. "Well. Aren't you lucky."

Ginny tossed her hair. "Oh, supremely. *There is no friend like a sister*, ah . . . something something something."

"Where are you off to for college, dear?"

"Nowhere," Ginny said. "For the time being. I will be taking a year off."

"Oh," the woman said, politely. "Traveling?"

"Working," Ginny said. "In a furniture shop. I'm going to learn to make tables."

"Ah," said the woman. "I . . . excuse me."

Ginny crossed her eyes and stuck out her tongue at the woman's retreating back, then threaded her arm through mine.

"That poem isn't really about sisters, you know," I said. "It's about lesbians. Or at least I think it is." We'd done Christina Rossetti at the end of our poetry unit, the last enjoyable thing to read before the unit on rhetoric and argumentation that presaged many drafts of college essays to come.

But there was no reason to think about that yet.

"Well, whatever." Ginny waved her hand in the air. We were making our way toward the tent with the sandwiches. "You know, I think I'm the first person to graduate from the Gregory School bound for a career of manual labor."

"This century, at least," I said. "Does that disqualify you from the Women's Alumni Association?"

"I should be so lucky." Ginny put a hand to her brow, scanning the lawn. A few yards away, the High-Strung Smart Girls were holding phones aloft, posing and reposing to get all five of them into a single frame.

"Do you want to—?"

"No," Ginny said abruptly. She turned on her heel. "Sandwich?"

"I'm not hungry."

"I *think*," Ginny said, "you should get one from *over there*."

She indicated a table at the edge of the tent, where Tate Kurokawa, in a blue button-down was standing, alone, and staring right at us. At me.

He waved.

"Gin!" Mom flapped a hand from the edge of the tent, where Almost-Doctor Andrews was waiting with his fancy camera. "Pictures!"

"Coming!"

Ginny flew off, and I circled around table by table to find Tate.

"Hey, Peach."

"Hey yourself."

He grinned. "Haven't seen you in a while."

It had not been a while. It had been approximately sixteen hours.

"Having some sandwiches?"

We both looked at his plate, which was heavy-laden.

"Obviously." He was wearing boat shoes with no socks, I noticed.

"That was a joke."

"Obviously." He chewed on his lower lip, an action I found attractive to the point of downright manipulative. But I, Plum Blatchley, was not about to grab Tate Kurokawa and make out with him right next to the cut-up fruit and cheese platters.

"Congratulations," I said. "To Benji."

Tate looked over his shoulder, where Benji was roughhousing with some other Sporty Senior Boys, ostensibly to take a picture.

"It's a miracle he graduated," Tate said. "Honestly."

"When was the last time someone *didn't* graduate from TGS?"

"Good point." Tate stuffed a sandwich in his mouth. "So do you guys go away or anything?"

"What?"

"For the summer."

"Well, Ginny's working," I said. "And I'm working. And my mother won a fellowship for an artist's retreat in Maine. Do *you* go away?"

"To see my dad. But that's just for a few weeks, or whatever. Just to get some sailing in." He picked at a second sandwich. "But you'll be here?"

"I will."

"So I'll see you around?"

"Yes," I said. "You will."

"Plum!!!" Ginny cried. She and Mom were waiting by the chapel entrance, holding their arms out to put me in place for a photo. I left Tate, for the time being, and went to be with them.

For once, I was not waiting for the future. For once, I was there on the green lawn in the breeze, seeing my laughing mother and my unruly sister, both happy and alive, and I knew I could not take either for granted, and that one day I would be old—if I was lucky, I would be old—and I could think back on this one day in June, this one day when there was light and leaf and light and love and we were together and all that glory was so ordinary we didn't think to be grateful for it.

Cripes. I'm no better at knowing how to end than to begin. I will go on and on until I run out of words or run out of brain. Such is my gift—to be insufferably long-winded.

But, yes, the occasion was drawing to a close. And we counted down, smiling, together, and the camera flashed.

One *is* never grateful for the glory of ordinary things. And yet—I was.

ACKNOWLEDGMENTS

Thank you first to Alyssa Miele, whose editorial insight and delightful revision letters guided this project from "draft completed in a frenzied state of anxiety" to "actual novel." Thank you too to Alexandra Cooper, a stellar editor and all-around publishing superwoman. To Uwe Stender, my agent-cum-Rilke-consultant, Frau Dornenberg says danke schön. Emily Rader, thank you for many exact and expert edits. Molly Fehr and Julie McLaughlin, thank you for a stunner of a cover—lucky, lucky me to see this beauty on the front of my book. Thank you to Kristen Eberhard, Janet Rosenberg, Meghan Pettit, and Allison Brown for all your hard work keeping every detail of this book on track.

To the gracious receivers of panicked chats/messages/texts, the metaphorical holders of hands, the truest of the true and the smartest of the bunch: Kate Brauning, Whitney Gardner, Katherine Locke, Aimee Lucido, Eric Smith, and

Alex Yuschik, thank you for being there and being brilliant.

Josh, thank you for reminding me to make my writing unpredictable. I love you.

Mom and Dad, thank you for absolutely everything in my whole life. Rory and Zero—alias Doug and Gizmo—good boys! Sit. Stay.

Finally, thank you to Alice Thornburgh, the Plum to my Ginny—you are a wonder of a sister. This book is for you.